FANTASY ADVENTURES™

Challenge dragons, battle hydras, avoid traps, and discover treasure... all with a flip of a card in Fantasy Adventures™, the collectible card game from Mayfair Games. Choose from over 450 unique cards filled with treasure, monsters, and heroes as you build a deck. Outwit your friends as you pit your deck against theirs. Cards feature art from some of today's top fantasy artists.

FREE
UNIQUE CARD OFFER!

To get your free Fantasy Adventures™ promo card, send a STAMPED, SELF-ADDRESSED ENVELOPE and a cash register receipt (price circled) to:

MAYFAIR GAMES
P.O. BOX 48717
NILES, IL 60714-0717

Absolutely no phone queries accepted. Please direct all questions to FA Questions at above address. Fantasy Adventures is a trademark of Mayfair Games. All Rights Reserved.

Name:_____

Address:_____

_____

City, State, Zip:_____

Daytime phone #:_____

Email address:_____

Cardmaster

Offer expires 9/1/97. No copies of coupon or sales receipt accepted.

C0-ATV-408

CLAYTON EMERY

CARDMASTER

This is a work of fiction. All the characters and events portrayed in this book are fictional, and any resemblance to real people or incidents is purely coincidental.

Copyright © 1997 by Bill Fawcett & Associates

All rights reserved, including the right to reproduce this book or portions thereof in any form.

A Baen Books Original

Baen Publishing Enterprises
P.O. Box 1403
Riverdale, NY 10471

ISBN: 0-671-87772-0

Cover art by Stephen Hickman

First printing, March 1997

Distributed by Simon & Schuster
1230 Avenue of the Americas
New York, NY 10020

Printed in the United States of America

Dedicated to
Mister Marc, our most dashing friend

Chapter 1

Fiends howled for his blood.

Byron ran, pelting down black caves with lumpy slimy floors that betrayed his feet. He slipped, cannoned into a stalagmite, pushed free, dashed on. It was pitch black in this endless labyrinth, yet somehow he could see. And smell. The demons stank of brimstone and smoke and ash, and the smell grew ranker as they drew closer.

There were dozens of demons. Some were small and naked like black chickens without feathers. Others were tall with two howling heads and skin like flaking tree bark. Still others ran on four legs turned backwards so claws ticked against scorpion-tough hides. Others had long drooping necks so their heads bobbled on their stomachs as they ran. The demons were hairy or naked, scaled or blister-skinned, horned or fanged.

And they could all run as fast as he.

Byron lurched around a boulder, skidded on shale oil, crashed on stone. His hands blistered on hot rock. His legs blundered into hidden holes filled with ashes and trash.

Ragged claws and hooks snagged his clothing. Paws, feet, curled tails groped at him. Demons lighted like a flock of vultures on a dead cow. With hoots and screams and croaks, monsters tore at the apprentice, tried to latch on, hold him. A demon with ragged yellow teeth snapped at his nose. A scaly tentacle slithered around his neck like a snake's kiss. Byron lashed out blindly, his hands slapping in slime and pus and drool.

His legs felt heavy, bogged down. The heat was roasting, and it was hard to breathe for all the smoke. Demons blocked his sight on every side. A monster with dripping jaws in its chest opened that hideous mouth to swallow him.

Desperate, Byron kicked, screamed, dodged. Slick with sweat, he squirmed free. Horrid hands yanked his hair and rasped his face as he burst through the stinking crowd and ran on.

Glimmers of light, yellow shot with red, showed far ahead, and he pelted that way. Perhaps it was daylight, an exit from this nightmare. Demons couldn't stand sunlight, he'd heard.

His feet crunched cinders and bone fragments. Smoke from dimly glowing pits suffocated him. He was freezing cold yet running sweat. He ran harder, feet banging bare stone, jouncing his spine and innards. But the glorious light loomed just ahead. He tore out of the tunnel.

The light was blinding. He squinted as his eyeballs dried. The tunnel emptied into a huge cavern with a black ceiling too high to see, and a floor that sloped down to the bowels of the earth. Fire roiled in the pit, and burning molten jets erupted. Byron felt the heat of the pit scorching the soles of his shoes. Drops of lava splashed him, stinging his hands and face, burning holes in his clothes and setting them smouldering. Billowing yellow-brown smoke made him cough and retch, his eyes water.

No escape. There was only this slope and nothing else.

Demons burst from the tunnel behind.

Jiggling, bouncing, jouncing, a tangle of gray and festered flesh, they slammed into the apprentice. The whole writhing mass, with Byron trapped among them, tumbled down the slope.

More heat, and now flame, as they rolled through patches of burning tar or metal. Demons screamed, sizzled, and died as gouts of burning sulfur from the pit ignited fur and scales and wings, made them living torches. They skidded headlong down the slope, unable to stop, the earth hot enough now to scorch flesh.

Byron's clothes caught fire; then his hair, crackling and spitting around his head, stinking and rank. His skin turned red, smoked, then burst into flame. He watched his hands sizzle to bare white bones that charred black as the screaming horde and the captive cardsmith toppled into the pit. A boiling gout caught them in mid-air, fused human and demon flesh into a burning pitchy mass.

Byron screamed as he fell, until he died.

Byron crashed on the cool, amazingly cool, floor. He opened his eyes. Alone. Safe. Lying on the cool wooden floor of the attic. Blankets entangled his legs, and he kicked them off. He'd been hot on this spring night, gotten snarled in blankets, had a nightmare, fallen out of bed. Just a dream. A nightmare.

He sighed with relief, but coughed, choked. He squinted at the hazy air. Had he left a candle burning? Was the nightmare not over?

Not quite. The house was afire.

Most junior of the apprentices, Byron got the attic, the highest part of the great house, musty and cramped, torrid in summer, freezing in winter, home to rats and cockroaches all year.

But not for much longer. Both ends of the attic blazed. Flames licked at the tiny lathed windows.

If Byron had a failing, it was massive curiosity. That both ends of the house burned nagged his brain for a second. Why was that significant?

Then a more sensible panic took over. He scrambled off the floor and smacked his head on the rafters, as he did four mornings out of seven. Cursing, clutching his sore pate, snorting smoke and sneezing dust, he fumbled on his trousers and shirt, grabbed up his cape and round hat. Fashion for cardsmiths required that every article be jet black, almost impossible to find and don at night in a smoke-filled room. He'd mention that at the next guild meeting—provided he survived the next few minutes.

His shoes, kicked under the bed, were black, too. He grabbed one and tugged it on, groped for the other, bumped it with his fingers. It skittered across the floor and dropped off the floorboards into the eaves.

Really cursing now, and coughing, Byron let it go. He had to get out or be cooked.

Crawling, he swung his legs through the trapdoor hole for the top rung, remembered too late it was missing, and fell. He touched the ladder just once, with his chin, before crashing on the floor. Damn Master Rayner and his parsimony, too cheap to have a ladder repaired!

The air was clearer on the third floor, but gray clots of smoke swirled when Byron waved his arms. The light was bad, only flickers of flame casting illumination and distorted shadows. Stumbling down the main corridor—clumping and padding with one shoe missing—he hollered, "Fire! Fire! Rouse all!"

No one answered. He stuck his head in a doorway. It was a bedroom for one of Rayner's mistresses: He had three and fistfuls of children. Bedclothes were tossed on the floor, the room empty. He found the nursery obscured by smoke. The children's short beds were empty, a cradle tipped over.

Dimly, he recalled his nightmare. The smell of brimstone must have been smoke; the demons' cries really the shrieks of women gathering children. No one had roused the lowly apprentice in the attic, he noted bitterly, but they'd been busy. Baskets and a doll strewn in the hallway attested to that.

Hunched under a curtain of smoke, Byron scurried for the back staircase, but it was a well of flame. Burning plaster crackled and spit, the smouldering carpet gushed dusty smoke. He turned and scampered for the front staircase. It billowed heat like a desert wind, hot enough to dry his eyeballs, but the flames from outside hadn't eaten through the wall yet. In blackness, he grabbed the brass banister for support, yelped because it was scorching. Afraid to fall headlong, he crawled backwards down invisible steps, sipping breaths rather than sear his lungs.

The second floor held the master's workshop. Below that was the kitchen, dining hall, and maids' quarters. In the cellar dwelt Rayner's other three apprentices, the piggish bastards who'd kicked him up to the attic. Byron heard no cries for help, assumed everyone had evacuated safely. Probably they clustered in the street in their nightclothes and watched the house burn, having completely forgotten the fourth apprentice.

No. Wait . . .

Halfway down the staircase, butt first, Byron halted, lost in thought. He pictured the house and grounds. The front and back of Rayner's grand house were of wood adorned with filigree and gingerbread and gold leaf and murals and a phony heraldic symbol: layers of paint that would burn like fireworks. The sides of the house, where no one could see, were plain brick without windows or doors, close-packed by gardens and olive trees.

The front and back had the only doors, and both were engulfed in flames.

So there was no way out.

Half-blind, drunk on smoke, and thirstier than he'd ever been, Byron blundered off the stairs onto the second floor. Rayner's workshop took up the whole floor. A hall ran all around it, so no walls touched the outside of the house, a provision against spies. It had a locked door, too, a provision against mistresses and children. Fortunately, Byron wore a key on a thong around his neck, so he might fetch anything the master demanded day or night.

The key scratched in the lock. Fumbling in the smoky darkness, Byron wondered if Rayner had been upstairs in bed or working in the shop when the fire broke out. Or had one of his spellcastings started the fire? Had he grabbed the most valuable supplies and run? That seemed natural, so it was strange the door was locked. . . .

Gasping, Byron shoved the door open, sidled around and shoved it closed, breathed fresh air. Obviously the master hadn't come into the workshop, for there was no smoke here.

No, he amended. Rayner had been here. Was still here.

Three guttering candles lit the room. The shop was a riot of mismatched tables and benches and bulging chests covered with thaumaturgical paraphernalia and tools and books. Sagging shelves were laden with crocks and jars and boxes and sacks of magic-making materials. At the center of the room was Rayner's own work table, which the apprentices were never allowed to touch.

Rayner sat on his high stool at the table, calm as ice.

Byron tiptoed over. Rayner was a big burly man, once an ox drover, now Waterholm's finest cardsmith. His thick shock of swept-back hair and spade-shaped beard showed glints of gray.

No, glints of *ice*.

Tiptoeing, the apprentice touched his master's brawny arm. It was cool and slippery, coated with a sheath of ice a fingernail's thickness. The ice refracted the candlelight, making Rayner glisten like a rainbow.

Horrified, yet fascinated, Byron prodded his master's bristling beard. The ice coating splintered, tinkled and chimed as it pattered on Rayner's icy lap. Under the glaze, Byron saw Rayner's eyes were open and staring, like a hibernating snake found under a winter rock.

But Rayner wasn't hibernating. He was dead, frozen solid.

Byron shuddered for himself as well as his master, for this was a common fate of cardsmiths. In some distant future, Byron's own apprentice might find him cold as an icicle.

He heard a thud and muffled crackling, remembered the fire. A pearl of water dripped from Rayner's nose. The temperature in the workshop was climbing. In a short while, Rayner would go from frozen to crisped.

And Byron would too, if he didn't find a way out of this flaming deathtrap. But first things first.

Rayner had died casting a spell on a card. The pasteboard square was still clutched between icy fingers. Byron picked up an iron candlestick and whanged the fingers, cracking the ice, and freed the card. A crude drawing in charcoal showed a round shape with a bite in one side. He slipped the card into his quilted doublet, vaguely wondering if Rayner had completed the spell. He should have, considering it cost his life. There were more cards scattered on the table: they might be finished or barely started. Byron grabbed them all and dropped them down his shirt.

Grimacing, the apprentice whapped the candlestick against Rayner's chest, fractured the ice sheath. Groping dead, cold flesh, Byron tugged out a key on a silver chain, snapped it loose. He slotted the key into a disguised knothole in the tabletop. Twisting, he felt a click, then pried up a board. Inside a secret drawer, handy to the master's hand, were more loose cards and a velvet pouch. He took them all. The pouch had the chunky satisfying feel of many cards inside, the master's hoard. It was Byron's only pay for three years of diligence, for Rayner hadn't believed in "spoiling" an apprentice with wages.

Congratulating himself, Byron ran for the door. He grabbed the brass handle and yelped. The door panels smoked, the paint curling. Wrapping his sleeve around his hand, he yanked the door open and almost scorched his eyeballs. The hall was a sheet of flame.

His time had run out.

Fighting panic, Byron fought to think of an escape. No way except the walls themselves. They'd have to do.

Circling the room like a madman, patting the walls above the crowded tables, he found the coolest spot facing the side of the house. Once, moving a table, he'd dented the wall and gotten a smack on the ear, been made to repair it. The walls were plaster mixed with horsehair over wooden lathes. Now Byron yanked the table aside, swept the shelves to send crocks and jars smashing, grabbed a big hammer from a worktable and, with desperate strength, pounded on the wall. Plaster crumbled, old wooden lathes snapped. A few more blows and he was smashing the opposite lathes. More plaster cracked and he saw the hall. Knuckles dinged and bleeding, his clothes white, nose filled with plaster dust, he bashed a hole big enough, dropped the hammer and wriggled through, tearing his cape in the process.

The hallway was hot and polluted as a furnace. Smoke roiled in clouds around the corners, sucked through the hole towards the fresh air in the workshop. Both halls burned, leaving Byron a single wall to escape through.

Solid brick.

Hissing, coughing, cursing, he wrenched Rayner's velvet pouch from his shirt, tore it open. Colorful pasteboard cards spilled on the carpet, some large as book covers, some small and square, a few round as big coins. Frantically Byron shuffled. Rayner had one special card he made often. Cheap and popular, people with grudges bought them—

Here it was. On a red-rimmed card, etched in black and washed gray, stone blocks cascaded from a castle wall. Crumble was the spell. With shaking fingers, in dim flickering light, Byron felt the rough bricks, found a slit in which to wedge the card. Madly he picked up the remaining cards and stuffed them in his shirt. When the spell triggered, he'd need to move fast . . .

But in his panic, he'd forgotten something else.

To trigger the magic, he needed the card's token, its secret ingredient. He recalled Rayner instructing a client in the card's use. Swearing, Byron squirmed like a singed rat back through the ragged hole he'd broken.

In the workshop, Rayner was rapidly melting. Soon, Byron knew, the man would topple like a shot duck. As the flames consumed the walls and floor, his skin would char, his skull and bones smoke, then ignite . . . just as Byron had burned in his dream. The apprentice shook his head. Better not dwell on it. He might roast for real, soon.

Scurrying around tables, he found a pot of white dust, sniffed it. Lime, used in mortar. Handy and cheap.

Grabbing a fistful of silky powder, Byron wiggled back into the dark hall. Flames ate the carpet at each end. If he didn't get out soon . . .

Careful not to spill, he crawled to the magic card wedged in the brick wall, trickled lime on it. He hoped Rayner hadn't changed the formula without telling him. . . .

Like a musketeer's "dragon gun," the lime sparked, then the card flashed and went white. Magic, bound into the card by Rayner's will, rippled outward from the card.

Impressed despite his distress, Byron grinned. Magic was always so thrilling.

Radiating from the card, as if dwarves wielded invisible hammers, magic crumbled the mortar between the bricks. The white lines cracked, crumbled, snapped, spat, trickled to dust. Unsettled, bricks cracked under the tremendous weight of the wall and roof above. The wall groaned, bowed.

Byron crawled back from the wall as red brick dust began to spurt. All the mortar within sight had turned to sand and sifted down like snow. Byron recalled that Rayner had guaranteed the card. Triggered in any one spot, the magic started a chain reaction that travelled through all adjacent mortar—all the way around a building or castle if not interrupted. Merchants bought the card to sabotage rivals' houses and warehouses and shops, or to sabotage their own and collect the insurance. A great leveller, the merest peasant could bring down a lord's castle—if he could afford the card. Funny that now lowly Byron used Rayner's card to destroy Rayner's house.

With a crunch and sigh, a shifting squashed stretch of wall bowed and fell out, leaving a gap big as a window. Fresh night air washed around Byron, the first he'd tasted in what seemed hours. But the clean air fed the fires around him, too. Flames licked near his hands, so he squatted on his heels, felt the warmth of the floor under his soles. The ceiling directly below must be burning.

Brick by toppling brick, the edges of the hole enlarged to engulf the whole wall. More bricks rained from above. Byron watched and waited, itching to escape, but the havoc of falling debris got worse. He'd hoped to climb through a hole and scramble spider-like down the buckled wall. Now, he couldn't dodge outside without being crowned or having his back broken, yet he was in danger of being buried under tons of rubble,

Then the floor buckled underfoot.

With the side of the house gone, giant roof beams lost their ancient footings. To a tremendous roar, louder than flames, roof slates cascaded by. Then furniture fell from the upper story: a bed, a cradle, a commode. Byron clung to the burning rug as floorboards twisted apart like an opened fan. Flames from below found new fodder and ate up the wall and across the floor.

Burned or crushed, Byron thought. He should have been a cobbler's apprentice like his mother wanted. They only worried about driving nails into their kneecaps.

He couldn't stay. He'd have to risk jumping. But it was two stories down onto broken bricks, splintered lumber, and razor-edged roof slates.

Gingerly, Byron inched along the floor to the lip. Tilted boards bobbed and creaked. Flinching from cascading debris, he peered outside. The cool breeze in his face felt like spring rain. Out in the dark street, people shrieked and shouted as the burning house spun fiery fragments and sparks all over the neighborhood. Bucket brigades hurled water, and people sopped blankets to beat out hot spots.

Pushing neighbors aside with swell-headed staves were guards in glittering helmets and breastplates. Not helping anyone, they pointed at the burning house and shouted at one another. Byron grunted. Why were *they* here?

The fragmenting floor suddenly slumped, and Byron was left standing on air. Then falling.

Byron had a moment to wish for a flying spell, then he landed with a crash and clatter and skitter.

One shod and one stockinged foot shot out from under and he sprawled in five directions at once. Muffled in his tattered cape, his head banged something soft, but the rest of him hit hard.

Jarred from teeth to toes, he bounced once on his spine, slid some more, settled with a groan and gasp. He knew more bricks or slates or burning boards might rain any second, but he couldn't make his arms and legs respond. I'm stunned, he thought, like a fish gaffed in the head. Panic flitted: what if he'd broken his back? Biting his lip, he forced his arms to move, waved weakly, managed to half-roll. No shooting pains ripped through him, though many small ones whimpered.

Like a whipped dog, the apprentice crawled off the rubble. It had partly buried Rayner's thick gardens. Brick dust and pigeon droppings and charred wood gave way to smells of mint and chives and roses. It was black in this jungle, but high above, both faces of the house blazed like beacons. Dimly he recalled that fact had seemed important when he awoke. Why?

And what next?

Voices.

"I tell you, someone dropped on these bricks!"

"Didn't! It was clothes or somethin'!"

"Merciful Malaga, it's hot! And I can't see with that damned bright fire!"

Stumbling steps, curses, clanking came Byron's way. Guards of the Bishop of Waterholm hunting within the grounds. He'd known them by their shiny helmets and breastplates glimpsed from above. Soldiers of the Prince of Waterholm wore armor painted red with three yellow lines. These glittering blue-garbed guards carried lead-headed quarterstaves, and Byron heard the sticks slash and stab, probing the garden greenery. A sergeant bawled, "Keep looking! That fox Rayner ain't been flushed yet!"

"He must'a burned by now! And which bloomin' idiot set fire to both faces of the house, anyway?"

Crawling under shrubbery, getting whipped and snicked by branches, still a bell rang in Byron's mind. Ah, that was the significance! If Rayner had tipped over a candle, or a cook had been careless at the stove, then the fire would have engulfed the center of the house, or one side. Not two places at once and not outside.

But, Tongue of Timur, why had the *bishop* fired Rayner's house? Committed deliberate arson? Granted, cardsmithing was banned by the church, but so were prostitution and smuggling and lottery games. Yet the church didn't fire whorehouses and docks and betting parlors.

Byron slithered under a rose bush, gagged on a thorny branch across his throat, pried it free. Against the damp earth, away from the fire, he was chilly.

Because they impressed their very spirits into magic-making, cardsmiths were always cold. Occasionally they froze to death.

His thoughts jumbled. It didn't make sense! Only a week before, the bishop *herself* had visited Rayner's house several times, been welcomed as a guest! Now she burned his house and ordered Rayner captured? What was going on? Was Byron snarled in some sour business deal?

Never mind, he thought. The guards were still hunting, and he had to escape. It'd be painful to be collared by angry guards with lead-heavy staves.

Blundering on skinned hands and bruised knees, gauging his path by shouts, and hoping half a burning house didn't crash on him, he wriggled through the gardens for the rear. A tiny gate in the wall gave onto an alley that ran towards the river. At the docks, he could board a ship and barter passage to anywhere with his hoard of magic cards.

Sliding under the knotted branches of a rhodo-dendron bush, Byron found the stone wall, scaled it and dropped into the alley. Checking his back trail, he saw the burning house lighting the night sky; but here overhanging trees and shrubs admitted only dabs of orange light. It was planned that way, actually: Rayner had a public and a private entrance for customers to choose. A few jigs and jogs, step-hopping with one shoe and one sock, and he'd be gone—

Two huge shapes flowed from the darkness to bracket him. Muscular hands grabbed his upper arms, which were neither great nor muscular, and hoisted him off the ground.

Someone small peered close. Byron glimpsed a

hooked nose, smelled garlic. He knew this man. Horacio, a penny-ante cardsmith, a competitor, a backstabber.

"It's not Rayner!" rasped Horacio. "It's a lousy apprentice! But tear his clothes off, see if he's got cards! It was magic crumbled that wall!"

Byron struggled, began to protest, froze.

Horacio added, "Then cut his throat!"

Chapter 2

Panic doused Byron like a bucket of ice water. *Cut his throat?*

Not here! he wanted to scream. Not now! Not me! I'm too young! I haven't done anything! I don't even *know* anything! Please—

A silky coo made all four men start. "And not hear what he has to say?" A woman's voice, oddly composed in this hellish living nightmare.

Horacio jumped like a spooked fox. The two thugs plucked weapons from their belts—clubs or long knives, Byron wasn't sure which. They still clamped his arms. Byron guessed they were sailors, for they smelled of salt and tar, sweat and rum. The apprentice scuffed his feet—one shod and one with holey hose— ready to run if they let go. . . .

Before anyone could move, Byron saw a silver flash, long but no wider than his thumb. A rapier blade. Old Horacio yelped, then screamed and fell down howling. The swordswoman had pinked his leg and put him out of the fight.

With a jolt of inspiration, Byron suddenly knew what she was, if not who. Maybe he'd get out of this predicament alive. Still hung up by both arms, he half-stepped to shift his weight. But even distracted by the swordswoman, the sailors pinned Byron close.

One grunted, "Cosh him, Ned."

The apprentice was flung backwards against the garden's stone wall. His head banged stone despite his hat and thick hair and ivy. The blow rattled him, made stars dance and wink before his eyes. A club whacked his shoulder. Byron gasped as if his collarbone had snapped.

Fortunately, his spinning head had lolled to one side, otherwise he would have been bashed on the crown. Despite his fog, he groaned and slumped down the wall. Evidently the sailors were fooled, for both let go.

They turned to fight a whirlwind of steel.

Byron saw the woman's outline in dabs of yellow-orange light cast by Rayner's burning house: she was neither tall nor slim, flamboyantly dressed in a wide hat and cape. The blade flashed again, and steel slapped aside a sailor's knife. "Me hand!"

The other sailor kept his distance, planted one foot forward, cranked the knife over his shoulder. He was going to throw it, Byron realized. Sprawled on his duff against rustling ivy, the apprentice felt heavy-headed, more clumsy than ever. His vision was patchy from his head caroming off the wall. Yet he kicked at the sailor to spoil his aim. He thumped the man's knee, but the knife was already flying.

A *clang!* resounded in the alley, and the knife pinwheeled into the darkness. Damn, thought Byron, she was canny to knock a spinning blade out of the dark air!

The sailors hefted clubs. "Rush her, Ned!"

Light as a deer, the swordswoman skipped backwards, landed in a patch of light. Byron saw red stripes and a yellow–flowered vest, colorful as a pirate. Something long and curved and clunky bobbled behind her hip. Then she bounced out of the light and was gone. The sailors stumbled into the circle and cast about stupidly, like fools in a stage play.

Byron realized she'd shown herself deliberately to lure the sailors on, for now she returned.

An arm and blade, and no more, flickered from the shadows. The rapier thrust through the second sailor's side just above the hip. He gasped at the cold slice. The blade travelled on to pink the first sailor, Ned, in the belly, and he dropped back in horror, clapping his hand over the wound.

Ned grew furious at these beestings from the dark. Howling, he dodged around the blade and charged the mysterious woman.

She kept her head, even leaving her blade lodged in the first sailor's side. As Ned charged around his comrade, she plied the rapier as a lever. The stricken man hissed as the blade through his gut wheeled him neatly as a team of oxen.

Stunned, trying to climb off the ivy, Byron wanted to whistle. A rapier was only sharp along its final six inches. Otherwise, the blade was dull; designed for neat surgical jabs, not slashing or hacking, which would only break the thin tempered steel. Byron had seen many swordfights in the streets and at fairs, and this swordswoman knew the sport to perfection. With a single blade, she pinned one man helpless, plied him as a shield, and threatened his partner.

The punctured sailor whined like a mouse caught in hawk talons. "Ned, back—off!" But Ned was angry. Swinging his club, he charged wide to circle behind.

The swordswoman's whistle pierced the air. Staggering to his feet, clutching the ivy wall for support, Byron wondered what she whistled up. It sounded like a summons for a dog—

The ground thumped in rhythm, then a hairy form like a werewolf exploded from the shadows. A brindled hound big as a man drove two huge paws into Ned's chest. Long white teeth snapped inches from his face as he fell backwards with the dog atop. When his back slammed the alley, the dog mashed its slobbery jaws against the sailor's. Knife and club had gone flying when the monster appeared. Ned could only grab for the dog's studded collar, but the animal twisted from side to side, snapping hard enough to sever cordwood, and the sailor flung his hands clear.

Another whistle, and the dog hopped off the sailor's chest, making him grunt explosively. Twisting her sword and shoving, the swordswoman toppled the wounded sailor onto Ned. He fell gasping and bleeding.

In all this time, Byron had barely collected his wits and regained his feet. Now a strong hand grabbed his upper arm. The wraithlike swordswoman hissed, "Come on!"

Byron was glad to go anywhere. Stumbling, he aimed for the blackest stretch of alley. A hot long shape jounced at his side, the giant dog. It had been silent while fighting, he noted, but now gave a gurgled query.

What did it want or warn? Byron wondered. Then

he tripped over a sack of bones and sprawled again.

Horacio, the ancient cardsmith, forgotten with his pierced leg, shrilled. "Stop! I want those cards!"

The swordswoman hoisted Byron upright—she was far stronger than he—and dragged him down the alley. But from the corner of his eye Byron saw a tiny flash.

He knew that sign. A magic card igniting.

Something cold and sticky clung to their faces, their hands, their legs. Byron was trapped head to toe, stuck tight. The dog snarled, the swordswoman hissed.

Behind them, Horacio crawled one-legged to the sailors, pounded them with bony fists. "Get them! Or do without your pay!" The bleeding sailors groaned as they fumbled for lost weapons.

Byron cursed as the cloying stickiness gummed his lips and tongue. Tasting, he knew what it was: a giant artificial spiderweb. He'd seen them before. This one bridged the alley, snarled in branches above and on stone walls and an iron gate. The magic-trained part of his mind noted it was a clever spell—not an actual spiderweb, but something similar probably woven from leaves or moss on the walls. You can't conjure something from nothing, he'd heard Rayner intone a thousand times, you can only convert one thing into another.

The swordswoman puffed as she slashed at the web, but it was more spun glop than sticky rope. When pulled, the strands snapped into wads of gum that coated them in lumps. Her blade would be coated like a taffy stick, Byron knew. Even the dog was caught, though it clawed massive feet to tug and shove in all directions.

Behind them, one sailor crawled on all fours, useless, but Ned gathered knives in both hands, murder on his face. Horacio slapped his back. "Kill all three and hurry!" The roaring bonfire of a house beyond the stone wall cast a macabre light on the old man's skeletal capering.

Where were the damned bishop's guards when you needed them? Byron wondered.

"Do something!" The swordswoman panted as she yanked at something at her belt. "Hold them off a second!"

"All right! I've got one trick!"

"One?" she bleated.

Trussed and half-hanging, Byron strained to suck the fingers of his right hand. The fake spiderweb tasted stale and peppery as moldy bread. Puffing on his fingers to dry them, he snapped them hard.

Flames danced on his fingertips. By their meager light, he glimpsed the swordswoman's round flat face and dark eyes. Twisting his wrist, Byron lit the spiderwebbing around his arm. Dry and musty, it sparkled like fireworks. Tiny blue flames crackled as he reached to free his companion. Better she got loose than he: she was dangerous and they needed help. Swiping with fire, he whisked the webbing off her shoulders. At the same time, he clenched his back against an anticipated knife thrust.

With a grunt, the fighter tore her head and chest free of the web. Leaving her sword dangling in the foul threads, she wrenched the long curve from her hip, cranked the object with a racheting sound.

Ned yowled as he charged, slashing the air with two knives.

Shouting back in a foreign tongue, the swordswoman

pulled a trigger. A pinwheel of sparks blossomed in the dark.

Her heavy pistol barked with a *ka-plam!* Ned was blown off his feet as if by an invisible wind.

Wondering, head ringing from the close explosion, Byron swiped with his burning hand to free himself, then waved near the dog, hoping he didn't ignite its fur. Huffing with pain, he snuffed his burning fingers against his breeches.

Cursing the fallen Ned, skinny Horacio shrilled and kicked the crawling sailor in his pierced hip. The man collapsed and Horacio shrilled louder.

By then, Byron and the swordswoman and monster dog were far down the alley.

"Where to?" she panted.

"I know—a place," the apprentice puffed. He saved his breath for running.

Warily they wound through moonlit Waterholm. They stuck to shadows, following Byron and the big dog's sniffing nose. Byron looked for pursuit but saw none in the silvery streets. Down to the river they slunk, then across one of many bridges. Passing from the rich side of town to the poor side, the prince's soldiers didn't detain them, assuming they were servants going home or to drink. Only if they'd tried to enter the rich side would they be questioned.

Below the bridge the River Wis thundered in its stone channel. North, the famous waterfall that named the city plunged eternally, shining white and alive by moonlight. Across the river, sloping up again, the streets were narrower and littered with garbage and filth, sleeping pigs and dogs and humans.

Pausing after trudging up steep cobbles, Byron gazed west. Past sparking chimneys and candlelit windows, far across the river, he saw that Rayner's grand house still burned. Numerous small fires ringed it; neighbors' outhouses and trees, probably. At this vantage point, many citizens stood with jacks in their hands and watched.

Slump-shouldered and staring, Byron wondered how he felt about his master's ruin. Curiously, he felt little. He'd lived there three years, befriended the cooks and maids. But Rayner had been a hard taskmaster, and his jealous mistresses had resented the apprentices, who in turn badgered one another, with Byron at the bottom. Now the servants would find new work while the mistresses were pitched out in the cold, and the apprentices were—what? Escaped? Crisped? Captured by bishop's guards?

Again: Why had they been attacked by the bishop? And why hadn't the prince's soldiers stopped them? As one of the richest (if cheapest) men in the city, Rayner had paid plenty in taxes. But the soldiers hadn't come to their aid. Was the prince in on the trouble, whatever it was?

But better worry about himself first, he cautioned. He was out in the cold, out of work, and perhaps hunted. Or perhaps not. But he could hardly ask a guard or soldier if he wanted to capture him. So how—

He groaned. Even thinking tired him.

"Are you moonstruck? Or will you stand here all night?" asked the swordswoman.

"What? Oh, no. Come on." He turned down an alley between two tilting houses, his holey hose seeping cold ooze between his toes. Under a rickety staircase, he rapped a signal on a door. A panel slid open. Steamy air flavored with wine and laughter gushed out. Byron couldn't recall the current password. "Uh, it's me, Byron from House Rayner."

The door unlatched and swung open. Byron squished inside on his soggy foot. The swordswoman jerked the door wider to admit her huge dog.

By a red lantern, the doorkeeper sneered at their disheveled clothing. They'd swabbed off some dirt and spiderwebs at a public fountain, but were still gummy and grimy. Then he rocked back on his high stool, squeaked, "No—no dogs!"

The swordswoman pushed past. "I'll buy her a beer."

From the top of a staircase, the cellar was packed, hot and steamy and noisy as a public bath. The far side sported a rude bar with red-glass lanterns. The floor was uneven flagstones jammed with plank tables and benches like a student's dining hall. Many roisterers were students who gulped weak ale and argued the day's lessons. Card players gambled and argued over bets and rules. Fops in flashy clothes cradled whores in their arms, while a few weary workmen nursed beers. And of course, there was a clot of cardsmiths' apprentices in black, most of whom Byron knew but didn't want to greet.

This was a card den, one of many scattered throughout the city. Illegal, like all aspects of cardwork, but thriving because of it.

He shouldered to a corner table, asked the patrons to slide along the bench, and collapsed against the wall. But the swordswoman gestured at him with a hooked thumb.

"What?" Byron croaked. Talking made him realize

he was parched from breathing smoke and running. It hurt to say that one word. He waved frantically at a barmaid.

The swordswoman plucked him up. "I get the wall. I don't like folks behind me."

Too tired to argue, Byron shifted around the table. He'd lost half a night's sleep, squeaked through narrow escapes and death threats. Temporarily safe and packed amongst hot bodies, he was gloriously warm, and only the promise of a drink kept him awake. Yet he couldn't sleep. He had to rest and run, or else answer questions in the church's dungeons. So much for the glamorous trade of cardsmithing, he sighed.

"I'm Cerise." The swordswoman signalled her dog under the table's end. "It means 'Cherry,' and spare me the jokes. Who are you?"

"Byron." He hoped the drink would come soon, and that he had the strength to drink it, and didn't drown by falling in face-first. He hoped, too, this woman didn't pester him with questions. "It means— I don't know what it means. Apprentice, uh, ex-apprentice to Rayner, late of House Rayner. Late house, too, come to think of it."

"Your master is dead?"

Byron jerked his head up. Laughter and gossip and shrieks and catcalls made a windstorm, so they had privacy after a fashion. "Uh, yes. But I shouldn't have said it. I'm so tired I'm slipping."

Cerise shrugged. "If Rayner's house burns flat and he doesn't show to stir the ashes, the whole city will assume he's dead. But did he die in the fire?"

Byron's initial slip made him wary. Never give anything away, was a magic-worker's first rule. "I'm not sure . . ."

She cocked an eyebrow. "Sure he didn't freeze to death?"

Byron squinted. "I didn't say that."

"You didn't deny it, either."

For the first time, Byron studied his strange companion.

Cerise was from the east, it was clear, from beyond the mountains. She was middling height and stocky, all muscle. Her face was round, her cheekbones flat, her hair straight and black and cropped at the shoulders, her eyes slanted at the corners. She carried blood from the Shinyar steppes or Kirthan frontier, he guessed. A long way from home. She wore a crimson shirt and yellow–flowered vest laced tight, a dark cape, red-striped pants, tall boots, a wide hat.

"You're a cardmaster," he said.

"You're a cardsmith."

Byron didn't argue. He wore the traditional costume of heavy clothes even in spring and summer: black round hat above a black doublet above black breeches above black hose above (one) black shoe. His hair, by contrast, was bright blond, cut in a bowl with shaved sides. As cardsmiths rose in prestige, they added silver thread to their outfits, but Byron didn't own so much as a bone button.

Cerise startled him by taking his hand. "Here's the proof. Anyone can dress in black, but your hands are like ice. And stained with chemicals and burns. But how did you ignite your fingertips? I've never seen that before."

Byron gauged how much to tell her—nothing would be best. But it was common knowledge a card*smith* was someone who made cards, as a tinsmith made punched-tin lamps, and a blacksmith made ironware. Except cardsmiths impressed their own life force into cards to bind the magic. As such, they were notoriously cold all the time, even in summer before blazing fires. He wondered again why anyone chose the profession. Cardsmithing looked exciting from the outside, but was actually soul-threatening drudgery. Still, only one person in ten thousand could harness magic, so men and women worked at it, and prospered . . . if they didn't die, or worse.

As for his snapping fire, that was unique. Only Byron could do it, and he didn't know how.

Cerise, on the other hand, was a card*master*, one of the flamboyant vagabonds who wielded cards for themselves and others, in small games of chance or the lords' Great Games. Most were also weapon masters to protect the cards and wealth they garnered.

But sitting opposite the table, cardsmith and cardmaster, Byron was again struck by the oddness of it. Cardsmiths were black, cold, and dour. Cardmasters were splashy, gay, and extravagant. The trades were linked by magic, but the practitioners were as different as peacocks and pigeons.

Their beer came in foaming pewter mugs. The barmaid, bosom prominent above a leather bodice, smiled at Byron. Cerise put down pennies while her free hand stroked the barmaid's rump through her thin dress. The woman absently slapped the hand away as if shooing flies, and departed. Byron watched the exchange with bemusement. Cardmasters supposedly kept a flashy oversexed lifestyle, too.

He sucked down beer but was still thirsty. He wanted to slink behind the bar and slide into a vat, soak up fluid through his pores like a toad. But he could only rest a moment before departing. To cover his agitation, and keep awake, he asked, "What's your dog's name?"

Cerise held her stein below the table so the dog could slurp ale. "Magog."

"Magog the Dog?"

A black glance flared under black brows, and Byron backpedaled. "Good name. Magog was a giant in legend, wasn't he?"

"Right. Now a legendary dog. Except she's a bitch."

"Uh . . . what kind of dog?"

Cerise pulled the jack away. The dog's tongue followed hungrily. Her shaggy head hit the underside of the table and knocked the planks up a foot. "A wolfhound. We used them at home in packs to destroy wolves. There aren't many wolves left."

"I believe you." Byron watched the dog yawn and flop on the stone floor with a crash. The dog was brindled with short curly hair, wore a studded collar four inches wide. The dog probably outweighed Byron.

Cerise still hadn't drunk. She drew her heavy pistol and tipped beer down the barrel. The pistol was long as Byron's forearm, chased with silver over dark wood, with a curious wheel mechanism on the side. She told him, "Wheellock pistol. They're new, expensive. Instead of slowmatches you have to light, you crank this clockwork spring and the wheel spins and spits sparks into a pan. More reliable. Ignites eight times out of ten in good weather. But the damned gunpowder corrodes the steel barrel if you don't flush it right away."

Having filled the barrel with beer, she poured black slush on the floor. It took three more flushes to scour the barrel. "In battle, the barrel gets so fouled you can't insert a bullet, so musketeers piss down the barrels."

The male ones, anyway, thought Byron idly. Machinery and weapons didn't interest him. He had enough trouble understanding magic. He watched Cerise dip a rag into her beer and wipe the pistol's pan. "You can drink that stuff too, you know."

"It tastes like dishwater. Back in Kirth, we serve our beer in oak jacks because it eats through pewter mugs."

Byron wanted to sigh. Why did travellers always malign the local beer? It tasted fine to him. He could have drunk a waterfall of it.

Cerise signalled for two more. The barmaids must have consulted, for a different woman served them. When Cerise stroked her backside, this barmaid smiled. The cardmaster threw half a crown on the table and chuckled, "Later." The barmaid took it and sashayed off.

The second beer set Byron's head buzzing. He'd been through a lot today—tonight—and cried for rest. But he couldn't nod off with a treasure trove of magic cards down his shirt. He had to crawl off and hole up. But where? And roaming the streets meant dodging the bishop's guards. He wasn't safe anywhere. He felt like a sparrow trapped in a storm and surrounded by crows.

"Yoo hoo." Cerise tapped the top of his head. "I saved your life tonight, you know."

"I know," Byron mumbled. He knew more was coming.

"So pay up. Hand over those cards."

Chapter 3

Byron stared at his strange tablemate. "What cards?" Three years of watching Rayner and keeping secrets had taught him how to dicker.

Cerise stared right back. "The ones you grabbed before the fire got them. You were the last one out, you must have been doing something. And that old goat said to strip your cards."

"Well," Byron lied, "I didn't get any. They were locked in a chest bolted to the floor and I couldn't find the key. It was smoky. And Rayner didn't keep many cards in the shop. He fashioned cards to order then delivered them to customers. Keeping cards around attracts *thieves*."

If Cerise took umbrage at the last word, she hid it. She purred, "I could take them, you know."

"Not here." Byron shook his head. "I've got a dozen friends within earshot. We apprentices stick together."

Cerise sniffed at the crowd. "My dog could eat their livers before they blundered off their benches." She changed tactics. "You've no gratitude for my saving your life?"

Byron shrugged, but thought fast. Was she after only his cards, or something else? Should he stay or bolt? "I'll show gratitude. I'll say thank you. Thank you. Why did you save my life anyway? For that matter, what were you doing in that alley?"

The swordswoman eased back against the wall, surveyed the boisterous sweating crowd. She did that constantly, Byron noted, as if she expected an enemy to leap up any second: probably it had happened before. While she shrugged her cape off, Byron wrapped his tighter around his shoulders. Cerise said, "I saw the fire and was curious. Lots of people came to watch."

"So . . ." Byron scratched his nose, found it crusted with a scab, though he didn't remember getting scratched. "Why not stand in the street instead of slinking around in a back alley?"

Cerise's Oriental eyelids drooped until her eyes were black slits. "All right, I'll give you something. I was on my way to see your master, Rayner."

"What? In the middle of the night?"

A shrug. "Magic works at any hour. He's rumored to have—special cards, much in demand."

"Piffle," Byron sniffed. "Rumors are thicker than fleas in Waterholm, and cardsmiths always have 'special cards.' "

But Rayner had acted queer lately. He'd spent nights alone, slaving over new magic kept secret from his apprentices. Rayner had gone out to consult other cardsmiths and their libraries, something rare in a competitive trade. And the bishop herself had visited a little while ago, something unheard of. The apprentice thought of Rayner frozen solid, sheathed in ice, hunched over a card powerful enough to die for. He shook his head to dispel the picture. "It's just talk."

"Talk on everyone's lips." Cerise didn't waste time in argument. "So what are your plans now?"

"Good question," Byron slipped. "Uh . . . I'll probably find work with another cardsmith . . ."

Cerise shook her head. "Not with the bishop's guards hunting you. And the prince's. Some of his guards grabbed an apprentice and handed her to the churchmen, so the prince and bishop have struck some deal. With you in the pot."

"Why didn't you tell me that before?" Byron pouted.

" 'Never give anything away,' right? And beware, for the night is young. Once the sots in this room hear there's a reward for your capture, how many friends will you have then?"

Byron grimaced as she echoed his thoughts. He huffed like a popped balloon. "I don't know what the bishop wants, but I hope not to find out. Once in her dungeons, her guards will damn me to hellfire while stomping on my fingers. So—it's the open road for me, I suppose."

Suddenly the possibility of bartering magic cards for a ship's passage seemed less likely. The prince's customs officers could easily check each ship's manifest and passenger list. Byron would have despaired, but he was too fuddled. He had a fortune in cards and temporary freedom, but no idea of his troubles, and no clue what to do.

Cerise cut into his thoughts. "Why not team up with me?"

"Hunh?"

The swordswoman patted her dozing dog. "Think. It's not the first time a cardsmith and cardmaster had paired up to seek their fortune. You manufacture cards, I wield them in games. I protect you, you provide for me, we both get rich. And I pay in gold."

Byron piffed. "I've *seen* gold, but never touched any. Rayner made me fight the seagulls for my supper, almost."

Cerise reached into a pocket in her wide belt, threw a coin down with a clunk. "How's that for starters? It's yours."

Byron slapped his hand over the coin lest anyone see. Carefully he peered in dim red light. It was gold, a full crown worth a thousand pennies. One side was stamped with a big-nosed king's profile, the other a spreadwinged eagle. "I can *keep* this?"

Cerise scritched a brindled head. "It's yours. A symbol of good faith."

Byron squirmed. This much "good faith" could buy him body and soul if he weren't careful. Reluctantly he pushed the coin back. "No, I'm sorry. I only take what I earn." That was true. Nights, after Rayner let him off, he'd mucked out privies and stables to earn beer and clothes money, when he could have easily filched supplies from Rayner's workshop and pawned them. But he'd maintained his pride and dignity. He had to: it was all he owned.

Cerise stopped scratching her dog, played with her beer stein, clearly nonplussed by this penniless apprentice refusing gold. "All right. I understand pride. I've got too much myself—it gets in the way of common sense. Tell you what, could I hire you?"

More dickering, Byron groaned. But he'd keep his options open. "Maybe. What for?"

Reaching into another pocket, she extracted a thin square pouch, withdrew a pasteboard card big as her hand. "I acquired some cards recently but forgot to ask their tokens. I'll pay you to tell me."

Byron peered from under his eyebrows, a habit he'd picked up from Rayner. " 'Acquired'? Cards are useless unless you know the tokens. They're just paint on paper. Anyone *buying* a card would be an idiot not to ask for the token."

Cagey, the swordswoman nodded. "True. But I won these in a game—"

"Stole them?" Byron interjected.

"All right," she sighed. "I took them off a dead man. And there was no way—"

"Did you kill him?"

Her temper flared. It was quick: Byron must remember that. "What business is it of yours?"

"Just curious. If we're partners, I needs know my partner's methods."

Her eyes slitted again. "Who said we're partners?"

"My question was first. Did you kill him?"

"No. Someone else did. A jealous husband burst into the den and hurled a bomb. People dove for cover, and I swept the table. The bomb killed the other players, and the husband, so I don't know what I've got."

"*Do* you kill people?" Byron might as well clear that up now.

"Are you always this curious?"

"Yes. Do you?"

She stifled a sigh. "No, mother, not if I can help it. Killing folks earns you a reputation as a mad dog. You make few friends and little money. And cardmasters are less likely to duel if they'll be killed and not just wounded. Recall, I only pinked those two sailors to stop them. I was forced to shoot the crazed one."

She had daring but sense, Byron thought, cool capability in spades. Perhaps she would make a good partner. . . .

He held out his hands. "Give me the cards. Let's see what you have."

Six cards Cerise didn't understand. Bunching his black cloak across the table as a partial screen and cupping his hands, the cardsmith studied them.

The first card was standard-sized, big as his palm, black with a trio of brass bells. Byron wet his fingertip, smudged some black paint, touched it to his tongue. "Tumult, a great din, or noise. Probably sounds like the rolling of war drums. The spell might confuse or deafen an enemy. But you'd have to pitch it amongst them and not your own troops." He handed it back.

"How do you know?" She didn't doubt, was just curious.

He showed the black fingertip. "Bells are always noise, but black signals a warning or destruction: these aren't marriage or victory bells. And these gold chevrons in the corners suggest military badges of an army."

"So, what's the token?"

"The paint has brass tarnish mixed in—you can taste it—so probably triggers when you rub it against something brass or bronze." The swordswoman sniffed the card, smelt nothing, folded it away.

The second card showed strawberries in the center and vines for the border. Byron held it to his forehead, flicked it to Cerise. "Healing. Some folks believe strawberries thicken the blood. The token is probably something you put on strawberries—milk or cream, maybe sugar. They're all healing substances in themselves."

"But how do you know it's potent?"

"Healers are warm, at least body temperature. And I'm always cold, remember?"

The third card was made of thin wood and painted like a dollhouse door. The card artist had even punched a tiny keyhole. Byron flexed the card, almost snapped it. "Supposed to be House Protection, I'd guess. Glued to the front door, it should keep the door locked to enemies, or jam in the frame if someone bashes it, or howl for help or something. But it's a fake. Too lightweight and dead. You'd sell this to a nervous homeowner who didn't know magic and had no way to test it." Cerise kept it anyway, no doubt to pass on.

The next card made Byron gasp, and he dropped it. It was red and painted with a gray rat's head. Gingerly, the cardsmith picked it up by the edges and stood up. Cerise asked, "Hey, where are you going?"

Byron didn't answer. Threading the packed room, careful not to touch anyone, he crossed to the fireplace and tossed the card in. It curled and smoked, the paint burst into flame. He jabbed a poker to make sure it burned completely, then stirred the ashes. Sitting down, he took her beer. "How long have you carried *that* around?"

"A few weeks. Why? What the hell is it?"

"Plague. Touch something dead or rotten to it, a piece of meat or a maggot or worm, and it'd kill everyone in this room."

"Oh." She thought a moment. "Sure it wasn't a

fake just to scare someone, or blackmail them?"

Byron killed her beer. "I didn't get close enough to find out. But generally, no, people who fashion black decks—decks for death—don't make spurious plague cards."

He frowned over the remaining two cards. One showed a severed hand on a light blue background. "Probably an Invisible Hand, blue denoting invisibility, like thin clouds against the sky. A hand of mana, magical energy, lets you perform a job at a distance. Get a kite out of a tree, unlock a jail cell, strangle someone. But the token . . . I don't know. Fingernail polish maybe? Or a gold or silver ring? I don't know."

He pondered the last one a long time. Bordered in grainy yellow-white, the center was blue with three brown fish. "Hmm. . . . These are freshwater minnows. The border has sand mixed in it. They say in the desert, water will sometimes mysteriously appear and disappear, and it always has minnows in it. So probably it's a Water spell, but . . ." He pored over the blue paint, scratched with a dirty fingernail. "No, I think it's guised."

"Guised? You mean trapped?"

"No. Trapped is boobytrapped to rebound against the wielder. This is definitely a Water spell: water would gush out of this card like a fountain. But it's only paint-deep. There's another spell etched underneath, I think. I wonder why . . ." Frowning, concentrating, Byron leaned close.

Suddenly a demon face—tiny eyes and red peeling skin—popped out of the card. Long ragged teeth snapped at his nose.

"Gaahhh!!!" Byron shrieked and reared back, thumped someone on a bench behind. The demon laughed and ducked its tiny head back into the card, gone.

"What the hell was *that*?" Cerise frowned while others craned to look. Someone muttered about drunks and hallucinations.

Byron flicked the card on the table. Fiends were hounding him during waking hours? Or was he asleep on his feet? Or were they just imagination? But if so, why imagine them?

"Hey!" Cerise called. "Are you deaf? Did a trap try to get you?"

"What trap?" Byron snapped. "Relax! Demons aren't after *you*! Uh, where was I? Oh, there's no trap. It's guised. There's probably something valuable hidden under the water. A sunken treasure or something. You'll have to trigger it and see."

"How? And what's this rubbish about demons?"

"Nothing. Forget the demons. Uh, just apply water, probably. Spit on it and you'll get gallons of water in your lap."

Byron's eyes roved the shadows for squat forms with glittering mischievous eyes. No, this was stupid: he was just dreaming with his eyes open. Still, he'd never dreamt of demons until last night. And now they were following him? Why? Since Rayner died? Had his master dreamed of demons? Had Byron had inherited his demons, like fleas?

Cerise sorted the five cards into her deck. All cardsmiths were crazy. She pushed across the gold coin, but pouted, "I expected clear answers, not 'probably this and maybe that.' "

Beset on all sides, Byron slumped. "Come back in a thousand years: maybe we'll understand magic by then. Anyone who claims to know magic is a liar. It's a new science and inexact, like mixing gunpowder. If cardsmithing were as ancient and simple as making toffees, there'd be card shops on every corner. Besides which, magic has different flavors in different lands. Here in Waterholm we've got rivers and streams up to our butts. Who'd waste time making a water card? Some desert sage fashioned that last one. And—"

"Cease!" Cerise objected. "You earned your pay, unless I discover you guessed wrong. But for the offer—forget it. I don't want a partner who gibbers about demons coming out of the walls."

Wrung out, Byron just shrugged. "Fine, swell. I don't want a partner who pours good beer down a gun barrel."

"Fair enough. Thanks for your time." The cardmaster clucked to her dog and, cape and weapons swinging, pressed through the throng. At the bar, she hooked the waist of the smiling barmaid, and the two women climbed the dim stairs. The dog galumphed after.

It was time Byron left, too. But when he tried to rise, he couldn't. Nerves, exhaustion, haunting, and ale had done him in. Making sure his doublet was laced tight and tails tucked in, the loose cards and pouch against his stomach, he cradled head on arms. Just a short rest, he promised himself, and he'd sneak out the city gates before dawn. . . .

Under a blazing sun in a harsh sandy desert, Byron was warm for once. But so were the demons.

Dozens ringed him. They were even uglier in eye-squinting daylight: gray scaly or sunburned red or blue-veined or bleeding. One demon had arms twisted back near his shoulder blades, as if he'd been tied

in a knot. Another showed ribs on the outside and
a beating heart. One was furred like a weasel, another
plated like a rattlesnake, one skinless. One lolled a
warty tongue down its chest. All of them laughed
huskily at the cardsmith in their center.

The demons hooted and waved branches from a
dead tree or switches of cactus. As Byron retreated,
seeking a way out of the circle, a demon swatted
him with a branch. Thorns stung his back through
his black clothes. Whirling, he was smacked alongside
the head. Demons chortled as he howled. When
he grabbed his head, a lizard-headed fiend jabbed
his belly, the sharp wood pricking skin. Another lashed
his stockinged calves. He still wore only one shoe,
and his unshod foot sank in soft sand that felt like
salt or alkali.

Blundering, stumbling, Byron glimpsed an opening
and lunged for it. The gibbering demons fell back
to let him pass. Byron brushed scales, smelt snake
musk and rank fur, then he was free. To run again.

But amidst mind-rattling panic, his eternal curiosity
threw out a plaintive question. Why let him pass?
Were they deliberately herding him? If so, where?
Why? What did they want?

Slipping and sliding, prodded and pricked by sticks
and switches, the cardsmith lurched across unending
dunes under a brassy sun. From the tops of dunes,
he saw nothing but more desolation. A flat stretch
spotted with rocks promised easier footing, so he
steered for it. Anything to get out of clinging sand
that made his legs ache.

The demons paced him, hobbling and hopping,
sometimes rolling, whapping him with thorny clubs
and laughing at the sport. The apprentice reached

the shale stretch and tripped along it. But rocks
skidding underfoot were treacherous, promising a
broken ankle, and painful to his unshod foot.

Blinded by sun and diamond-hard reflections, he
could barely make out a dark crevice splitting the
earth ahead. Maybe if he ducked in there, he could
hide. Keep them from surrounding him, anyway.
Perhaps wriggle through some hole and escape. But
the demons saw the crevice and rushed to block
him. Panting, but encouraged, Byron put on a burst
of speed.

But near the edge of the crevice, he realized he
couldn't see bottom. This wasn't some rain-cut gully.

Sliding on shale, he tried to brake. Horny hands
grabbed for him. The crumbly edge fractured under
their weight, gave way.

Spinning end over end, spattered by sand, with
demons littering the air, Byron tumbled into the
canyon.

The sun was cut off, and the chasm darkened.
Far down, Byron saw bottom. Jagged rocks.

The last sound he heard was his bones shattering. . . .

The cellar door flew open with a crash.

"Repent, sinners!" A voice screeched, "You who
would dabble with the Dark Ones' designs! The hour
has come—*oof!*"

A dark-robed cleric topped the rickety stairs. She
held a bible high, as if warding off demons, and
railed against the heathens who gawked up at her.
But only for a moment.

Byron struggled to wake up. He had to tug free:
a long splinter at the table's edge had impaled his
doublet and pricked his belly. The dream thorns,

he thought muzzily. The salt reek was sweat. The sound of his breaking bones must have been the door being smashed. But who . . . ?

With a yelp, the priest was bowled tumbling down the stairs. The room exploded with shouts as a dozen burly bishop's guards thundered into the card den. The stairs shuddered as their boots tromped the treads.

Each guard wore a shiny lobster-tail helmet, breastplate, and tunic of blue emblazoned with the church's symbol: a swell-footed cross with a circle atop, reminiscent of the priests with their flowing robes and tonsured heads. Because church members couldn't spill blood—directly—each guard carried a shoulder-high staff of rowan wood with a bulging head drilled and filled with lead. They couldn't stab or hack you, Byron knew, but they could break every bone you owned.

Pandemonium erupted as patrons screamed and dove in every direction. The bartenders aided the panic by smashing the red-glass lanterns to plunge the room into darkness.

Shoved and butted, Byron scrambled up, assured his cards were safe in his shirt, and faced towards the far stairwell. He'd been in raids on card dens before. They always came at dawn, when the patrons were groggy from a night of drinking and gabbing, and always in spring when the bishop and prince needed to repave the roads. Captives spent the summer in ankle chains resetting cobblestones and dodging the lash.

Cardsmithing, -mastering, -playing, -painting, buying or selling were all banned by the church: a bother to card wielders and a great source of profit to the city elders.

Byron was not graceful, but he did possess an excellent memory. Fixing the invisible stairwell in his mind, he ran for it—straight across the packed tables.

The first leap brought a crash and clatter of mugs. On the second table he trounced someone's hand and almost fell. At the third, he tripped over someone's back, skidded, and regained his feet. But if he'd guessed right . . .

He had. The screaming, shoving, and shouting was horrendous, but he heard cheap clogs clattering up the stairs. Crouching low, he slid off the table and joined the throng that stank of sweat and grease and beer. Jammed on all sides, he wiggled up the stairs like part of some giant centipede.

The first floor was lit by tallow candles in tin sconces on the walls. Most patrons spilled left and right to hop out windows into the muddy alleys. Byron heard their outraged cries as guards stationed outside clobbered the culprits with leaded clubs. But the students and apprentices and cardplayers outnumbered the guards, and their sheer driving weight forced the "bluebellies" back. Someone cheered as a guard caught a drubbing, and someone else threw a flagon.

Byron rounded the corner and disappeared up the next flight of stairs.

It was quieter here, though noise echoed and rebounded. Barmaids and whores and the pub's owners stumbled out of doors. From one door popped Cerise and her monstrous brindled hound. The swordswoman buckled on her baldric of scabbards and holster, whirled on her cape and wide hat. Behind her leaned the barmaid in a blanket. "What's going on?"

"Raid!" Byron panted. "Bishop's guards!"

"Are they after you?"

"Hunh?" Byron gawked. In the excitement, he'd forgotten he was hunted—maybe. "No! They wouldn't break down doors just to get me! I'm not that important!"

The barmaid's blanket drooped as she pointed to a ladder. "They'll round up everybody. Take the western window. It runs across the rooftops. It's how the altar boys come in."

Cerise laughed, grabbed the girl's hair on both sides and kissed her, snatched Byron's arm and slung him towards the ladder. "You heard her! Go!"

Byron grabbed the rungs. "What about your dog?" And why should he worry about it?

Cerise boosted his rump so hard his head banged the trap door. "She can climb ladders better than you! Go!"

But Magog spun towards the black well of the staircase, rumbled deep in her throat.

"Repent!" squeaked a voice, vaguely familiar. From the stairwell popped a blonde head: the young priest who'd been trampled by the guards' onslaught. "Repent, you sinners! The day of judgement—*aaaah!*"

Magog barked like a cannon blast and the priest jumped backwards down the stairs.

But not for long.

"*Halt in the name of the bishop!*" boomed another voice in the stairwell.

Three bluebellies clattered into the hallway, clubs and armor and boots forcing Magog to give way. The last one, a blue-plumed officer, pointed a silver-headed mace at Byron.

"*That's the one we want! Seize him!*"

Chapter 4

Cerise, the fighter, hopped off the ladder and ripped out her rapier. *"Hyaaah!"*

Byron, apprentice cardsmith, scampered up the ladder like a squirrel, pawed the trap door up, and scrambled into the dark attic. He reflected the night's adventures had begun with him falling from the attic down one ladder, and here he was falling up another ladder into an attic. No matter what happened, he thought, the day had to be better.

The attic was stifling hot and jammed with crates and broken furniture, but a clear path down the center led to a shuttered door with a thumblatch. Byron duckwalked down the low passage and wrenched the door open to fresh air.

Outside, dark night remained, but streaks of yellow and red creased the eastern horizon, casting a pale growing glow. A steep ramp nailed with crosspieces for traction sloped to another house peak, met a walkway that angled along the roof, then bridged a narrow alley to intersect other walkways and staircases and tiny balconies and flat roofs. In most of the poor part of town, where ramshackle houses were unsettled and tilting and piled upon each other, the streets and alleys were so narrow neighbors could shake hands across them. It was natural to interconnect the buildings with these catwalks: partly to stay off the muddy and dangerous streets, partly for airy spaces and privacy and relief from the heat, and partly as escape routes from the bishop's guards.

Of course, the guards knew the catwalks too.

No sooner did Byron stick his head out the hole than two guards tried to flatten it with clubs.

"Yipes!" The apprentice whipped back inside to thump against something warm and hairy. The something clamped giant paws on his shoulders and clambered over him—Magog, who really had climbed the ladder. Because the outside passage was small, the dog scampered low. Byron was smothered by a sliding bellyful of hair, had his groin stomped by two heavy paws, his mouth stepped on by a rear paw, then grunted as back legs pushed off from his stomach. Guards yelled as the brute burst from the attic snarling and biting.

Byron rolled over in a flurry of dust and dog hair. Howls on the catwalk turned to screams. What now? Tattered cape entangling his elbows, he crawled back for the ladder. Maybe all the guards had gone outside—

He bumped heads with Cerise vaulting the ladder.

"Ouch!" Byron rocked back. "What are the guards doing?"

"Bleeding." With one brawny arm, she shoved

Byron backwards so his knees collected splinters from the rough boards. She clambered out and reached to slam the trap door . . .

. . . And the priest popped her head up.

Byron noted she had blonde hair cut in a bowl shape like his, but also a churchman's tonsure: a shaved spot on the crown of her head. It was, he concluded, the stupidest haircut he'd ever seen.

"You sinners!" The girl shook her bible. "You traffic in magic, committing all the sins flesh is heir to—"

"Not all, but close!" Cerise slammed the trap door on the girl's tonsure.

"*Ow!*" The girl skidded down the ladder, but her big bible stayed wedged under the trap door.

Cerise swore as the priest popped back up like a groundhog. "Ow! You—jeez, that smarted!—blasphemers! You'll burn in . . . hell and damnation, you gave me a lump!"

In the confined space, Cerise couldn't hold the trap door and wrest the bible from the girl's determined grip, so she bunched the priest's robe in her fist and hauled her bodily into the attic. "If you won't go down, you'll have to come up!"

The swordswoman dragged the squawking priest across her lap and stuffed her in Byron's face. Flustered, Byron backed until he felt cool air on his naked toes.

Besides all his other troubles, he reflected bitterly, he had to look out for another shoe.

Outside, guards' screams were drowned by snapping and snarling. "*Move!*" Cerise boosted the priest's fanny so she bonked heads with Byron. The apprentice had to back onto the catwalk. He hoped no one cracked his spine with a leaden club.

He was just in time to see Magog put the last

guard to flight. The others had leaped over the side, Byron presumed. The lone guard, tunic and sleeves in tatters, pelted down the catwalk ahead of the charging dog, jumped for the roof catwalk, missed his footing in heavy boots, slid howling down the roof, tore loose the gutter, and disappeared with a scream that ended in a thud.

Byron turned on the narrow walk to ask Cerise what to do next, bumped noses with the red-faced priest. "Assaulting the bishop's guards is a sin! You'll be flogged—*ulk!*"

Cerise snagged the girl's robe, yanked her over backwards, put a booted foot on her midriff and stepped over to Byron. The cardmaster nodded thataway. Alternately thumping and padding with one shoe and one bare foot, Byron jogged down the catwalk. Magog waited up ahead, ears perked, tongue lolling, tail wagging. She was having fun.

"It'll be light soon!" Byron panted over his shoulder.

"Should we hole up in an inn, or try to escape the city right away?" Cerise called. "I've got to retrieve my baggage and pony!"

"I don't know!" Byron trailed a hand along a slate roof and skittered along a wobbly board. "If the bishop wants me personally, she could order a house-to-house search!"

Nimble as a cat, Cerise used only her arms for balance as she skipped behind. Byron reached an end gable where six brick chimneys lumped together and tried to guess which way to go. Cerise called, "The bishop probably doesn't want you. You're nothing. She must want your cards. Rayner's cards."

"Thanks for the compliment. Why are you helping me? I thought we weren't partners!"

Cerise shielded her eyes against bright slanting dawnlight, peered across the rooftops. "Someone's got to take care of you."

"Or my cards?"

"Them too. But no more blithering about demons."

"You'd blither too if—never mind. Which way—"

"Get down!"

A heavy hand mashed Byron flat on the walkway. A blob smacked the chimney beside him, rolled down the roof and clunked on the catwalk. Byron hefted the dark ball, found it heavy. "Lead."

More missiles smacked into the chimney. Pressing him flat, Cerise yelled in his ear, "They're sling balls, you idiot! They'll knock your brains out!"

Squatting, she pointed to a distant catwalk. Two buildings over, three men in blue tunics tucked bullets into sling pockets and wound up. The heroes ducked as the balls rocketed and ricocheted, one smacking Byron's back and stinging like a sword thrust. The slingers vaulted a roof and slid down the other side. Closer, they reloaded for another volley.

At the same time, Byron saw a flicker off to the right. From the card den attic boiled more bluebellies. Before them scampered the tonsured priest, now somewhat worse for wear.

Cerise nodded toward the roofline behind them. "That's the only way out."

Byron blinked. "There's no walkway!"

"Can't be helped." Cerise grabbed slates and chinned herself, swung a leg up and over. "It's only three stories! Come on, Magog girl!"

Hearing her name, the dog barked happily and jumped after her mistress, who slid out of sight with a whoop. The dog, aware something was wrong, yelped in sudden fright.

Byron yelled, "Wait—" A sling ball clipped his ear and smacked into the chimney. "Wait for me!"

He scrambled on the slippery slates, up, over— and out of control.

Byron watched Cerise fly off the roof; she gave a triumphant shriek while Magog gave a surprised yip.

Dragging his hand down slates to slow his plunge, Byron had a stomach-flipping moment airborne. Then he crashed on wood.

Cerise was plunked beside him, hands sprawled. Magog staggered to four feet. Scarcely believing their luck, Byron peered around groggily. They'd landed on a balcony. Flowerpots lined a low railing. Behind them was a window where a goodwife, caught preparing breakfast, goggled. The smells of brewing tea and frying bacon were overpowered by a stronger smell welling from below. For the moment, Byron couldn't identify the odor.

"My, that was fun!" Cerise babbled. "Not that I want to do it again—oops!"

Hammered by three falling bodies, the balcony creaked. Byron gawked as the platform pulled away from the building with a steady screech of nails. "We better get—"

"Inside!" Cerise cut him off. She grabbed the edge of the window, shooed the goodwife back. "Ma'am? If we might enter your kitchen, please? Oh, come now, we won't hurt you! Hey, put down that knife!"

Gingerly, Byron inched towards the window. Magog, disturbed by the pinging of nails, pushed after her mistress. Her shaggy rump knocked Byron aside, and he slid towards the outside railing. The balcony squeaked louder. "Cerise, hurry—"

A skidding and clattering sounded from the slate roof above. Byron looked up at a flutter of blue skirts and white petticoats, then the blonde priest crashed in his lap. She chided, "Ha, caught you! Now you'll pay for—*What's that?*"

That was the sound of the balcony quitting the wall. The priest's final weight was too much. Flowerpots tilted into space and disappeared. The floor slowly became a wall. Arms full of female, Byron slid into the railing. It broke like matchwood.

All four fell.

Byron had time to wonder what lay below, then recalled what the strong odor was.

Oh, yes. Manure.

They plowed into a mountain of horse droppings, feet first, and sank to their waists. Luckily, the cascading balcony crashed just behind them, or it would have killed all four. Magog gave a happy yelp and rolled in the pile, then shook herself, spraying the three humans. Still holding a breathless priest, Byron looked around, amazed he was alive.

Before them, wedged between tenements, was a public stable, a three-story barn with triple doors wide open to admit hay and air and light. Framed in the big doors was a stableboy with a pitchfork who stared open-mouthed.

Cerise struggled free of the pile, shedding straw and muck. "Boy! Where can we hide?"

The stableboy looked around. "I—don't think—"

"We'll pay in silver!"

His eyes bugged wider. "Right-o! This way!" He dashed inside.

Byron let go of the priest and plucked his legs free. The priest tumbled off the pile and landed on her head. But she was up quickly enough. "Ha! The gods protect me! I've stuck to you and now—"

"Cerise!" Byron called. "What do we do with her?"

The swordswoman whirled, fury on her swarthy face. With one sweep she drew a dagger and flicked it before the priest's face. "Cut her throat?"

The priest goggled at the long blade. Then her eyes rolled white and she fainted.

"Good enough." Cerise sheathed her blade. "Bring her."

"What? Am I supposed to carry her?"

"Or else make her disappear." Cerise herself disappeared into the dark barn.

Cursing and fuming, Byron squatted, gathered up the girl, and stumbled into the grass-sweet dimness.

"Having seen you in action," Cerise hissed, "I'll re-open the offer. Shall we team up?"

Byron couldn't see the cardmaster or anything else. They lay under a mountain of loose hay. It was cool and sweet and comfortable except for chaff sticking to their skin and trickling down their necks. But having finally rested, he didn't mind. And screwed into the straw like a squirrel, he was almost warm.

They'd hidden all day, undiscovered, for the stableboy had lied like a madman and pointed the bishop's guards down a maze of alleys. Byron had slept the day away, too tired to wake even from demonic nightmares. The priest lay silent because they'd shredded her petticoat and trussed her in a white cocoon.

"Maybe we shouldn't team up." Byron tilted a bottle of cheap wine the boy had fetched, drank thirstily. It tasted like timothy grass. "It'd be dangerous to be seen with me."

Cerise snorted, sucked hay into her nose and choked. "Nothing west of the mountains scares me. I need you to manufacture cards. But no more blather about demons."

No, Byron agreed, he'd keep that secret. No point telling people he was haunted.

"I'm just an apprentice. I make cards for students and fops and jugheads. Love cards, cheaters for passing exams, prank cards. Trifles."

"If you can fashion *any* kind of card," Cerise persisted, "you're one in ten thousand. That makes you valuable, so people want to rob you. If we team up, I get cards and you get protection."

Byron was silent. He had nothing to lose. He had to leave Waterholm and the bishop's reach, but wandering the countryside was as dangerous as lingering in town, but for different reasons.

Unless, of course, Cerise killed him for his cards and left his body in the first ditch.

"Well?" Cerise whispered from the darkness.

Byron sighed for an answer. "You're persistent, you know that?"

"Slack-arses don't survive long on the Kirthan frontier."

Between them, the priest grunted under her gag. Curious, Byron reached for it. Cerise cautioned, "Shout, missy, and you'll have two mouths."

The priest gasped, sucked hay, retched, coughed, spluttered, "*I'm* persistent, too! I'm not letting you go without a fight!"

"Fight?" Byron asked. "What kind of fight?"

"A fight for the right!" the girl snapped. "The gods on high have chosen me to show you the light! Saint Wiltona guides my vision, Lord Ashkaga my right arm, Grand Francesa my heart! This is my gravest mission! I'll turn you from your evil ways, even if I must pursue you to the ends of the— *mumf*!"

"The ends of the what?" Byron asked.

Cerise cinched the gag with strong fingers. "We'll leave this one here when we slip out. They'll find her in a week or so when she starts to stink."

Byron nodded absently. He had bigger worries than addle-pated priests. "If we teamed up—*if*— where would we go?"

"Ah!"

"What?" Byron jerked alert at danger.

"No, silly. 'Ah, I figured that out.' Look here."

Sweeping her arm through hay overhead, Cerise cleared a shaft to admit late-afternoon light from the topmost barn door. She fished in her shirt for her pouch of cards, unfolded a paper. Opening it with a crackle, she pronounced, "There's a Great Game to be held in late spring in Thallandia. I have an invitation to partake!"

Byron grunted as he studied the invitation. It was calligraphed by hand with a gold-painted border and illuminated letters at every paragraph. At the bottom was a gorgeous heraldic device, a circular chain broken at the bottom, holding a sheaf of rye and a sickle. He skimmed. The language was flowery and, since cardplaying was forbidden by the church, deliberately vague.

" 'Gentlebeings, we greet you!' " he read. " 'For

the glory of men, women, fays and gods; for the betterment of all; for the pure beauty of life; we invite you to compete for honor and fame and prizes against all comers . . .' Blah, blah . . . 'Fair such as never seen . . . Jongleurs and jugglers, jesters and jousters . . . Food of the richest variety from the corners of the world . . . Games of skill and chance . . . Marvelous prizes to stun the imagination . . . Fair play for all . . . In the fief of Thallandia, thou shalt be the guests of Duke Stanwin the Bold . . . At the Eagle's Road in the White Bone Mountains . . .' "

He read to the bottom. "Why is this a personal invitation? It doesn't have your name on it."

"Of course not!" Cerise hissed, "but it was *handed* specifically to me! They never put down names in case they're intercepted."

"Funny it doesn't mention the word 'cards' anywhere."

"It's in code! 'Gentlebeings' means cardmasters."

"If you're gentle," replied the cardsmith, "I'd hate to see rough."

"Shut *up*! Here. 'Games of skill and chance.' They just can't spell it out. That would give the bishops license to ride down and sack the place!"

"They can do that anyway." Byron scooted on his elbows to pluck hay off his chin.

"Not in the countryside, they can't, you great booby. A bishop's jurisdiction only encompasses a city's walls. You'd need a cardinal to sic his guards on a mountain fiefdom."

"There must be a church at the fief, with a monsignor or prelate. Where are they while the Great Game runs? Tied up in a barn?"

The priest lying between them hummed and tossed, but they ignored her.

"That's someone else's problem," Cerise snapped. "Haven't you ever been to a Great Game?"

"No. In three years, there's only been one Great Game nearby, and Rayner wouldn't take us apprentices, the cheap prick, rest his soul. He came back fuming and broke, and boxed my ears for a week."

"See? Exciting things happen. And aren't you curious to see cards put to work?"

Byron was, but wouldn't admit it. "The very words 'Great Game' still make my ears throb. But—"

Cerise waited. "But what?"

Byron tilted the invitation to catch the failing light. "This heraldic symbol at the bottom. . . ."

Cerise craned to see. "Duke Stanwin's, called the Bold. What about it?"

"I've seen it somewhere before—" Then he remembered, too late. Damn his blabbing tongue!

"Where?"

"I forget."

"Liar."

Byron sighed. It was strange, he thought, that Cerise had asked about curiosity, Byron's greatest flaw—or asset. Curiosity was the sign of a keen mind, he'd heard. Right now his curiosity bump needed scratching, badly.

"Here." Handing Cerise the invitation, he rolled over, showering hay and chaff that glittered in the dusklight, fished sticky loose cards from inside his shirt. Dusting them off, sorting, peering, he finally found the right one. Sliding the others into the purse, and swearing he'd find a better hiding place soon, he showed the card to Cerise. "Look."

Inside a gold border lay a broken chain, sheaf of rye, and sickle. Cerise compared the card and letter.

"That card was in your master's deck? Why would *he* have a card showing Duke Stanwin's device? Thallandia is forty leagues from here! Is it a magic card?"

"No, common." Meaning not enchanted. "I don't know why. Perhaps Duke Stanwin commissioned Rayner to fashion cards, and this is some password or calling card. Maybe you'd present this to a banker to get paid, or the messenger who collects the cards."

"Do you think *that's* the card the bishop's guards lust for?"

Byron tapped the card against his forehead. "I don't know what to think. I'm dizzy with thinking. But it's fate's own clue, isn't it? As holder of this card, I should journey to Thallandia, shouldn't I?"

"And as your rescuer, I should go with you," Cerise pronounced.

"Why not?" the cardsmith shrugged. "It's that or go home to mother. One place is as dangerous as another."

The priest gave a strangled *mummf*. Byron asked, "Look, we can't just leave her here. She knows where we're going now. What shall we do with her?"

Cerise considered. "Chop her up and feed her to Magog?"

Chapter 5

In the end, they lugged the priest along.

They moved after dark. Cerise had been staying in an inn called the Riverweir. She slunk there by dark alleys, paid her bill, retrieved her baggage and horse and returned to the barn. Byron hadn't owned much, a spare shirt and some books, and they had burned up with Rayner's house, so he had nothing to gather. Cerise gave him money to buy clothes and essentials. From a pawn shop came a cast-off gentlemen's shirt stitched in red, long brown trousers and riding boots, a knit hat and poncho, so Byron could pass as the cardmaster's servant.

The stableboy pointed out some solid-colored horses belonging to the bishop herself. Cerise let the boy stash more silver under hay, then bound him hand and foot and dropped him in a grain bin. His boss would find him in the morning, a victim of horse thieves.

The struggling priest they rolled in a tarpaulin.

So, on three good horses lashed with saddles, blankets, food satchels, and a bound priest, with a dog big as a pony trailing, and a bribe to the prince's guard to pass the gate, they disappeared down the eastern road in pitch blackness—towards Thallandia.

Late morning found them miles down the road. It was a bright spring day, the air scented by plowed earth and growing grain and the chuckling river at their right hand. Regular rain had settled the road dust and a breeze swept flies away. Waterholm lay near the coast where the River Wis thundered out of the foothills, and higher up, the White Bone Mountains. The horses climbed steadily. At the pass through the mountains—the only pass—lay Thallandia and other small fiefs of the king.

Despite saddle sores, Byron enjoyed himself. He'd never been this far north of Waterholm before, and he saw new things at every turn of the road. Gradually it was sinking in that he was embarked on a real adventure. It was all the better that they passed other travellers plodding to dreary work: farmers in carts bound for market, barefoot students with satchels of books, woodcutters with faggots, a girl driving geese with a willow switch. (No one noticed that the priest was tied to the saddle horn, for Cerise had tucked her robe over the ropes, and the priest didn't dare speak for fear of having her throat cut.) Far back and far ahead they saw other colorful vagabonds going in the same direction, and Byron wondered if they were cardmasters bound for the Great Game.

"We should stop soon," Cerise said. "Let the horses rest and we can eat."

They plodded through a deep intervale where the river narrowed, with steep hardwoods on either side. Byron nodded to a jumble of rocks. The lower ones formed natural tables and chairs, and scorches marked fire pits.

Cerise hopped off her horse easily, while Byron almost fell off stiff-legged. He hadn't been on a horse more than four times in his life. There wasn't need in the city, where he could walk for miles. Riding stretched different muscles that shrieked and burned and trembled in his thighs and calves and rump.

Without comment, Cerise untied the priest's hands and dragged her off the saddle. The girl too almost fell. Cerise left her tethered to the horse by a long lead so she couldn't dash off. But after the girl had squatted in the bushes, she could stifle her anger no longer. "You'll be sorry you kidnapped me! The lords of heaven will vindicate me! Jomarc the Punisher will visit you with boils and hives and shingles until your days are a living hell! You'll—"

"Shut up," said Cerise, "or we'll hang you from a tree upside down until your face turns purple and your empty head bursts. And you won't get fed."

Miraculously, the girl shut up. Her growling stomach betrayed her. Cerise untied her tether from the saddle horn and led her to the rocks. Meekly, she sat and accepted the food Byron laid out. But they left her hands tied, with a trailing rope that might be quickly stepped upon.

They lunched on cold tongue, fresh flat bread, apricots, olives, and white cheese, drank spring water more sparkling than wine that trickled through the rocks. With loosened girths and rope hobbles, the horses foraged after green grass, accepted a handful of oats from a sack on Cerise's saddle. Magog wolfed some tongue and went sniffing off through the woods.

After an interval of munching and lounging, Cerise talked. She had to raise her voice over the noisy river, which rattled and gabbled around rocks here. "We'll keep her a while longer, drag her higher into the hills. Maybe we can sell her to someone at the Pithian Crossroads. We can't release her here, for she'd scurry back to Waterholm and blab our whereabouts to the bishop."

Byron nodded absently. Fresh air and exercise and odd hours of sleep left him dozy. He was content to let Cerise lead. He had his own, magical, concerns to work out, with precious few clues.

"You don't have to talk above me as if I were a child," the priest objected. "I'm not a tree stump."

Cerise and Byron regarded her. The swordswoman said, "Congratulations. That's your first civil word since you began hounding us. Till now you've only spouted claptrap dogma like a parrot on a perch."

"It's not claptrap! It's the holy word of the lords of heaven, and you—"

Cerise squinted, pointed, "That maple branch should hold your weight . . ."

Stifled, the priest munched more cheese. Actually, she stuffed it with both hands. Byron studied her. "The church doesn't feed their priests overmuch, do they?"

"No," the girl conceded. "They reckon gluttony a sin. We acolytes are supposed to mind spiritual matters, not worldly ones. May I have more bread?"

Byron handed the loaf. "Acolytes, yes. But I never

saw a prelate or monsignor who didn't have to cinch his or her beads low to encompass their bellies. I suppose once they've starved their way to holiness, they can let worldly goods enter." He grinned impishly.

The priest objected without conviction. "It's a sin to criticize one's superiors."

"Convenient for the superiors," Byron returned mildly.

Cerise leaned against a rock lazily, yet stropped her sword with a whetstone and watched the road in both directions. "Keep feeding her. It's got her quiet."

"You don't have to call me 'her' as if I were a sow. I have a name."

They waited.

"All right, I'll tell you. It's Veronica."

Cerise sniffed, but Byron smiled. "A lot of name for such a small girl."

"*Sister* Veronica, actually." She tilted her nose, which was speckled with freckles. "I was given a long name because I was the runt of the litter, my mother said. She was a lacemaker, but grew crippled in her hands and couldn't work, and we had no food, so I was sold to the church."

"What a bargain," Cerise muttered. "I'd have thrown you back as too small."

Veronica looked hurt, so Byron changed the subject. "My family runs a fulling mill, making cloth, in a village down towards the sea, but I was too clumsy for the work. I was always in danger of toppling into the hammers or getting my arm caught in the belts. But I had my little trick—" Byron snapped his fingers and produced fire, then blew it out "—so my father brought me to the cardsmithing guild."

The two women looked inquisitive, so Byron

elaborated. "The guild watches for any sign of magic. They had me sit at a table and take a test. A journeyman handed me a deck of cards—all kinds in a jumble, all frayed and dirty—told me to separate them. Most boys and girls just do it any old way, but I went through carefully and made two piles. The journeyman checked, then brought out a cardsmith to see. He fetched a different deck and bade me do it again. Some of the cards were charmed, you see. Some were healing cards that felt warm, or crop-growing cards that smelt of earth, or whatever. I picked out charmed ones just because they felt 'different.' Later, I learned only one person in ten thousand can sort them properly. They bargained with my father, then Rayner bid for my services."

He grinned at Veronica. "Rayner didn't believe in feeding apprentices much either. But I slipped cards to the cook so she'd win games with her friends, and she'd slip me food—her own brand of magic."

Cardsmith and priest looked to the cardmaster. After a while, Cerise began, "I grew up on the Kirthan frontier. My family—there were thirty-some of us, uncles and aunts and cousins—voted to leave the stockade post and build a ranch near the steppes. My grandfather was an old scout and knew a valley where the water flowed year round, with woods nearby. So we moved there, built a fortified house of stone, and prayed the Shinyar stayed away.

"They didn't. There'd been drought in their land so they've pushed west, this way. We were the first Westerners they encountered. I was camped in the badlands, chasing stray horses and cattle, when I saw smoke, a lot of it. I rode hell for leather, but I was too late. Or too early."

Her voice took on a harsh edge, and her hands flexed on the sword. "The Shinyar hid in the grass under camouflaged blankets. As soon as my father unbarred the door and stepped outside, they shot him. Most of my family were killed early on, some in bed, I guess. But some survived, for a while. They lashed my mother and others to the fence posts, and took turns all day torturing them, men and women, laughing the while. They cut off their ears and noses and every other part. When my family tried to close their eyes, they cut off their eyelids. Finally, when it was dusk and my family couldn't scream any more, they punctured their throats and drank their hot blood out of mugs. Then they roasted my family along with our pigs and cattle and ate everything. . . ."

In a faraway voice, Cerise finished, "I could do nothing, nothing at all. So I herded my strays to the stockade post, sold them, and moved west. Along the way, I learned how to gamble. I'm good at it. Unlike many fops, I have nothing to lose except my life . . ."

It was quiet in the grove except for the peep of goldfinches in the trees. Byron reflected that his troubles weren't as overwhelming as he'd thought.

Cerise spread a blanket under a tree to nap, putting Magog on guard. Since Veronica was still tied up, she lay down, too.

Byron climbed, ostensibly seeking a flat place. Instead he found a pocket in the rocks and sank inside like a rattlesnake. For the first time since— could it be?—a day and a night, he had a chance to look over Rayner's cards. Bits of hay fell out when he untied the purse.

Forty-seven cards. Closing his eyes, the smith shuffled them into two piles. He was glad to see the magic pile three times higher than the common.

He sorted the unenchanted deck first.

Five cards were blank, but ready for enchanting, steeped in Rayner's secret solution of thirty different minerals and herbs that let the cardmaster bind in magic—though no one knew why it worked. So Byron could improvise five cards if necessary.

Eight commons were painted and worthless. Two souvenir cards showed the Waterholm Winter Festival, one depicted the Wis Waterfall, a wedding keepsake portrayed a bride and groom, and so on. Byron kept them for painting over later. The last was Duke Stanwin's heraldic symbol—its purpose a mystery.

Of the thirty-four magic cards, only a dozen were finished, painted. Most he recognized as standard cards for merchants or wags. Two depicted Crumble as a collapsing castle. A Ship Protection showed a carrack in safe harbor. A Test Gold card showed a real and a fake coin. A Serpent Staff was obvious. One prank card showed the devil bending over and laughing, another a buffoon slipping off a bridge, and Babble was a card students sicced on unliked teachers. Detect Lie showed a man with a forked tongue like a snake. Others were Banish Gloom, Find Gold, and a Palm Leaf for healing.

That left twenty-two unfinished cards, dull white with charcoal or lead sketches. Some he knew, and Byron had bought a small set of paints to make these presentable. Two more Crumbles. A Garden Pests Begone. A Charm Against Plague. A Mist. Explode. Charm Beast. And more.

Then came the confusing ones whose secrets had

died with Rayner. Rayner was no great hand at drawing or painting, and Byron couldn't even guess the picture on some, let alone the spells they signified. A pair of bug-eyed weasels entwined. A donkey with what might be a seagull sitting between its ears. A girl dressed in flowing clothes—a gypsy? A cup of broth or tea. A thorn tree. A boat in a storm. And those were the clear ones.

Handling carefully, Byron studied the one Rayner had been working on when he froze. The pasteboard had sketched an apple with a bite missing. Byron squinted, sniffed, shook, tapped. "What's the rest of it?" he asked the card. Or the dead Rayner.

Although methods might vary, a cardsmith generally fashioned a card by sitting down with a blank card and a charcoal or lead pencil, entering a trance, then imagining the spell he/she wanted and slowly sketching it. The image helped the smith concentrate, bind the spell into the card, and remember the spell afterwards.

Having successfully enchanted the card, the smith usually scraped it clean, sharpened the image with a pencil, then passed it to a card artist. Good card artists were as much in demand as good smiths, and commanded high prices. A final card could be elaborate or simple, but had to be visually appealing. A client paying through the nose for magic didn't want a dull white card scrawled with charcoal; they wanted flash. With his big hands workworn from years as an oxdrover, Rayner had been a poor artist. His bitten apple looked lopsided and squashy, and the leaves atop could have come from a tomato.

A pathetic thing to die for.

Byron scratched his sunburned neck. He knew

the card was magic, for it practically crackled in his hand, but what was the spell and what color should the apple be? Red could mean poison or passion. Green might mean sourness or youth. Yellow might mean beauty or gold. And what was the token? Apple juice? Cinnamon? "Apple, apple . . . A magic apple what? Or a tomato. But who ever heard of a Magic Tomato card?"

For a second, he wanted to curse magic-making and all its roundabout secrets. But the dead Rayner might be listening and hovering nearby, so he kept quiet.

Disgusted with his ignorance, he examined another card. Smeary, it showed two mountains with curvy lines between. A mountain stream? Or pass? Could this be the Eagle's Road near their destination? Had Duke Stanwin commissioned this card? What could it mean? Strength? Solidarity? Isolation? It could be anything, with any token at all.

Once again, he heard his mother scold his father for not apprenticing him to a cobbler. *Everyone needs shoes! And you don't dabble in the black arts to make them!*

"No, Mama," Byron muttered, "not black arts, just murky gray ones."

With a sigh he picked up another card. A single smeary eye stared back. "Lovely. True-seeing? Invisible Spy? See Through Walls? Clear Up Hangover?"

A snow-capped mountain bore a line of tall grass at its feet. "Feed Goats? Grow Barley? Build a Snowman?"

On another card, two crooked men's faces stared pop-eyed at one another. Byron guessed it was some form of Detect Lie. But the token?

"Always," he sighed aloud, "always it's the token!"

Tokens, good and bad rolled into one. The secret ingredient that triggered the card and, without which, the card was useless. A cardsmith couldn't experiment with an enchanted card, because if he/she accidentally triggered the card, it would be used up, dead. And with some cards, such as Plague, the smith could end up dead.

There was no avoiding it. He'd have to show the unknown cards to a master cardsmith to learn their tokens, as Cerise had shown her half-dozen unknowns to Byron, and give up the best cards as a fee.

And for the love of the gods, which of these cursed cards did the bishop want so badly? *If* the bishop in fact pursued him for cards and not some other nonsense.

His head hurt. If only he'd become a cobbler as Mama wished . . .

"Byron! Where are you?"

The cardsmith sat up with a jerk. He'd lost track of time, dozed off. The sun slanted west. Time to move on. Keeping the cards sorted, he stuffed them in the purse and down his shirt, then climbed out of the warm rock pocket. Stiffly, for he was covered with welts from slingballs, scrapes and splinters from falls, and sore muscles from riding. "The rewards of adventure," he reminded himself. He wondered if he could soak in a hot bath anytime soon.

Veronica was muzzy-eyed from her nap, frustrated by the rope on her wrists. "You can untie me. I won't run to the bishop."

"Of course you will. It's your duty." Cerise tightened the girth on her saddle. Her beast was a shaggy plains pony, roan-red with a golden mane, incongruously named Powderkeg. Byron and Veronica had fine black horses with white stockings: the bishop's buyers preferred solid-colored animals. Byron wondered if they shouldn't trade down to less conspicuous mounts. The stableboy had told their names: Byron's gelding was Moldano after a mischievous fairy; Veronica's mare was Byzer after a sea god.

The blonde priest with the tonsure staggered up, tugging at her wrists. "My duty is to convert heathens such as you! And lure you from your wicked ways, creating cards and gambling with them! The gods sent me to minister you, and that's what I'll do!"

Cerise checked Veronica's mount, boosted the girl into the saddle and retied her lead. "Fine. Preach. Until we hit the crossroads. Then we'll sic you on some other poor sinners to heckle. We've had an earful and don't want to be greedy."

"But you won't listen!" the girl wailed. Cerise hunted for a gag in a saddlebag, and Veronica talked faster. "How can I convert you if you won't attend me?"

"Ah, the eternal struggle," Byron chuckled. "How can I turn you into me if you insist on being yourself?"

"That's not it at all!" the girl shrilled. "It's just— seeing truth, is all."

Byron grinned. "The eternal quest! For truth, whatever it might be!"

He spoiled his teasing by vaulting into the saddle and pitching over the other side to crash in dust. The women laughed, and Magog barked.

"You know," Cerise hitched her baldric of heavy weapons straighter, "we'll have problems with you, too."

"Me?" Byron brushed himself off. "Why me?"

"You're hopeless. So clumsy you'd blind yourself with your thumbs blowing your nose. And we'll be fighting before long. No one rides the roads long without bumping into something ugly. But, Pithcur's Arm, with a sword you'd stab yourself, or me, the first time you drew!"

Byron mounted carefully. "I'm just a little stiff. And fighting is for fools. A cardsmith doesn't need a keen blade, but a keen mind. I—"

Plumped in the saddle, he found no reins. He'd forgotten to loop them over the saddle horn first, so they dangled on the ground. Grumbling, he dismounted.

"A keen mind, yes." Cerise donned riding gloves. "We'll have to teach you some dull weapon. A flail, maybe. If peasants can thresh grain, you can. But I don't know much about staff weapons—"

"I do!" piped Veronica. "Churchmen aren't allowed edged weapons, as you know. So guards use clubs, captains carry maces, and the bishop has a ceremonial sceptre. A priest—that's me!—wields a quarterstaff!"

The cardmaster stared. "How much training have you had?"

"Lots! We got extra food if we did well, and it gave me an excuse to thwack the snotty proctors!"

Cerise reached up, gave a yank, and pulled the girl squealing off the saddle. Untying her, she said, "Don't try to run or I'll hamstring you. Grab that stick and show me." She drew her sword.

The small priest flexed her wrists, hissing at chafes, but picked up a sapling someone had dragged down as firewood. "It's not the right length, but it'll do."

She gripped the stick properly, one small hand in the middle, one a quarter way up the shaft, the longer half pointing right.

Cerise bowed with her sword, paused, lunged experimentally for Veronica's middle. The girl neatly turned the shining blade without uncovering herself. "Good!"

Magog, delighted at the new game, galumphed around the two. Humming to herself, Cerise stepped back, lunged for the middle again, feinted and swept back to jab at her thigh. But Veronica tapped the blade aside, followed with a stroke at Cerise's shoulder. The swordswoman hoisted her sword to parry, but Veronica feinted herself and swung for Cerise's hip. Another click fended off the staff. "Ha!"

Before Cerise could return to the poised position, Veronica swung hard at the end of her arms. Cerise ducked the flailing boom. In a wink, she was behind Veronica with the swordblade alongside the girl's ear. "Oops."

But she smiled. "Not bad. You could protect yourself against the average slew-footed bandit. If there were only one, which is unlikely. But not bad. You could teach Byron some things. But then, so could Magog."

"Hey!" yelped the cardsmith.

"So may I accompany you?" Veronica asked brightly.

Cerise rolled her eyes. "Not if you spout dogma all day."

"I could restrain myself, convert by shining example." The girl tilted her freckled nose in the air. "That should suffice to please the gods, I think."

"You just want free meals," laughed Byron.

"My payment for teaching you the quarterstaff!"

Byron laughed again. "By the forge of Allion, she's got pluck!"

"Good enough," said Cerise. "I was tired of tying you up anyway. And we'll need pluck *and* luck. So let's pluck ourselves loose of here and move on. We've miles to go to the crossroads and a decent inn."

The three mounted, Veronica unfettered for once. Reining tight, Cerise warned, "Another thing, and listen closely. Past the crossing, the road to Thallandia will be busy. Remember, good cardplayers play close to the vest. Don't tell *anyone* where we're bound or why. Besides bandits circling after loot and pig-ignorant superstitious peasants terrified of witches, there'll be gods know how many cardmasters and smiths converging on the game, sizing up the opposition and looking for advantage. So keep the talk light and inconsequential—discuss the weather. It's enough to watch for stabs in the back or coshes on the head without my worrying about blabbermouths spilling our secrets. Got it?"

The two nodded. Veronica feigned buttoning her lip. Byron hardly needed to be told: cardsmithing was dangerous enough without arming your enemies with secrets. But he said, "Good advice. We'll keep alert."

"You better. This road will be the most dangerous place in the kingdom in the next few weeks. And it's not the dangers you know that kill you. It's the ones you don't know."

With that encouraging word, the cardmaster kneed her pony onto the road, whistled her dog. Meekly, cardsmith and priest clumped after.

Chapter 6

Past the Pithian Crossroads, the road bore east towards Thallandia, and traffic picked up. Hundreds of folks of every stripe journeyed to the dukedom for "The Spring Fair." Many, of course, were actually going to the Great Game, but no one mentioned it, for the Church had many ears. Byron wondered how anyone could truly believe the churchmen didn't know about this game. But he played along like everyone else.

The three travellers found the inns of the crossroads bursting at the seams. A room, or even space on the common room floor, was unthinkable. So they bought food at outrageous prices and camped outside of town with scores of others.

Along the road, they once passed a vendor of musical instruments. Veronica sighed and admitted she knew how to play the flute. Feeling sorry for her, Byron bought her a flute. The girl was so grateful she cried. Cerise approved, muttering that if Veronica were playing she couldn't be preaching, but both enjoyed the girl's glad and sad tunes as they plodded along.

Two days down the road found them camping out still.

Campfires were strewn throughout a pine forest on either side of the road that threaded a shallow valley through the foothills. The horses were hobbled in a rocky clearing where they could crop weeds and grass amidst boulders. Byron was alone, nursing bruises and painting cards by the light of a fire made from fallen pine boughs. It snapped and crackled with pitchy knots. Because the soft wood burned quickly, Byron had to keep feeding the fire. He was sore through his shoulders and arms.

Cerise had instituted a "training program" where every morning, noon, and evening, while practicing her own swordsmanship and exercising Magog, she oversaw Veronica instruct Byron in the quarterstaff. They'd cut staves of ash, long and straight, light but strong, and whack each other for three long hours a day. Or Veronica whacked and Byron got whacked. The priest avoided rapping Byron's head and fingers, but his shoulders and arms and ribs and hips ached. Frantic as a frog in boiling water, the cardsmith flung his staff this way or that, managing to deflect or block some strokes. Fighting, Cerise intoned, was more than mere hitting; you must read your opponent's moves and react without conscious thought. In short, your eye caught a flicker of movement and your body judged where the blow would fall and knocked it aside first. "It must be automatic," she emphasized. "If you take time to think, you'll be too slow and get killed." So practice, practice, practice.

Byron did and, over days, took a pride in not getting thwacked so often. He even had a goal: to survive a full minute without being batted. Eventually, Cerise promised, she would assume his training, teach him to fend off sword thrusts. "Oh, joy," he'd muttered, "I can hardly wait."

This evening he was alone. Cerise was off gaming with other cardmasters, using common cards, to sharpen her wits. Veronica was off singing hymns with a clutch of blue-robed priests.

Byron sat still and painted Rayner's unfinished cards. He was no card artist, but he could mark a straight line and fill in blanks, even paint details such as eyeballs if he went slowly. He'd finished the known cards and, after deliberating, had decided to paint some unknowns. There was a danger he might paint things incorrectly—paint a mountain alpine blue when it should have been black and red like a volcano or such. But maybe by decorating the cards, he'd see them in a new way, and learn their purpose. And they all had to be painted eventually.

Another project was to assemble tokens for the cards he did know in a small leather pouch he'd bought: a pinch of lime from a brickyard for the Crumbles, a snake fang for Serpent Staff, a tuft of Magog's fur for Charm Beast, linen (as in a gauze mask) for Charm Against Plague, and others. Of course, he didn't know the tokens of many cards, so the purse was fairly flat.

"Hello, the fire!" A fluting voice interrupted his reverie. "Care for some company?"

"Eh?" The forest was black, with straight pine

trunks sidelit by campfires sprinkled like lightning bugs. Staring at white cards by a bright fire, Byron was blind until a feminine shape was silhouetted against a yellow glow. He jerked upright from the tree, wincing. "No! I mean, yes, surely! Come and sit, share my fire! Ouch!"

The woman chuckled in her throat. "Does it hurt to admit company to your inner sanctum?"

"Uh, no. I'm, uh, glad . . ." His voice trailed off.

Once in the firelight, he could see the woman was stunning. Her hair was dark and long except for twin gold streaks that framed her face. She wore a leather jacket embroidered with blue swirls, a white silk blouse with blue piping, dark breeches knee-length and baggy for riding, and good boots. A brass-hilted rapier and dagger at opposite hips marked her as a cardmaster. When she smiled, firelight glistened on moist rouged lips.

Accustomed to his stunned expression, which she'd no doubt seen on men hundreds of times before, she smiled graciously, nodded at his handiwork. "You're an artist?"

"What? Hunh?" Byron looked at his brush and paints and water pot as if he'd never seen them. "Oh, those. No, I'm a—bookbinder."

The woman chuckled again, throatily, and Byron liked the sound. "Bookbinder" was a common code word for cardsmith, a dodge when travelling. In the superstitious countryside, where peasants imagined witches and ogres and werewolves behind every tree, cardsmiths passed themselves off as bookbinders, often carried leaves of pages to sew or illustrate at odd moments.

Of course, right now Byron wore a servant's clothing,

not the traditional cardsmiths' black. Besides feeling exceedingly shabby next to this glittering woman, he worried she might not believe he was a real cardsmith.

Primly, she lowered her shapely bottom onto a fallen log. "I'm a mercenary, myself. Sword for hire, risking all."

"Mercenary" and "risking all" were codes for a cardmaster. Other phrases were "Life is a game," "I travel decked for adventure," "I seek to trump death," and so on.

"I am Ingrid, from the Black Forest." Her eyes glowed golden in the firelight, like a cat's.

"Byron, late of Waterholm."

Both chuckled at their transparent disguises. The woman was bewitching, but Byron tried to remain on guard. Cardmasters lived by cards, and cardsmiths usually carried a bundle. In some ways, he was a sheep travelling amidst wolves.

"And what do you work on, Byron late of Waterholm?" She nodded casually towards the card drying near the fire.

"Oh, not much," he confessed. "I'm painting to make this card prettier, if less clear." There was no harm in admitting he owned cards he didn't understand. Everyone did.

"May I see?" Red fingernails took the card. It was one of the few round cards, and depicted a mountain with a line of tall grass along its foot. "You've no clue?"

"None. My master—" Here he played his cards close to the vest, for this was business. "—bid me take a passel of unknowns to 'the fair' and see if any other 'bookbinders' can identify them."

"I think I know this one." Ingrid handed it back. "Does it feel cold?"

A cardmaster could only guess. A cardsmith, Byron could tell. "Yes, it's cold."

"I'd guess a Blast Crops. The snow on the mountain signifies frost. That's wheat, with little tufts atop. A rival farmer would plant it by night in a neighbor's fields, feed it the token, make the dew turn to ice. For spite or to drive up local prices. If he retrieved the dead card before his neighbor found it, all the better, for there'd be suspicion of magic but no proof."

Byron nodded eagerly. It made sense, and cards for damaging a rival's produce had been a major product of Rayner's. "But the token?"

Ingrid shrugged, her dark-and-light hair shimmering in the firelight. "Well, it couldn't be ice. Water, maybe, but that's risky because dampness might trigger the card prematurely. I'd guess you'd feed it kernels of grain in the field. That would be simple to remember and handy."

Byron nodded again. "Yes, I'll bet you're right." Picking up his brush, he daubed the wheat heads white for frost. Blowing it dry, he handed the card to Ingrid. "There. Take it. A gift."

Pleased, she smiled but hesitated. "Are you sure? There's no need—"

"No, take it." Byron felt gallant presenting it to such a beautiful woman. "If you hadn't come by, it would just be pasteboard painted wrong."

Careful not to smudge the drying paint, Ingrid accepted. "But I must pay you something. Cardsmiths are not generous, usually. Here."

She craned forward and pursed red lips. Byron got a luxurious view of soft breasts heaving in her blouse, then she kissed his mouth, a blow as stunning as Veronica's smack with a quarterstaff. Byron sat back gasping and blushing. Ingrid chuckled. "There. We're quits. And I'm still in practice. I haven't kissed a handsome man all night."

Handsome? His mind rang like a church bell. "Um, well, thank you . . . I haven't, I mean, I don't— Oh, I don't know what I mean."

Ingrid hitched her baggy trousers higher, showing her calves and knees. "Have you other cards you don't comprehend? Perhaps we can interpret and . . . reward each other some more."

"What? Oh, sure—" The idea of another electric kiss made Byron want to pull out every card he owned. But he balked. Showing his full hand was a bad idea. "Um . . ."

With a shake of his head, he regained his senses, but the kiss still tingled on his lips. Stealing a glance at Ingrid, he saw her pout and smile, ready for more. How many cards, he wondered, would it take to get her clothes off?

"Who's this?" a voice barked.

Byron jumped. Cerise strode into the firelight, hands on her sword and dagger pommels, ready for a fight or anything else. Her brindled hound pranced after.

"Oh, it's—she's Ingrid. She's a—one of us."

For no reason Byron could see, the women took an instant dislike to one another.

Cerise sniffed. "Hardly one of us. With those overblown udders, she's too topheavy to fence properly."

"True," Ingrid replied regally. "Better to be built more like you. Nothing up top, heavy in the thighs and butt, low to the ground."

"Those bleached strands around your thin face must be a distraction in a fight."

"And your hair, black and coarse as a horsetail, would make a good handle."

Cerise stepped back, as if needing room to draw steel. "Those brass-hilted toys must sparkle nicely in a battle. Did your mother buy those?"

"Yes, unlike yours, obviously scrounged in a pawn shop." Ingrid stood, balanced on the balls of her feet. "What a clever shopper you make."

"I should paint my lips, perhaps. It's to cover up pox blisters, correct?"

The women were circling now, and Byron gathered his cards and paint set before they were trodden in a brawl. Ingrid sneered, "I could help you make up, sweetie. The more of your face we disguise, the better for all."

"Perhaps we should fence," Cerise hissed back, "and see who comes away pricked."

Byron couldn't help compare the slinky brass-glittering Ingrid to the plain-steel Cerise. One was a tiger, the other a pitbull.

"Getting 'pricked,'" Ingrid advised, "is the least of your worries, I should think."

"No doubt you avoid trouble by flopping on your back and surrendering."

Magog barked at the darkness.

In a brisk trot and swirl of skirts, Veronica burst into camp, flush-faced and laughing. "Hi, everybody! I just came to get my flute! We've got a round going! Everyone's chiming so well in harmony—oh!"

The glances of the feuding women shrivelled the girl like a dandelion pitched in a fire. The priest burbled, "Uh, who's this?"

"No one," Cerise snapped. "She's not here."

"True." Ingrid dusted her seat with her hands for Byron's benefit, put her nose in the air. "I think I'll take some air away from the kennels. The smell of bitches in heat is thick." She paraded away, hair swinging, while Byron goggled and the women glared.

"What the hell was she after?" Cerise swung on Byron viciously. "Or don't I know? She was working you like a pump handle to spill cards, wasn't she?"

"Hunh? What? No, of course not!" Byron put his paints down, put his thumb squarely in the pot of blue. "Hell!"

"How many cards did she take you for, you gull?"

"Just one," Byron shot back. "She identified a Blast Crops card and I gave it to her. It was useless anyway. We won't be near any farmlands."

"You idiot! You never know when a card will come in handy! If you're playing a Great Game and your opponent's army nears a field, wouldn't a Blast Crops spell be handy to delay his army and force foraging for food? One card can win a kingdom!"

"Maybe . . ." Byron conceded. "But cardsmiths have to share knowledge to learn—"

"Share spit, more like!" Cerise spat. "She'd lock lips with you, catch your crotch, then club you over the head! You'd wake with a purse empty as your skull, and only red lips to show!"

Veronica giggled, and Byron touched his mouth with a blue thumb and withdrew red-daubed fingers.

Cerise snorted, "Try to keep your wits, will you, Byron? Think with your head and not your cock? You're no use to me without cards, no more than a blacksmith without iron or a tinsmith without tin!"

Byron scrubbed his mouth. "Hey, I'm not indentured

to you! I accompany you of my own free will, like Veronica here, and you can't order me around!"

"You're right," Cerise admitted. "But we made a pact, you to produce cards and me to protect you. Part of protecting you is to warn about snakes that might slither into camp, pop a few buttons off their blouses, and dazzle you with mounds of female flesh. An attack isn't just stabbing a stranger in a dark alley, you know."

"I—know," Byron conceded. "And you're right. I was tempted to show my other cards, but didn't. Now you've protected me and I've learned my lesson and there's no harm done. Does that suit you, Mother?"

Cerise grunted a laugh. "A jackass was your mother, and a mule mine."

Veronica lectured in a sing-song, "But even a jackass and a mule can learn if you smack them in the head. You've both learned to keep a sharper eye out. Now shake and make up."

Cardsmith and -master looked curiously at the small priest, but they shook hands.

"Great!" piped the priest. "We're all still friends! Bye now! Don't wait up!" Clutching her flute, the girl flounced out of the firelight.

Cerise shook her head. "You people make me feel old."

"How old are you?" Byron asked. With swarthy skin and a face lined by a lifetime outdoors, it was hard to tell.

"I'm twenty-six," Cerise snapped. "And I hope to live to one hundred, though I'll get gray shepherding this flock."

Byron wasn't listening. "I'm nineteen. I wonder how old Ingrid is . . . ?"

"*Aggh!*" Cerise spat into the fire, snatched up her cloak, and stomped off into the darkness.

Once again Byron ran from demons. But this time he couldn't see them.

He was swallowed by jungle, as Byron had heard travellers describe. A green hell higher than he could reach, plants and trees with fleshy fronds were packed so thick a bird couldn't have flown through. The cardsmith beat at leaves large as clothes on a line, broke through them or clambered over, more swimming than running in a sea of green.

All around he heard the thrash of leaves as squeaking pattering monsters hunted him. They were close. He could smell their rotten breath and urinous stink even above the fuggy muck of jungle. He rammed past a bush hung with red flowers like bloody organs that dripped sickly-sweet sap on him. Razor-edged grass sliced his hands and face. Insects by the millions covered his skin, turned it black, and burrowed into his wounds to feast. And all around demons hooted and panted and yodeled.

What did they *want*? And why *him*? He was nothing, had nothing! He wasn't even a superior cardsmith, just an apprenticed hack who conjured schoolboys' pranks and mushy lust spells. Someday, maybe, he might be a real cardsmith but, for now, he was useless as a three-legged horse. Why did demons pursue him? And what would they do if they caught him?

He grabbed the scaly trunk of a pepper tree, clambered over the knotty roots, hopped into grass that clutched his legs and hands.

A claw snagged his collar from behind. Hooked nails like iron scratched his neck, plucked at his hair. A demon shrieked in triumph. Not daring to turn, Byron flailed behind his back, knocked loose demonic arms that sloughed dead skin like a corpse's.

Panting, his heart near bursting, Byron beat aside a cluster of slimy vines across his path, plucked his feet from mud, jumped onto the shiny leaves of a plant big as a fountain that had upright tendrils and stagnant water at its center.

Before he could dash across the tiny pool, the plant gave a lurch. Twenty long leaves snapped up around the cardsmith to shut out light. Too late, Byron felt wiggly tendrils tangle his feet. White hairs along the leaves sprang up to prick his clothes and skin like needles. The stagnant water, warm and reeking like blood, gushed up his legs, to his waist, his chest, his neck.

A cannibal plant, he realized. It shut tight to form a natural vise, gushed water or sap to drown its prey.

Him.

He felt the thick leaves drum as the bony fists of demons pounded on the outside. He was wrapped tight as a mummy, punctured like a butterfly on a pin. Sap bubbled around his chin, clogged his mouth, shut off sound. His nostrils filled . . .

. . . and he drowned.

"Wake up! We're attacked!"

A boot thudded his ribs. Someone jerked his blanket off. With it tangled around his head, he'd been bathed in a fog of his own sweat. Groggy, still frightened, Byron crawled off his bedroll.

He was chilled by dark night air. There was no fire, only dull coals. Cerise had kicked it apart. Veronica was off her bedroll, a quarterstaff in her hand, but didn't know where to strike. Cerise, with Magog, crept out of camp into the dark. She'd take the fight to the enemy rather than wait for an attack.

The forest was a madhouse of noise, an echo of the demonic shrills in Byron's nightmare. Men and women shouted in the woods and on the road. A musketoon blatted and Byron heard buckshot shred branches. Someone gave a shout of triumph and someone else shrieked: a sword thrust and hit, he guessed. Only, who was attacking? And where?

Then a madman rushed from the dark.

As if still dreaming, Byron felt the drum of feet through the forest soil, heard Magog bark and Cerise shout, saw a huge form loom against the darker forest. A red flash glinted on a curved edge: the light of coals reflecting on a sword edge.

"Byron, duck!" hollered Veronica.

With his clumsy feet glued to the ground, Byron threw himself backwards and hoped his head didn't smack a tree. As he crashed to earth, the silent giant swept the glint down at him, and the cardsmith rolled frantically. A *chuff* announced a sword or axe slamming the forest floor, just missing him.

A surprised grunt came from the giant. Byron heard him pluck the weapon from the soil, kick out right and left. His toe tagged Byron, still rolling towards the dying fire. The apprentice sensed the giant whirl, heard air hiss around the weapon as it stroked upwards.

Panicked, Byron rolled clear over the firepit. Hot ash and smoke puffed in a cloud. A coal stung his hand like a wasp as he scrambled up and ran. The giant clumped after him—

—and Magog exploded from the dark.

Mouth open, teeth flashing white, horrendous barks ripping the night, the dog bounded to fasten bone-crushing jaws on the giant's arm.

At the same time, Veronica grunted as her quarterstaff walloped the giant's head. With a groan, he collapsed backwards onto the dying fire. When he hit, Magog skipped free with a satisfied "Whuff!"

Byron latched onto a tree trunk and spun around the other side like a squirrel. He ought to grab his quarterstaff and join the fight, if there was anyone left to fight. But he couldn't see it or anything else, and knew nothing about fending off swords. He'd only get killed. But he couldn't do nothing—

"Byron!" a hiss at his elbow made him jump.

Cerise coolly assessed the battle. "Something's wrong! That brute passed five other camps to come directly for *us*!"

"Hunh? Why?" Byron clutched his pounding chest. He was unused to people trying to kill him. He forced himself to think. "Does *he* want my cards, too?"

"Anything's possible!" Cerise's voice waxed and waned as she turned to scan the forest. There was more shouting on the road. Another firearm exploded and a mule whinnied in fright. "I'll bet that busty bitch Ingrid pinpointed our camp!"

Why her? Byron wondered. Was this more of the raid on Rayner's house? Could the bishop's guards have come this far?

He jumped again as someone crowded his other side. Veronica, her blonde tonsure a dim halo. "What do we *do*?"

Cerise swore in a foreign tongue. "I wish I could *see*!"

"See?" Byron had a flash of inspiration. "Ah! Wait!"

"For what?"

Off to their left, a clash of steel on steel resounded. Some authority hollered, "To me! To me!"

Byron fished in his shirt for his purse. Luckily, he'd sorted the cards into order. The ones on the bottom of the deck were blanks. He plucked one out and held it before his eyes, a dim squarish glow, clawed out a crayon, squatted with his back against a tree. "Cover me! Give me a minute!"

"Why?"

"I'll let you see! But wait!"

Cerise grumbled. Byron didn't hear.

Staring at the near-invisible card, he sank into a trance.

Chapter 7

Phantom cats danced around Byron.

Sure-footed, they padded under a crescent moon from the gardens, tiptoed along a slat fence, oozed through a bed of sunflowers, hopped light as thistledown from olive trees. All kinds of cats came calling, as if Byron had thrown fish scraps out the back door of Rayner's grand house. But there was one particular cat he wanted of the throng that milled and slunk and purred around his knees.

There. A lean gray cat with glowing yellow eyes. This was a real cat Byron had known, a regular to the kitchen door, an alley scamp that Byron admired for its calm staring eyes that bored into his soul. Squatting, he fixed his mind on the cat's eyes, yellow with a vertical slit. Slowly in this half-dream state, he raised the white card alongside the cat's head.

He'd fashioned this card once before while sitting

on the kitchen stoop, but then the cat was right by his feet. Now he had to coax his imagination to bring the cat closer. Frowning, scarcely breathing, he struggled to *press* the power of the cat's eye onto the blank pasteboard. It was hard as carving a name on a tombstone with a hammer and chisel, as pounding steel on an anvil, as hauling grain sacks up a ladder, but he kept at it. Unknowing, his hand scrawled with the crayon.

A chittering gurgled in the air. The cats turned, ears flicking, searching.

From all over the garden, demons came scuttling to mind Byron's business, scrabbling along gravel walks on twisted feet, skittering down the house walls with ragged claws, peering over his shoulder, whispering dark secrets.

"Go away!" he muttered. The monsters laughed. One tugged his hair, another pecked his ear. "Go away!"

"What? Who?" asked a feminine voice close by.

The cats disliked the demons. Some hissed, yowled, turned tail and bounded off. Some bit the demons, scratched them. The wretched scabby twisted demons clawed back. When they found Byron attended the lean gray cat, they began to circle.

Byron didn't understand. How had the demons invaded his concentration? For this was not dreaming, this was magic-making. Wasn't it? Why were they muddling his spell? Why were they only knee-high, cat-sized?

"Get out of here!" he rapped. "Shoo!"

Popped and bloodshot eyes turned his way from their circle around the gray cat. The other felines had fled. Surrounded, the gray arched its back and spat, tail puffed up like a sausage.

Desperate, Byron clung to the spell, fought to concentrate, to bind it, but demons danced over and around him like fleas. The damned cat's eyes became slippery as peeled grapes. Byron twitched his shoulders, jerked his legs to shoo the small demons like flies. But it was hard to move his legs and arms, for they were stiff with cold. He clamped his jaw to keep his teeth from chattering. The cold sweat on his brow would make a good token, his mind rattled.

The cat spun in place, scratched, leaped—

Byron's mind leaped with it, caught the essence, the wildness, of the cat's eyes. For a blurred second, he saw through the animal's eyes, saw demons level with his whiskers. This was bad, he reckoned. Any minute he'd suck up the cat's mind and lose his own. Why was magic so damned hard? Shaking himself mentally, he grabbed the cat's eye and *burned* the image into the card, squeezed, clamped, pinned it until the mental glue dried. And let go.

Released, the cat vaulted a wall and disappeared. The demons cast about stupidly, then ran for the flowers and bushes. Byron fought to remember where he'd been. He didn't know, and it frightened him.

He gasped for air, gagged, snorted, smelled pine. Oh, yes, he lay on the forest floor, cheek on dry needles.

Cerise bent low. "Balthazar's Blood, what happened to you?" She mashed a mosquito at his ear and another on his neck. He was glad for the human contact. He's spent enough time with demons and cats.

"Here, take it . . ." A croak. He tried to hold up the card, but strength had run from his arm like blood.

Wondering, Cerise plucked the card from his grasp, held it aloft to catch the light of a distant campfire. "It's—what? An eye?"

"Forehead. Sweat. Hold it to your . . ." Weakly Byron pawed the ground, tried to sit up. He felt cold as if lying in snow.

Game for any advantage, the cardmaster shifted her sword, touched the blank card to her forehead. A sharp puff made her gasp.

"Shield of Voltara! I can *see!*"

Cerise stared about in wonder. The world was a new place.

The black-drenched night had flushed silver, as if the moon had crept from behind clouds. Yet the moon had set an hour ago.

Her eyes felt cool yet itchy hot at the same time. She wanted to rub them, but feared to interfere with the magic. Instead the fighter tried to orient herself as quickly as possible. The magic wouldn't last long, and the whole forest needed help, it seemed.

Gradually she sorted out images. The world was flatter, as if seen underwater. But every tree trunk, every jag in the rough bark, was crystal clear. Blinking, Cerise saw a carpenter ant struggle up the bark, a black ant on a dark gray background.

Turning, she saw pine needles underfoot, fallen pine cones, a buckle torn from someone's shoe. In her camp, the fire was a bed of glowing coals. Beside it, Byron pushed up with his arms like an invalid. Veronica stood open-mouthed with her quarterstaff ready, but obviously couldn't see much. Cerise could have tweaked her nose, as if she were invisible. Lying at the edge of the camp was the brute who'd charged them. He had on a long, tattered smock and deerhide trousers and brogans, was strapped about with a baldric and various pouches. Four feet from his hand lay a wicked-edged war axe. For a second, Cerise wondered why he'd attacked them personally, then she pushed it from her mind.

Magog yipped, whipped her tail happily so it batted her mistress's leg. Out on the road, swords clashed and clanged, men and women bellowed. But now Cerise could see that no one pressed an attack, as if offering a diversion.

Yet a hundred feet off, another party had been singled out for attack. Pushed by enemies, the defenders retreated this way.

Cerise hissed to Magog. Padding silently, the two dashed across the forest floor.

As near as she could tell, a half-dozen bandits—four men and two women—had beset three travellers. At the center was a tall young man, a noble by his expensive clothing, who fought with a heavy cut-and-thrust sword and a buckler, a round shield strapped to his left forearm. Guarding his left was a gray-haired woman who fought like a tiger, and behind him a podgy man, probably a squire, with a thick-bladed hunting falchion and round shield. They fought well against twice as many, but all three were bleeding. Cerise wondered who the nobleman was, that so-called robbers battled so hard to kill him.

Then she plunged into the fight.

The squire had the hardest time, beset by two men who wanted to carve through him and stab the nobleman from behind. Whistling low to her dog, the swordswoman circled toward them. She had to beware not only of backthrusts from the bandits, but of the defenders breaking free and stabbing as they went, as well as watch she didn't trip over Magog or jab her accidentally.

Easily as beheading a chicken, Cerise slid behind a bandit and neatly hamstrung him with a forward slice of her rapier. The man gasped. He barely felt the sharp cut but suddenly could not stand on that leg. He crumpled, grabbing air. With her marvelous cat's-eye vision, Cerise whisked a return stroke under his chin. The man gargled blood as his throat was cut.

Missing his companion, the other bandit whirled, dancing out of distance of the squire's short falchion. Cerise saw his head whip right and left to gauge where she stood. But normal night vision counted for little under these trees.

Magog caught his heel and he stumbled, cursing. Cerise noted he was dressed rudely as the other bandits, in linen and deerhide, but was neatly shaven. Odd for a "woods beast."

Off-balance, unsure where the real enemy lay, the villain took a mighty swing with a short sword. It would have cloven Cerise to the spine had she stood still, but she sidestepped easily. When the sword ended its arc, too high to nick Magog, she jabbed for his breadbasket, thrust upwards. Her thin blade punctured his liver and lung and the man squeaked. He grabbed blindly for the offending blade and sliced his palm and fingers. Dipping, thrusting, Cerise nicked his heart. The man rolled backwards over her wolfhound and fell unmoving.

"Good girl!" whispered Cerise.

"What's— Who's—" His assailants felled, the podgy squire was confused. "Who's there?"

"A friend! Friends!" Cerise moved on. Anyone could claim to be a friend, and to stand still in battle was fatal.

The gray-haired defending woman hissed. She was locked blade-to-blade with a bandit who tried to shove her off-balance. At the same time, a female bandit thrust at her side, and she had to fend that blade aside with a gauntleted hand. In two seconds, she'd stumble back and be lanced through the guts.

With a snap of her fingers, Cerise sicced Magog on the bandits belaboring the nobleman. Then the swordswoman leapt to aid her sister in steel.

Keeping well back, Cerise angled her blade between the two assassins. She snapped down her tip to sever the cords in a man's hand. He'd been sweeping wide when his suddenly-powerless hand released the sword. Flying, the blade bounced off a shield and cartwheeled. The sword pommel thumped against Cerise's breast.

Startled, she jumped back. Overconfident, she had gotten too close, might have lost an eye. Magicked or not, she must be more careful.

Wary, she resumed the attack, slashing at the other bandit's face. The woman sensed her somehow, by smell or body heat. She jerked her sword up to slice Cerise, but the frontierswoman easily parried her blade. With her superior cat-vision, it was like fighting a blindfolded opponent. Her thin steel slashed the bandit's face, cut the bridge of her nose, destroyed an eye. Shrieking, clawing at her ruined face, her elbows went up. Cerise lunged beneath, slid between the woman's ribs, punctured her heart. The woman keeled over and hit the forest turf with a thump. Pounding sounded: the bandit with the sliced hand running.

The bandits ganging the nobleman heard their companions' screams. A female bandit disengaged and backed into the gaping jaws of Magog, who bit hard on her calf. She tumbled with a whoop.

The last bandit, male, cried "Andromeda!" with the distress of a lover. Confused by the dark, he spun the wrong way. Because he looked capable and dangerous, Cerise flicked her sword hilt straight up to the prime position, stabbed him behind the ear. A major artery severed, he gushed blood and fainted.

Sprawled, the last female bandit wrestled to stab Magog with a dagger, but the canny dog hung onto the woman's lower leg and jerked her backwards with mighty tugs. With cat's eyes Cerise saw the dagger flare silver. She smacked the blade with her own, but the bandit clung. Grimly, lest her dog be stabbed, Cerise sliced her sword tip across the woman's knuckles. All four fingers were cut to the bone, and this time when she smacked the blade, it sailed into the dark. "Magog, hold her!

"Hold! Put up your swords!" Cerise called to the defenders. "I'm a friend! The bandits are dead or defeated!"

Despite a bleeding palm, the elderly swordswoman snatched the shoulder of the nobleman and shoved him onto his duff. She squatted into attack position. "We don't know that! Put up *your* sword and we'll believe!"

Tough, Cerise thought, and trusting no one. A woman after her own heart. Backing out of range, Cerise raised her sword to the tierce position: hilt hip-high, blade upright and ready to snap down. "I'm Cerise, a friend. The bandits attacked our camp, too."

"Then why are you here?" demanded the defender. "And how can you move in the dark like a wraith? And what's that with you? A dog?"

In her excitement, Cerise had forgotten Byron and Veronica. She hurled answers to placate the woman. "A wolfhound. I needs check my camp! Gird for more bandits, for they aren't simple bandits! Magog, come!" She dashed off.

An armed horde had invaded her camp.

Byron had finally sat up, shivering. Having conjured, he felt he'd slogged ten miles through a snowstorm.

Someone big stumbled into him and swore. Veronica had been blowing up the fire with ashes in her eyes. Now, she bleated as six bandits dashed from the encircling darkness.

Bumped, jolted, Byron instinctively grabbed in his shirt for his pouch. If he'd sorted properly, his most offensive card was third in the deck, but he was dizzy, frozen-fingered, and couldn't see. He counted down, caught a card and tugged it loose.

Tall rough legs and unsheathed swords surrounded him. Strong hands pinned him.

"This the bastard?"

" 'At's him! Move out! Someone kill that priest!"

Weighing little, Byron was hefted easily by four brawny hands. He slumped to make it harder to lift him, but they dug in thick fingernails. He twisted and squirmed until someone banged a fist alongside his head.

Past spinning stars, Byron glimpsed Veronica diving for her quarterstaff. But a boot tromped it flat and another kicked her sprawling. A sword flashed up, then down to stab the girl—

And was deflected with an earsmashing clang.

Flower colors and brass flickered in the firelight. Dimly, Byron recognized the cardmaster Ingrid, her matching sword and dagger spinning like fireworks. The woman who'd made to stab Veronica got a blade slice between her wrist bones. She screamed as blood pinwheeled. The man opposite her leaped back, thumped a tree, had a chunk shorn off his nose as Ingrid's sword flashed.

The cardsmith lost sight of the battle as his abductors jogged into the forest. The burly men grunted as they trotted, and Byron's lungs were squeezed in rhythm. Vaguely he thought: This is good, in a way, because it confirms my and Cerise's fears. Someone really *is* out to get me, even this far from Waterholm. But he still didn't know who or why, unless it was still for dead Rayner's cards stuffed in his shirt.

And one miraculously still clutched in his hand.

More than anything, Byron wanted to get warm and sleep. He was only barely conscious. Magic wasn't worth it, his mind meandered. It took too great a toll on your body, left you feeling sick or wasted, or else froze you solid. And all for money, of which there was never enough to keep you warm. Magic got you killed in too many ways.

Like being kidnapped into the forest by bandits, he recalled.

Ah. He should do something about that. Oh, yes, the card in his hand. Wouldn't Cerise be impressed when he triggered this one? And Ingrid? They might have flashy weapons, but he had pieces of cardboard with pictures. And magic behind them. Sometimes.

Fighting for breath and clear thoughts, Byron dragged his hands up to his chest. His captors, busy dodging trees and uneven ground, didn't notice. With regret, Byron recalled how he'd once triggered this spell accidentally and paid the price. But it couldn't be helped.

Hands and body jiggling, he dug a dirty finger in his nose, then smeared it on the card.

For a second, nothing happened, and he wondered if he'd plucked the right card from the deck. It would be stupid to wipe snot on a Garden Pests Begone card.

The card warmed suddenly, puffed, then gushed a billowing green-yellow cloud that enveloped them all.

Byron tried not to breathe, managed for ten seconds, then his lungs flexed. He snorted in clouds of Devil's Fart.

Rayner made this card often, in large batches, for pranksters, students, and other oddballs to set off in church, at family reunions, at parties, or in alleys to incapacitate people with fat purses. Byron had helped fabricate them, steeping them in manure, piss, rotten eggs, sewer gas, and other vile substances. Sniffling from a head cold one day, he'd wiped his nose and picked up a card at the wrong time, filled Rayner's workshop with the stench.

This time was worse.

One whiff and Byron vomited. He folded in half, puking up dinner and every other meal for the past few days. He bounced on turf as his captors also curled into spewing, strangling, gagging balls. Byron rolled onto his face and got a mouthful of pine needles. He crawled blindly, but the stink was everywhere, inescapable. The air got worse as one of the bandits shit his trousers.

Never, thought Byron while retching, his stomach a knot of agony, never again would he trigger this spell. It was too horrible and too humiliating. Soul Destruction was a balm compared to it. Better he died.

He crawled, made a foot, kept going. Maybe in a year or so he'd be free of the putrid scent.

Over his own heaving, he heard shouts. Then more folks retching. His rescuers had run smack into the cloud. Wonderful. He hoped one of them would miss with a sword thrust and kill him. Anything to stop the gut-wrenching pain.

But the cloud would blow away on a breeze, and now he felt one on his fevered brow. Voices got louder. He was still crawling, his stomach still spasming. He fell face down, breathed the clean sweet aroma of pine and earth, forced his guts to relax. Slowly, slowly, he could breathe again.

A snuffling sounded, then something hot and slimy lapped his face, clogged his nostrils. Magog, delighting in wretched odors.

From above came a voice. "Is he alive?" Veronica.

"Hard to say." Cerise. "He smells dead."

"Insults," Byron gasped. "Always insults. I'd have to die to—*blagh! Get away!*—get a compliment around here."

"What shall we do with him?" Veronica piped.

"Tie a rope onto his foot," Cerise suggested, "and drag him into the stream."

And despite Byron's feeble protests, that's what they did.

Sometime later, the cardsmith hunkered by the campfire, naked and wrapped in two blankets but still shivering. Dawn was not far off. He'd slept a while, demons mocking his puking with flaring nostrils, protruding tongues, and bulging eyes. His only consolation was that he'd handed over his purse of cards before they'd dunked him.

"Not that the damned cards do me good," he groused. "They'll get me killed yet."

"You saved our lives with that Cat's Eye spell," Cerise stated.

Veronica fried bacon and dripped the grease on bread. "Want some?"

Ingrid handed him a tin cup of rosehip tea. "Drink up. You'll feel better."

The smells flipped Byron's stomach and drove him back under the blankets. But after a while his native curiosity, his curse, prodded him alive. Throat sore, he croaked, "Has anyone figured out the object of that raid?"

Cerise's and the nobleman's parties now ringed the fire. Byron was introduced to the nobleman, Stanwin the Younger.

"Stanwin?" he rasped. "Like Duke Stanwin who's hosting this fair in Thallandia?"

"My father," replied the young man proudly. Young Stanwin was square-jawed, keen-eyed, white-toothed, sun-tanned, handsome and handsomely dressed in a brocaded green doublet and wide hat with ostrich feather, silk trousers and polished boots, and a wolf-edged cloak with the family broken-chain crest embroidered in gold thread.

Naked, baggy-eyed, haggard and wet, Byron felt like a drowned sewer rat in comparison. Maybe the man was a louse, he hoped, and spent all his time fighting and drinking and wenching and contracting odious diseases. But Stanwin shattered this hope. "I've been away, spreading goodwill with neighbors in my father's name. I've visited the homes of knights and peasants, listened to their problems and tried to help them, pitching in to dig a drainage ditch or erect a dam or repair a mill, seeing the women and children and elders aren't forgotten, that everyone has enough to eat, arranging for physicians, that sort of thing. It's been wonderful fun, but now we journey home for the the Great Game."

Byron groaned inwardly. Maybe the man kicked dogs when no one was looking. But Magog took to Stanwin immediately, laid her shaggy head on his knee. Chuckling, he scritched her head, and she thumped her tail in delight.

With Stanwin was his pudgy squire, a middle-aged man named Yves who could cook and clean and sharpen a sword edge. And Molly, Stanwin's "combat trainer." That explained her clothes, Byron thought, like a cardmaster's only simpler, gray leather armor and trim breeches, a rose-colored cloak, a hat with the brim turned up on one side. Despite her gray hair, Molly seemed no more than forty years old. Watching her slow but stealthy movements, Byron decided she was like Cerise, a coiled spring, quick to strike as a rattlesnake.

All three, Stanwin, Yves, and Molly, wore red-stained bandages.

Cerise, her eyelids heavy from a night without sleep, answered Byron's question. "We think the raid was two-fold. Stanwin's party was attacked by double numbers and slashed viciously. Obviously an assassination. But you were grabbed and hustled off like a prize hog. So, at a guess, we play two games at once: kill the nobleman and capture the cardsmith. But why two goals from the same thugs?"

Before Byron could answer, Cerise added, "Come see this." She caught his arm and helped him rise. Byron clutched his blankets with numb hands. Not wanting to separate, the party moved together deeper into the forest.

On the sward lay nine bloodied bodies, male and female bandits dressed alike. Very much alike, Byron thought, as if their rude foresters' clothing were a uniform. He wrinkled his nose: either Devil's Fart lingered in his nostrils, or someone had charred flesh.

Cerise nudged the foot of a cleanshaven man. "No beard. Odd for a hill bandit. Odder still, Stanwin recognizes him."

"Aye," said the nobleman. "Ferdinand, once in my father's bodyguard."

"Eh?" Byron rasped. "What's he doing out here?"

Molly answered, her voice low-pitched and melodious. "That's what we wonder. Is he just a renegade, run off from the Duke's household because he committed some offense? Or did someone send him to hide in the forest to assassinate us returning home? And why should members of his party try to abduct you, whom no one's ever seen before?"

Mind whirling, Byron blinked. They'd left intrigue behind in Waterholm without solving it. Now, they weren't even to Thallandia and interrupted an assassination. He saw sleepless nights ahead.

He asked, "Is this all of them? How many ran off?"

Cerise kicked two more feet, a man's and a woman's. Byron saw their bellies were scorched as if they'd tumbled in a fire. "We don't know how many ran off. There were more villains creating a diversion on the road. These two were left behind. I staked them down and shovelled coals onto their stomachs. They claimed only Ferdinand knew who they worked for. By the time their skin charred through to guts, we believed them. Then they died."

Byron winced, but remembered Cerise came from the frontier, had seen her family tortured and eaten. He was glad he'd passed out. Suddenly, he wished he was back in Waterholm, sitting in a pub and flirting with barmaids, his only worry whether Rayner would be in a good mood today.

"There'll be more before this is over," Molly growled. "We'll find who's at the bottom of this conspiracy if we have to carve our way through the jousts and the Great Game!"

There were mutters of agreement. As one, the fighters plucked their swords and shot them home in scabbards.

They have heaps of weapons, Byron thought, and I have a stack of pasteboard cards, half useless, half unknown.

If this was adventure, then life with grumpy old Rayner hadn't been so bad.

Chapter 8

"Well, it's not hard and it *is* hard. Rayner said it was like cutting out your own liver with a dull knife. I mean, how many other trades require you to sacrifice your very spirit? Does a knifemaker have to open his veins to temper blades, or a cobbler peel off his own skin to make shoes? But you get better with practice. Or worse, because you try bigger spells— Am I babbling?"

Ingrid laughed throatily and set Byron's spine atingle. "No, not at all! It's fascinating to see cardsmithing from the other side."

Cerise warned from ahead, "You'll be seeing it from under my boots if you don't stop pestering him for trade secrets."

The combined party plodded through a hilly pass with grass and sheep on both sides. In the distance were tree-covered hills, ever-steepening. The rocky road had climbed steadily for days, leaving the horses gasping. But they were almost at their destination.

Other pilgrims jammed the road ahead and behind, singing, laughing, promising themselves and others fun and riches. Their party was led by Stanwin and Molly. Skinny Veronica rode as close to the nobleman as possible, occasionally tooting her flute. Yves and Cerise plodded in the middle while Ingrid and Byron bumped along in the rear.

The blonde-and-brunette swordswoman Ingrid had attached herself to the party. Even Cerise had to admit she'd saved the lives of Veronica and Byron, and the party could use another sword to guard Stanwin and Byron's cards.

It was no longer a secret he carried the magic items, nor that someone—possibly the bishop and perhaps someone else—pursued the cards. They'd pored over the deck and talked long around campfires. They guessed about unknown cards, replayed the varied attacks, discussed Ferdinand, bodyguard-turned-bandit, and hashed over conspiracy theories, but still had no clear story or clues. Often they discussed the upcoming Great Game: Duke Stanwin had invited two neighboring lords to participate, but no one, including Young Stanwin, knew the game's stakes. Wild rumors muddied already-murky waters.

For days, Ingrid had clung to Byron, questioning him about cardsmithing, complimenting him, laughing at his jokes. At her urging, and within the party's comparative safety, he'd redonned his cardmaster's uniform: black doublet, breeches, hose, cape, small hat. Ingrid thought him "handsome and dashing." Cerise ground her teeth at every sexy chuckle.

Now Ingrid called ahead, "Are you his mother, Cerise? You're old enough."

The frontierswoman craned her head around. "This mother will turn you over her knee and spank your plump backside."

"Is that how you get your fun?" asked Ingrid innocently. "Some of us prefer men."

"Yes, any man, no doubt. But keep prying at my cardsmith, and we'll see what kind of meat you can eat. You and I will cross swords some day, and I'll needs put flowers on your grave."

Ingrid rolled her eyes and sniffed. To Byron she whispered, "Pay no attention. She's jealous because she can't catch a man's eye."

"I don't think she wants it," Byron murmured. "Or any other part of a man. Cerise doesn't need anyone. She's independent as a wildcat."

Byron was embarrassed when the feuding women tore shreds off one another. He didn't want his friend Cerise slandered, but also didn't want to lose Ingrid's attention. Flattery or not, he enjoyed it. And so far he hadn't spilled any great secrets—he hoped.

Ingrid set his head spinning with another compliment. "I have to say, Byron, that I prefer your company to Young Stanwin's. You're much more polite and interesting, and so much more—exciting!"

Byron felt himself blushing. And doubting. No one was more courtly or considerate of man or woman than Stanwin, heir to Thallandia. Secretly Byron guessed she wanted his cards. But at her prompting, he carried on, voice low.

"Basically, a cardsmith can imagine anything he or she wants on a card. It all comes from whether you can 'see and bind' magic—whatever magic is.

Scholars spend years arguing about the source of magic. Does it come from within a magicmaker or from without? Is it someone's life spirit, ripped from their brain or soul? If so, can anyone learn to bend magic? Or is it part of nature, like water in the air or gold in the earth? If so, could anyone find a 'vein' of magic and mine it? Is there some simpler way to control magic we haven't discovered yet?

"And why can some people perform spells without cards, like my finger-snapping fire? Not much of a power, mind you, but it's unique. And handy. Another of our apprentices can make beer go flat by sticking her finger in a mug. Fun for a joke, but useless otherwise. One fellow I know can make birds fly to his hand like Saint Catania; we don't even know if that's magic or not.

"Magicking is so sporadic, too. The rate of success in fashioning cards is atrociously low. Rayner was a great smith, practiced for years, but he still only managed one or two cards every third night. Sometimes he'd concentrate until veins bulged in his forehead but yield nothing. The magic wouldn't come, or faded too soon. He hit about one in two tries with spells he knew, and perhaps one in four with new ones.

"I can hit one in three with spells I know, simple ones like that Cat's Eye card. Except that spell bound quicker this time. Magic seems easier all of a sudden. As if I'd inherited Rayner's power when he died, which doesn't make sense. Or I've gotten better since—" He stopped, barely clamming up in time. He'd almost blabbed, "since I started having demonic nightmares."

A new, curious thought struck him: Could the nightmares actually be a *good* sign he was growing in magical power? Could the demons be *helping* him while pursuing him? If so, what was their price? Nothing is free, Rayner had intoned often, especially magic.

If Ingrid noted his halt, she ignored it. "So, Byron. Can a great cardsmith imagine anything, then?"

"Hunh? Oh, no, no. For one thing, you can't conjure something from nothing. You can't make bricks without clay, or fire without fuel. You couldn't just conjure a dragon; you'd need tons of meat and bone and blood. There are stories that far in the East, in Karzakhan and Valay, dragons are fabricated from these big lizards they capture on an island. But then I've heard stories of sea serpents in the Wis Waterfall, too. I suppose you could fashion, for instance, a minotaur if you could merge a man and a bull. No one's done it yet.

"See how it works? A cardsmith doesn't really *make* something as much as *convert* it. The simplest cards change intangibles like emotions: apathy into lust, a lie into true-speaking, silence into babble. A step up is to change one thing into something else. Old Horacio trapped me and Cerise with a 'spiderweb' spun from leaves. The Blast Crops spell lowers the temperature to turn dew into frost. Normal vision into cat's vision. Pure air into Devil's Fart. Even a Fountain card doesn't create water; it turns dirt into water. It's a good thing, too. Simpler spells require little magic or life force.

"For instance, people came to Rayner all the time asking for a Shower of Gold card. Think: If Rayner could fashion gold from thin air, would he risk his life and sanity fabricating cards in the dead of night? And what would a customer pay for such a card?

Diamonds worth more than the gold? People are foolish about magic sometimes.

"Instead, he'd sell them a Transmute Lead to Gold card. Alchemists say lead lying in the ground eventually purifies into gold; that's why they're both so heavy. Rayner's card made the purification happen quicker. Mercury, *quick*silver, was the token. But he charged barrels of money for the card, and only made it once or twice a year, it cost him so much life force.

"A cheaper, easier spell was Sniff Out Gold for prospectors to take into the mountains. The gold is already waiting to be discovered. The customer just needs help to find it—"

"Home!" boomed a voice. *"There she lies! Thallandia!"*

Past a final rise, the whole valley of Thallandia lay before them. Young Stanwin reared in his stirrups and shouted for joy. Transported with happiness, he hopped off his big palamino and trotted to a nearby ridge just to drink in the sight of home. The others copied, letting their horses rest from the climb.

Thallandia was rugged and beautiful at the same time. The valley was miles wide, a rolling jumble of hills and rills dotted with farms and plowed fields and stone walls. The last habitable place in the kingdom, for past the valley mountains rose like a misty blue curtain eastward.

Trees clustered along the lower slopes of the mountains, but eventually failed, leaving only snow and stone high up. The peaks were peculiar, crowding the skyline but broken in their attempt to encompass the world. Great gaps like hatchet blows had chopped the ridge in a hundred places, until the skyline looked like the backbone of a primordial monster. Snow filled each crevasse but, torn by eternal winds, left only long white streaks to mark each cleft. From these stripes of white on gray came the name White Bone Mountains—that, and the spectre of death on the other side.

Byron shaded his eyes and stared. The mountains, he knew, were a barricade against the east. Past them, the land fell again to a vast rugged plain, then to steppelands and badlands. From that grim world streamed the hordes of the Shinyar, torturers and cannibals, incredibly savage—and moving like locusts this way.

Out there Cerise had been born, Byron reflected, and out there all her kinsfolk had been massacred. He glanced at his companion, saw her staring heavy-lidded without emotion. But her jaw clenched, and her hands flexed on her weapon hilts.

Scanning, Byron marked the deepest cleft, the Eagle's Road, the only true pass through the White Bone Mountains. It was open only four months a year, when howling winds tempered by summer sun blew out the last shreds of snow to permit tiny humans and their mounts to creep through. There were years, and had been decades, Cerise said, when the weather didn't soften and the pass stayed closed. But in past years, she added, with drought in the east, the Eagle's Road was clear almost six months. Pushed by lack of water and graze, the Shinyar could stampede through at any time.

If so, they had to thunder through Thallandia.

Byron dropped his gaze. The actual pass was still ten leagues, or thirty miles, distant. No one lived in the pass except soldiers on post. The first thing a traveller, or invader, found upon descending was the Keep at Thallandia.

Gateway to the West, home to the Duke of Thallandia, the keep was massive. Cut into living rock and heaped high above it, the castle spanned a gap wide enough for only a single horseman to ride through. On the left was the castle proper, block and tower and tier upon tier until it looked half a mountain itself. Across a thick bridge above the gap—barred with triple portcullises of hardwood and iron—was more castle, home to five hundred soldiers. So important to the kingdom was this gap that the Duke was lent troops from the various fiefs north and south and west, each bivouaced at their lords' expense for the protection of all.

Still, for all the castle pennants snapped bravely in the eternal wind from the east, and for all the soldier's shields ranged along the walls displaying diverse colors and designs, the Keep at Thallandia seemed a toy against the forbidding mountains— and the threat of thousands of hungry Shinyar beyond.

In the shadow of the castle was the town Thallandia, sturdy houses of stone and wooden beams and stucco. And before the town, sprawling across the three roads leading to farmland, was a new, temporary "town"—a great fair of striped tents and stages and ramshackle shops and jousting lists and tournament fields and corrals and haystacks and much more. Byron smiled at the sight, for all that colorful bravery seemed to dare the Shinyar to invade the graceful west.

He smiled for himself, too. No matter his troubles, of thugs hunting him by day and demons plaguing his dreams, here he'd find adventure and joy and that most precious thing, further knowledge of magic and its secrets. And if he could get Ingrid to stay close by, day and night, things would be about as fine as life could get.

Then a gust of wind from the east swirled by, chilling him, so he tugged his cape around his chest. The biggest problem, he thought, was how life and magic conflicted. Rayner, who had loved life and wine and women and song, had practiced magic and frozen solid as those mountaintops. Practicing magic brought Byron demons in his dreams, and cards in his shirt that thieves would kill for. Maybe it would be good if someone stole all his cards. . . .

"Hoy!" A voice broke his thoughts. "Molly, do you see?"

"I see!" echoed the combat master. "It's not good, milord!"

Byron peered from under his hands at the castle. Now he saw. Above each bright flapping pennant was a small black flag. "What does that mean?"

Molly swung to the saddle. "It means someone important has died! *Hyaah!*"

The young nobleman already rode hell-for-leather for the castle. The party scrambled to chase him.

Portents of evil increased as they galloped headlong through the sprawling fair. For as people recognized the young noble, rather than cheer and wave their hats, they grabbed their faces and hair and sent up a hideous weeping and wailing—a valley-wide cry of mourning.

Stanwin never stopped for the castle guards, only called to clear the way. Six companions rode hard on his heels, hooves clattering and striking sparks on cobblestones, Magog galumphing full tilt with her red tongue lolling out.

As Stanwin vaulted from the saddle, male and female guards rushed from all around, many weeping, tears dripping from the men's proud mustaches. But they attended their duty even in sorrow, dropped halberds and lances across the paths of the six companions. Choking with emotion, Stanwin yet remembered his manners. "These people saved my life—they are to be treated as guests with all courtesy."

Then he raced up the narrow ramp into the keep, to the main hall. Six ran with him.

Home, the handsome young nobleman reverted almost to a child. "Father! Father! Where are you?"

Around him clustered butlers, maids, cooks, all in ancestral green and chain-and-rye sigil. From an upper room bustled a roly-poly man. His baggy breeches, long flowing vest, and golden chain around his neck hung with a gold key marked him as the keeper of the keys, the chancellor, the lord's right-hand man, who oversaw the day-to-day workings of the fief and, absent a lord, made all the decisions. Stanwin clapped the small chancellor on the shoulders and held on. The young noble was crying, his tears matching the chancellor's. He cried, "Chancellor! Clement! Please, my friend, tell me the worst!"

"Would I were the lowest peasant in the fief," the man lamented, "than the one to bear bad news! But your father, good Duke Stanwin, may his name always be treasured, has—has—"

He broke down, and Stanwin had to shake the rest out of him. "He's—gone, sire! He passed away not a fortnight ago, quietly, in his sleep! Such an ignoble death for him who rode through combat, through showers of arrows and forests of steel! But he was old, good Stanwin, and the winter was long and the wind off the mountains strong enough to snap flagpoles! He got a cough in his lungs—and he—he could not fight it, sire! It was quick! No man could lay him low, but the night wind stole his breath, the invisible thief we all fear—and now—and now he is no more . . ." The poor chancellor couldn't continue, and thumped his head on Stanwin's broad chest, and cried like a baby. As did the nobleman, holding his old friend and family retainer as if he, and not the son, needed the comfort.

Molly, Yves, Byron, Cerise, Veronica, and Ingrid, and even Magog held their breath lest they interrupt the sacred moment. Feeling like an intruder on this family scene, Byron wished he were somewhere else.

"Oh, Lumpkin!" crooned the chancellor, making the others start at the childish nickname. "Your father was so proud of you! In his last days, when he was failing, he talked only of you! He laid plans, charged me with a hundred tasks you might address. Ah, Lump, you'll—"

The round man froze, straightened as if he'd been lashed. Hastily he backed away, ran pudgy hands over the untidy brown curls that covered his head. "But what am I saying? Pray, sire, please forgive me! I've forgotten myself!"

"What?" Stanwin stood with open hands, shaking his head. "What? Clement, what is it?"

"Sire!" The man's eyes were round as saucers. "I've been manhandling you like some child! But that cannot be! As of two weeks ago, as now, you are a lord! Sire, you are the new Duke of Thallandia!"

❖   ❖   ❖

Hours later, Byron sat on a bed wider than he could reach with both arms and half again as long. The bed was laid with fresh linens, and wolf- and sheepskins were heaped on a carved chest at the foot. By candlelight, he scanned the walls hung with glowing tapestries recalling fabulous deeds—hunting unicorns, trumpeting to battle, sailing the green ocean against monsters—and in a carved wardrobe hung cloaks and gowns edged in ermine and mink. The cardsmith took off his dusty boots and laid his round hat on the bed. He didn't even care that, because of crowding on this second guest floor—which had forty-some rooms, he'd heard—he had an inside room, against the hill with no windows, while Cerise had an outside room. Just having a comfortable bed was a luxury! But he'd have to ask for a fire in the small hearth: even in warm spring weather the cardsmith felt chilled.

Cerise knocked, entered. She'd shed her cloak but retained her weapons, which rattled as they swung around her. "Not sleepy, eh?"

Byron shook his head. "I can't be comfortable in this room. It's too fancy for me. I feel out of place as a cockroach on a dinner table."

Cerise nodded and, turning her scabbards out, sat opposite him, six feet away. Magog padded in, plomped her big head on the pile of skins. "I know what you mean. I've stayed in fancy inns and manors, but nothing like this. Wait'll you see dinner. No doubt seventeen courses and five sets of cutlery."

"A spoon and bowl would suit me. Some stew and black bread."

More nodding. "Aye, we're peasants at heart, and I'm glad. Castles are grand to look at, but hell to live in. The smallest crofter's cottage in the valley will be warmer and snugger than this rockpile in winter. The winds will howl through these spaces. It's no wonder the lord died of lung rot. It's that or overeating usually kills them."

Byron nodded absently. "I've never had a nobleman with his own fief for a friend before."

"Nor I, but don't fret. Now that he's duke, he'll be busy sunup to sundown listening to gossip and complaints and lists and reports. And when he snatches a few minutes' peace, it'll be to ride with hounds or go hawking, or to select a bride, for lords must be married. Nobles hang with nobles, not gutter rats like us. In three days, he'll have forgotten our names."

Byron didn't think so. Stanwin had too big a heart. But the man would be busy as a salamander in a fire. "We'll still be valuable in the Great Game."

Cerise scritched her dog's head, and the tail beat the stone floor. "Valuable resources, yes. Hired help like horses and hounds. But we'll be rich if we play our cards right."

Byron hopped off the bed, too excited to rest. "What's your room like?" Cerise laughed and waved graciously at the door.

They crossed a wide hall flagged with blue stone that curved out of sight in both directions, for the massive castle followed the contours of the stony hill it had been carved from. Cerise's room was much the same, only with windows. Byron could see over the castle's outer curtain, squinting as the sun set behind the ragged forest to the west. Beyond the town the fair was booming. Noise perked up with sunset as families came to frolic after a day of tilling

and planting. Flutes and tambours and horns colored
the wind as a parade formed. The old duke might
be dead, but he'd been a stranger to the transients
out there. And now the commoners of Thallandia
had a new duke to protect them, so their lives were
complete. On with celebrating.

"The Great Game will go on, won't it? The terms
must have been agreed upon last fall, and nothing
can alter them. Poor Stanwin, excuse me, *Duke*
Stanwin will learn to swim by being pitched in
midstream."

"Aye." Cerise stood by him. He smelled her natural
outdoors perfume, an odd blend of sage and spice,
leather and camp smoke and horses. "Let's hope
the duke left him a strategy on how to play. There's
more to a Great Game than flipping cards on a
table."

"He's got other worries, too." Byron spun too quickly,
and Magog growled a warning. The cardsmith backed
away. "Easy girl . . . One of the duke's bodyguards
was raiding as a bandit. If someone in this castle
ordered the attack on Stanwin, then he's in danger
here, too."

"Perhaps, but you can't jump at every shadow.
Men have been cashiered in the past and become
rogues in the woods." Cerise took out her dagger,
tapped the point on the windowsill idly. "But the
other side of the card *is* a conspiracy. Where there's
a court, there's court intrigue, even if it's just vying
for favors or land grants or tax exemptions. Honest
Stanwin will be a sheep amongst wolves. It's lucky
he's got such a loyal chancellor to watch his back
and help him over rough spots."

"I wonder . . ."

"Wonder what?" Cerise's swarthy face was ruddy orange in the setting sunlight.

"I wonder if the duke died naturally."

Cerise's dagger stopped its quiet tapping. "You mean, was he—murdered?"

Byron sighed. "Yes. That's what I mean."

Chapter 9

Crowded by new ideas, Byron talked fast. "The duke died of lung rot! It's possible to cause that magically!"

"There's a card for everything," Cerise frowned. "But this man was ancient— Hist!"

A girl came in the door. " 'Scuse me, sir, ma'am, jus' fetchin' t'water." She hoisted a heavy ewer and poured fresh water into a redware bowl on a commode, that the guests might wash before dinner.

Byron tried not to stare. The girl was pretty in a simple way, dark hair drawn neatly to the nape of her neck. Her maid's outfit was a white chemise with green bodice and skirt and a bright white apron pinned before.

Suddenly he had an idea. "Um, wench . . ."

The girl's dark eyes flashed.

Byron grunted as Cerise's hard elbow banged his ribs.

"*Rose*."

"I'm—*ouch*—sorry, miss. Rose. I'm just a—*oof*—common oaf let loose in the castle. No more manners than this dog."

Cerise snorted. "Fewer."

"Uh, right." Byron tripped over his tongue as the girl stared pointedly. "Uh, please, can you tell me if there were any, uh, rumors about the duke's death?"

"Rumors, sir?" She was deliberately vague and blank, the perfect servant.

"Oh . . ." Byron forged ahead. If anyone had suspicions, it would be the household staff, who knew everything. "We were just curious if, oh, anyone thought the duke's death were too sudden, or strange."

The maid bit her lower lip. She glanced out the door, into the hall, but remained silent. Byron knew why: if she were caught spilling royal secrets, she could be discharged, even whipped or imprisoned.

Cerise took over. "Rose. We're friends of the new duke. We saved his life; undoubtedly, you know that. But we're new here, and so is he. If you know anything that might help Stanwin, please tell us. I give my word we'll keep it secret and you'll come to no harm."

The girl fidgeted. "It's not that. We all know . . . something is amiss but . . . no one's sure what to do or say about it. And it wouldn't help much now. Poor Lord Stanwin is dead and buried in the family crypt—"

"Might we see his chambers?" asked Byron.

"Eh?" The girl blinked. Her eyes, the cardsmith noted, were green. "Why see them? Sir?"

"We might learn something." Byron waved a hand. "But I can't tell what until we look."

The maid nodded, then crooked a finger. Cerise

shrugged her baldric higher on her shoulder, called to her dog. They followed the maid into the curving hall, but rather than turn to the wide central staircase, she passed into Byron's room. At the back wall, she tugged a heavy tapestry aside. Behind it was a wooden door set flush. It opened silently on oiled hinges.

Inside was a dim winding passageway with tiny windows at far ends or high up, the distant light tinged red with sunset. The back wall of Byron's room was square-cut blocks. The opposite wall was rough-hewn, dimpled as a cave wall. Every surface except the floor was whitewashed to spread the meager light.

"A secret passage!" breathed the cardsmith. "Just like in old stories!"

"Hardly secret," Rose smiled and led left. "It's just the servants' hall."

"The what?"

"We're not supposed to be seen if possible. The main stairs are for nobles and their guests." Her tone was bitter: she might be a commoner, but she had pride. "So we use these back stairs. They connect to the kitchen and cellars and run behind half the rooms all the way to the third floor. They're handy to fetch linen and cordwood and water and—other uses."

Byron followed close behind the girl. He liked her smell, like fresh flowers and milk. To keep her talking, he asked, "What other uses?"

"Night traffic is one," she replied blandly.

"What kind of—oh." Meaning lovers could come and go through the back stairs without being seen in the hallways. Byron thought back to Cerise's words.

There were more types of castle intrigue than politics. "But how did they get here?"

"The castle was hacked out of the mountain in the old days, cut higgledy-piggledy where the stone was soft or there were caves. Over time, they squared off the rooms by building neat back walls. These irregular passages were left over. In some places they enter caves, but those are sealed. The lifeguards check regularly for tampering."

"Tampering by whom?"

"Enemies." The girl hiked her skirts and mounted a stair, half cut, half constructed. Byron watched her hips sway from side to side, tried to guess what was skirt and what girl. The whisper of petticoats was exciting, too. Cerise must have seen his gaze, for she poked him in the back.

Up another story, the maid turned without wavering. Byron found the passages confusing, for they had odd widths and turns, and the floor wasn't always smooth. He stumbled more than once.

Rose paused at another wooden door, peeked through, lowered her voice. "These are the old duke's chambers, but you must be quiet. The hall door is closed, but there's a guard posted outside."

"Why post a guard at a public door but not a secret one?"

The girl shrugged. "Tradition?" She crooked a finger and led them inside.

Dark with encroaching dusk, the bedchamber was grand and vast. Byron could have thrown a rock and not hit the end. The walls were lined with tapestries, the floors thick with rugs. Glossy furniture was painted with the family crest. A magnificent bed was heaped with skins. Brass and silver candlesticks were bright, but already a layer of dust had settled, giving the room a neglected air.

Rose whispered. "He died in that bed. Chancellor Clement had it pulled apart and repainted to kill any sickness. So it's ready for Young Stanwin, I mean, the new duke. But he ordered his baggage carried to his old chambers across the hall." Stanwin hadn't yet mentally displaced his father, Byron thought. Lady Stanwin had died years ago, and Young Stan had no siblings. He was a lord now, but a lonely one.

The huge bed stood away from the wall upon a raised dais like a small stage. As he circled the huge bed, Cerise followed, Magog padding behind. The swordswoman offered in a hiss, "It's away from the wall so no one can strike from behind a tapestry. And raised so guards can peek underneath for assassins."

Byron nodded. He reflected it was too bad the chancellor had had the bed repainted, for any traces of card-invoking tokens would be obliterated. But there might be something. . . .

Behind the broad headstead, he knelt to examine the stone floor. He peeped under the dais, saw Rose's feet in black slippers at the far end. Certainly no one could hide under there—

A hairy muzzle snuffled his ear. "Magog!" A long tongue licked in his mouth and made him sputter. The dog was curious why Byron knelt at her level. Pushing her wet muzzle aside, Byron studied the floor. Magog snuffled alongside.

The dog sneezed. Again. Snuffled, and sneezed again. With a whimper, the wolfhound jerked back from the cold stone. Cerise caught her muzzle to silence and comfort her.

Still on all fours, Byron watched the dog for a long minute, then resumed his examination of the floor. The flagstones were blue-gray slate, uneven with gaps between them up to a finger's width. Tracing drool, he found where Magog had snuffled. Wetting his finger, he dug in the crack.

Cerise hissed, "What are you doing, hunting ants for dinner?"

Byron showed a finger tinged with yellow-brown powder. He sniffed it and snorted. Curious, Cerise sniffed it and sneezed. "Plah! What is it?"

"It's trouble. And proof. But not magic." The two women crowded close to stare at his dirty fingertip. "This is the spore of a mushroom called puffball. You've seen them. They litter the forest floor in autumn. If you step on them, they puff out a little brown cloud. Those are spores, mushroom seeds. Deadly poison if you breathe enough of it. One tiny whiff set your dog, big as she is, sneezing."

Green and black eyes were round as the women stared. Rose squeaked, "You mean . . . ?"

Byron nodded. "I'd guess someone collected these last fall, then stole in by night, and puffed them into the duke's nose while he slept. They'd rot your lungs just fine with no magic at all. But the assassin spilled some powder, and it settled into the cracks in the floor."

"But who could have done it?" Rose squeaked. "I mean, who would want to kill such a wonderful man?"

"Lots of folks," said Cerise.

"So now we've another unpleasant task," Byron stated.

As night stole over the land, the adventurers sat on Byron's bed. Veronica had joined them in her blue robe with spraddle-footed cross. Having helped with inside knowledge, the chambermaid Rose had joined their ever-growing party.

Byron said, "Someone has to tell Stanwin his father was murdered."

"No." Cerise scratched her dog's head in her lap. "We don't *have* to tell him, and we won't until it's necessary."

Byron blinked. "Not necessary to tell him an assassin stalks the castle unpunished?"

The swordswoman shook her head. "No. While the Great Game is on, with strangers everywhere, Stanwin will be guarded more closely than usual. And to tell him now would distract him. Poor Stan's got enough trouble playing host and overseeing the Great Game. If we announce his father was murdered, he'll throw everything to the wind and turn the dukedom upside-down looking for the killer. The game would be ignored, yet nothing would be solved. Alerted, the assassin would just go into hiding, or his/her bosses would kill them. Better the four of us keep the secret and quietly ferret out the assassin and plot, whatever it is. We have an advantage in knowing there *is* an assassin, and *that* knowledge is power."

Byron frowned but nodded. "When *do* we tell him?"

"When we've got the conspirators hanging by their heels."

"Poor Stanwin," Veronica sighed. "It's broken his heart to learn his father is dead. How will he feel when he finds it was a vicious murder? The poor dear . . ."

The three stared, and the tiny priest blushed clear to her shaved tonsure.

Cerise teased her to lighten the atmosphere. "Why then he'll need someone to hold his hand and cradle his handsome head to her bosom."

"He is *so* handsome!" Veronica blushed until her face matched the red tapestry borders. "But don't worry. He'll never notice a skinny nothing like me."

Byron joked, "Maybe if you let the hair grow on your crown—ouch!" The priest slugged his arm.

Rose stood and smoothed her apron. "It will be hard to do nothing to help Lord Stanwin."

Cerise brushed dog hair off her red-striped breeches. "We shan't be idle. We'll be the busiest in the castle with *two* tasks: to win the Great Game and scotch a conspiracy. Rose, you better stay close to me. We need your sensible head. I'll ask the chancellor for your services during my stay: it's common enough to be lent a valet. Would that suit you?"

"Oh, yes!" piped the girl. "I hate working the scullery and toting water and wood! It's boring!" Byron admired her spunk, and the way she smoothed her bodice down her ribs.

"Fair enough. Let's meet here after dinner to work out a plan—"

They were interrupted as Ingrid swept in without knocking. The cardmaster had switched her leather jacket and riding breeches for a long white gown cut low to reveal an expanse of round bosom. From a silver chain around her slender waist hung a long stiletto with an ivory handle. Her dark hair was piled atop her head so the blonde strands that normally framed her face spiralled upwards. She licked rouged lips. "Byron, will you please escort me to dinner? You're alone, I see, except for hired help."

Cerise hissed through her teeth, Veronica *tsked*, and Rose stiffened as if kicked. Byron blushed, hastily scrubbed his hands at the commode and slicked down his bowl haircut, wetting his black sleeves. "Oh, certainly. I'm ready, I mean. Not alone. This is—"

He meant to introduce Rose, but Ingrid hooked his arm and towed him out. "A scut from the kitchen, yes. Good for hard labor, but too coarse for a gentlemen such as you. Forget her."

Dragging Byron beside her, Ingrid turned the corner.

Rose huffed. "*Who* is that?"

Cerise flexed strong hands on her baldric. "Don't bother to learn her name. She's not long for this world. I think I'll slit her tongue—like a snake's— before I split her gullet."

"May I hold her down while you do it?" Rose asked.

"I'll offer a prayer to speed her to Hell," added Veronica.

"Done. Rose can have her bleached scalp for a dustrag and Veronica the skin off her bosom for a bible cover." The frontierswoman chuckled and patted the girls' shoulders. Then she batted at her worn and stained clothing. "Well, I got most of the dog hair and road dust off. I guess I'm ready for dinner. Come on. And pull your noses out of the air. You'll trip on the stairs and break your necks."

The heroes' after-dinner meeting was postponed, for Chancellor Clement held one of his own to explain the stakes for the Great Game. Byron propped both elbows on the table and tried to stay awake. He was murky from too many courses of food and rounds of wine. Ingrid sat by his right, Cerise by his left, Veronica opposite. As the duke's favored guests, they were close to the head of the table. All around sat the duke's friends and relatives and advisors. As the game officially started tomorrow, this was the last time the duke would be "alone" with supporters. Hereafter, he must entertain the lords of the other two fiefs.

One relation was Edric, the duke's closest cousin, who also lived in the castle. A skinnier Stanwin, he would have been handsome had not easy living and drink wasted him. Though barely twenty-some, his eyes were sunken, his cheekbones prominent, his hair flat and greasy, his breath foul as a cesspit. Still, he was a gracious and jolly drunk, and regaled his neighbors throughout dinner with stories of Young Stanwin. ". . . One time he saved my life, he did! Waste of effort, eh? We were swimming, and I was showing off, as usual. Slipped and bashed my conk, sank like a stone. Lumpkin dove off that rock like an otter and dragged me out, pumped me dry as a loofa sponge. Maybe that's why I'm dedicated to soaking up the wine and brandy now! Oh, he's a noble one, Lumpy is. Glad someone in the family is responsible and not me! I'd do anything for him. Except get sober, of course. Pass that carafe, would you please . . . ?"

At one point, Byron had interrupted Veronica's mooning at Lord Stanwin, nudging her elbow to request the bread. "And what will your official position be during the game? If the church bans all cardplay, and we've gathered for just that purpose—"

"I'm an observer." The priest wiped her mouth primly with a napkin. "I'm to prevent sin in, um, small things. There will be a prelate or monsignor to oversee the larger, uh, undertaking."

Byron squeezed her forearm, offered her more honey. "Well, keep tucking there. Maybe if you put some meat on your bones, Stanwin will be able to see you. Right now you're thin as a shadow." The girl shot him a black look but ate heartily anyway.

Byron glimpsed Rose, pressed into serving at table with so many extra guests. She smiled briefly at the cardsmith, then frowned as Ingrid tickled his chin with a painted fingernail. By the time Byron brushed Ingrid's hand away, Rose had disappeared into the kitchen. He didn't see her again.

When the table was clear, and fresh mugs of ale and sweetcakes fetched—Veronica took four—Chancellor Clement stood up at his place. His pudgy, ringed hands fluttered, alternately clasping before his ample stomach or smoothing down his curly dark hair, a habit he didn't know he had.

"Milords, miladies, attendants, retainers, relatives, friends. As your humble servant, I wish to sketch for you the broad picture of the Great Game which commences tomorrow. There will of course be a thousand details, but we'll burn those bridges when we come to them." He paused for laughter, then continued. "In the main: As you know, Thallandia guards the only pass through the White Bone Mountains, the Eagle's Road. Our fair dukedom spans some ten leagues along the foot of the mountains. To our north," he trailed a hand at the right wall and everyone instinctively looked, "lies the fief of the Countess Lenda, the land of Skurage. To the south runs Romney, managed so ably by Otto, an earl. Both are good neighbors. Oh, we have occasional quarrels over straying herds and such, but there has been no bloodshed for thirty years while Duke Stanwin the Elder, may he rest in peace, ruled.

"But of course, peace never lasts. Through the Eagle's Pass, our scouts report seeing more and more of the encroaching Shinyar, the savage hordes of the steppes, mindless and rapacious as locusts. From travellers we know of enduring droughts on the steppes and a scarcity of food. So it's only a matter of time before the Shinyar brave the Eagle's Road and ride here, into Thallandia." He pointed straight down at the floor. Men and women alike put hands on their weapons, as if the invaders would burst through the flagstones.

"That's why I'm here," Cerise hissed. Byron understood. Her frontier family had lived beyond the pass, but not for long.

"Duke Stanwin was a wonderful man," Clement went on, and everyone wondered if he'd changed the topic. "He gave his all for his dukedom and her people, assured no one went hungry or homeless, nor died in battle if it could be avoided. And when there were battles, he led his troops personally. His like, may he sit at the right hands of the gods, will not be seen again. Until, of course, the younger Stanwin makes his mark upon the world." He smiled at the young duke, who blushed at polite applause. "The Duke of Thallandia is traditionally the Guardian of the Eagle's Road, and Lord Stanwin saw its posts and forts were kept in good repair, its soldiers drilled razor-sharp. He oversaw other soldiers from Skurage and Romney and the Pithian Crossroads and Waterholm and elsewhere, all garrisoned here. But Duke Stanwin was a thorough and thoughtful man, and he worried these preparations were not enough."

Everyone hung on Clement's words. The fat man smoothed his hair as he got to the meat of the matter.

"To this end, Duke Stanwin called a Great Game, and persuaded Lady Lenda and Earl Otto to partake. For he put up the grandest stakes he could imagine—the lordship of this fief, his ancestral home!"

Byron blinked. Cerise stirred. Veronica squeaked. The drunken Edric awoke with a snort. Clement waited for quiet before resuming.

"After years of study, Duke Stanwin concluded that the might of Thallandia, even reinforced with visiting troops, was not enough. For the Eagle's Road to stand intact against invasion, *all* the resources of the mountain fiefs must be consolidated. We need the fields and forests of Thallandia, the sawmills and shops of Romney, the vineyards and orchards of Skurage, *and* all their industrious people, *combined*.

"Duke Stanwin loved his dukedom and his people, but he loved freedom most of all. He decided the mountain fiefs must be united for mutual protection, for the protection of the entire kingdom. But not by the usual method, warfare. The duke knew if he tried to conquer Skurage and Romney, there would be blood spilled and bad blood left behind, with no winners, only losers. Three tattered fiefs made into one would be too weak to withstand the Shinyar. So he turned to another method—the Great Game.

"He proposed, and Lenda and Otto accepted, that they bring their best cardmasters and play one game for mastery of the three fiefs, winner take all. Whosoever wins becomes the new Duke of Thallandia, Guardian of the Eagle's Road, Defender of the White Bone Mountains. The two losers—and there must be two losers—would retain their titles, but pledge complete and total obedience to the will of the winner for now and every generation to come. Lords they'd still be, but vassals to a new duke—the High Duke of Thallandia.

"So much did Duke Stanwin believe this unity was vital, he was willing to give up his ancient home and homage and swear to serve on his bended knee the new High Duke, or to take on that awesome responsibility himself. But now, what men could not accomplish, overwork and winter's chill have done, and the elder Stanwin is gone to greater glory. So it's up to us, Duke Stanwin the Younger and us, his friends, to carry out his plans.

"Tomorrow commences the Great Game. You've heard the terms. They are fixed and inviolable and must be played to the last card. Will you join me in a toast and a pledge?"

Clement snapped his fingers, received a fresh mug of ale. As he hoisted it, the dazed guests copied. "To success! To the memory of Duke Stanwin, long may he reign in the heavens! To the strong right arm and quick wits of Duke Stanwin the Younger! To you, our friends, who'll stand by him through every travail! And to the dukedom and the people, who will see history made here in the next few weeks! Let us all do our best!"

Everyone drank, then babbled, minds awhirl with the ramifications of the game, except Cousin Edric, who'd passed out again. Byron said, "Imagine! Putting up a whole dukedom in a Great Game! That's the highest stakes I've ever heard of!"

"I've played for higher, elsewhere," Ingrid interjected coolly. She poured fresh wine while laying a hand on Byron's thigh under the table.

Cerise snorted and poured herself ale. "I've heard of higher, but never been in the thick of it. And thick it will be, like fighting in a bowl of porridge. Our friend the chancellor's said much, but there's as much unsaid. And yet to be revealed. . . ."

Byron lowered his voice so Ingrid didn't hear. "Like the identity of an assassin or two?"

"That and a lot more." Cerise drank off her ale.

Dreaming, Byron swam without getting wet.

There was no water, only dry white powder underfoot and a cool blackness dotted with stars overhead. Craning around, he decided this was the moon, where the air was cold and thin as at mountaintops, so philosophers guessed. The cardsmith jumped in great bounds like a chamois and fell to earth slowly. When he landed, his feet raised clouds of fine dust that swirled like fog. Moving his arms, they could barely grasp the air, and he often spun full around trying to take a small step.

And here too, in this dream, were demons.

They capered like apes far behind him. As they ran, they pushed off and floated high like grasshoppers. Their shrieks and hoots were high-pitched, like bird calls. But they came for Byron, to catch him and—what? Kill him? Eat him? Turn him inside-out? What did they want?

There were scores of demons on this dead world. Some had long necks like giraffes, others horned

noses or long pendulous lips. One looked broken
in half, cracked in the middle, so it scuttled on all
fours sideways like a gray crab. One fiend had stripes
like a zebra, and a black upright mane that grew to
its eyebrows. One had fingernail claws so long they
curled back on themselves like a boar's tusks.

Byron ran, but a glance over his shoulder showed
the demons surrounding him again. In seconds, it
seemed, they closed into a ring that contracted. A
cloud of dust rose like a fog bank around a ship,
until he had no way out except straight up into the
black white-pointed sky.

He skidded to a halt, powder clouds rising around
his shoulder, looked this way and that, saw only demons.
Shuffling and stuttering, he circled until he couldn't
see for dust. A long hand with webbed fingers reached
for his hair and he ducked. An eagle's talon snagged
his cape, but he tore free. A demon grabbed his
arm and opened two mouths, one above the other,
to expose razor teeth to sever his arm. Byron heaved
and shook the monster off.

But dozens slunk and clawed at him. Shrieking,
Byron hunched low as the ring closed tighter. No
way out, he thought numbly. Except up. Where he
could jump like a demented frog.

As a smother of acid-reeking bodies grabbed, Byron
squatted, gathered his legs under him, and leaped.

It was startling how high he rose. One second
he was mobbed, the next he was free as a dove and
peering down at howling frustrated demons. He kept
rising, too, higher and higher, like a balloon. When
would he drift back down?

He didn't, but kept going, until the moon was no
bigger than a pumpkin, then an apple.

What now? he wondered vaguely. Where would he land?

Something bright made him squint, something overhead like a street lamp. Twisting, he saw it was a star. No, a sun. Close now, too bright to look at.

He shielded his eyes, but felt the heat on his scalp. Sweat broke out on his neck. He tried to turn away, but the heat was everywhere, all around. If it got any hotter—

It did. He was roasting. He pulled at his cape to yank it off, found it smoking. His hair caught fire. He beat it with burning hands, but the heat built.

Breathing flames, Byron screamed as he fell, until he died.

The cardsmith screamed and screamed, then landed with a smack.

His head hit something hard and cool. A flagstone floor. Still trapped in throes of nightmare, he felt around frantically in the dark. Where was he?

Oh, yes. In a bedchamber in the castle at Thallandia, a guest of the duke. Safe.

Tangled, drenched in sweat, he kicked free of the blankets. Some servant had come in the night and built up his fire. The logs in the small hearth blazed merrily, fully engulfed.

Byron wiped his sweating forehead. "A fine guest I am, screaming in the night. They'll make me sleep with the pigs—"

The door to the hall cracked open. A curvy feminine form was silhouetted by candlelight. A trill: "Byron, are you all right?"

A whisper of skirts, a whiff of flowery perfume,

and a cool hand touched his brow. Gratefully, he caught the hand, glad for human contact.

"Thank you, thank you," he croaked. "Is it—Ingrid?"

The cool hand was snatched away. "No, it's Rose!" The chambermaid. With a catch in her throat, the girl whirled and dashed from the room.

Byron lay on the cool floor, then thumped his head on it, hard, three times.

"No," he groaned. "No. Pigs would be too good for me."

Chapter 10

The next morning would see the Great Game begin. But first the fair would begin.

The nobles from the houses of Thallandia, Skurage, and Romney assembled on a canopied stage before the largest tournament field, until recently a pasture of rye. As "privileged" commoners, Byron and Cerise and Ingrid stood behind a rope barrier alongside the stage. A band of twenty instruments whomped and umpawpawed and tweedled as the crowd milled into place.

Before the stage gathered most of the populations of the three fiefs plus hundreds of lowlanders and vagabonds. Byron was amazed: he hadn't known there were so many people in the world. Over fifteen thousand, someone guessed, maybe twenty thousand. They filled the field in bright or drab colors like an immense flock of birds lit from the sky. All strained to see Stanwin, the new Duke of Thallandia.

Sweating with stage fright, the young duke jerked out a halting speech with Chancellor Clement's gentle prompting. The duke welcomed everyone and thanked them for coming, hoped all would enjoy the sights and tournaments, held out the hand of friendship to locals and strangers, and so on. The happy crowd gave him hearty applause and three cheers, then laughed and applauded louder when he blushed—Stanwin's humility and shyness endearing him to the crowd more than any speech could.

Similar speeches from the cool Lady Lenda of Skurage and the bristly Otto of Romney elicited more applause, then the Grand Marshall of the Tournament took the stage and announced the day's events. The entire fair would run ten days or more, with much jousting, juggling, and jongleuring. As the various bouts and contests were announced, the crowd melted away to get the best seats or spots at the ropes.

The band pounded out a wheezing beat as, surrounded by guards and retainers, the nobles and their servants retired to the castle—where the real reason for this gathering would take place.

Everyone assembled in the War Room.

This chamber occupied the entire top floor of the castle, which made it long and wide enough to support a tournament of its own. Originally it had been designed with wide windows and strong mounts for ballista and other siege weapons, a refuge if the castle were inundated by enemy hordes—a place for last stands and final battles.

Which Byron thought appropriate, for here the
fate of three fiefdoms would be decided.

The room was well-lit by open windows on three
sides, the walls hung with tattered banners and portraits
of stern-faced battlers. Unlike the lower floors, the
back wall was not screened with a smooth wall, but
showed the original carving and hacking and lumps
and niches of its half-cave construction, all whitewashed.
In two fireplaces near either end, despite the spring
warmth, small blazes of birchwood crackled. Rich
oriental rugs lay in rows down the floor. Forming a
huge rectangle was a dark polished table, the open
center of which was big enough to corral a dozen
horses. Two more tables near the windows were
heaped with food and drink.

In addition, near either end of the room and at
the center front wall were tables overhung by the
banners of the three noble armies: "refuges" or
"safe havens" where the house members could
convene and rest and discuss without being overheard,
and they were guarded by men and women with
halberds. Myriad square stacks surmounted each
table.

The suspense of impending battle heightened as
the players swirled into the room and gravitated to
their respective tables like generals and war councils
on a battlefield—which this was, in a way.

Byron glanced around the room, tried to avoid
catching the tension. He'd have little part in actual
playing, after all. Cerise, hip-tilted with her sporty
weapons and massive brindled dog by her side,
looked calm and composed, but Byron knew she
was tight-drawn as a bow and arrow. Rose, dark-
eyed and beautiful, stood behind her, ready to serve

in her maid's green-and-white outfit without the apron. Veronica hovered nearby, swamped in sin but unsure where to start correcting it. Ingrid, once again in leather and breeches, brass hilts gleaming, watched everything, including Byron. And before them all stood Duke Stanwin in a magnificent green doublet with gold thread, a new hat with jaunty feather, and snow-white, skin-tight breeches. With him was Chancellor Clement in his pendulous vest of office, Molly, his trainer, and his valet Yves, who looked uncomfortable in a new white shirt that squashed his double chins.

Last of all entered the game judges. The Grand Judge was a blocky woman with swept-back white hair and a white gown to match, trailed by three more Judges, two women and a man in white. They would oversee the game. Drawn from academies all over the kingdom and paid lavishly, their decisions were final and their integrity unimpeachable—it had to be, for proof that they'd taken a bribe would see them burned alive at the stake. Behind the judges minced three young pages with white tabards hanging front and back. Apprentice judges, they would act as scorekeepers.

They weren't in the room long before the Grand Judge mounted a small dais and called the participants to gather round. Everyone complied, for all were eager to start play.

But first, the Grand Judge announced they would receive a blessing! Veronica squeaked, and Byron teased her. "Odd to receive a blessing from a church that bans cardplaying."

Yet here came a prelate into the room, with a floor-sweeping gown of blue with the thick-footed cross painted in gold. Tonsured like Veronica, the man looked unhappy as he took the dais. Gruffly, he led a prayer. "Gods of the heavens, lords of creation, spirits that are with us always, bless us and our work here today and for the days to come. Upon the heads of these nobles rest the fate, perhaps, of our kingdom and all civilization. Give them strength and wisdom and courage to—fight fairly and well, so that thy greater glory may be spoken and thy people protected. Amen." With a huff, he swept from the room.

As Veronica pouted, Byron teased unmercifully. "So the church blesses our 'work' without mentioning what it is. Do you think he misunderstood our purpose here?"

"Better the church watches to keep sin to a minimum," the girl snapped, "than be absent. A priest is needed most where sin is the greatest."

"Then you won't be bored," Byron smirked. "I wonder if Duke Stanwin would let you bless him up close, perhaps by laying hands on his— Ow!" The girl's bony fist hammered his arm. Rubbing, the cardsmith attended the Grand Judge.

In keeping with her neutral stand, the Grand Judge didn't welcome anyone, but simply stated the rules and stakes of the game: Winner to become High Duke, the two losing lords to swear eternal fealty and obedience. The game would commence when she announced, momentarily, and would continue until two houses had exhausted all their resources—represented by cards—and could no longer continue. Play could run all day and night, or if all parties agreed, could be suspended for a rest. All cardplay must take place at the great table. Judges would circulate continuously to monitor play, but would avoid the safe tables. Judges could handle any cards in use to test for magic, for only common (non-enchanted) cards could be played. Any cardmaster caught with magic cards at the table would be stripped of that deck, which would be burned, and the ex-player ejected from the game permanently. Any questioning of the judges, quibbling, hair-splitting, or whining could yield a heavy fine, strippage, ejection, or all three. Any duels involving weapons were to take place outside the room. Any rogue or questionable cards (that is, new or non-standard) had to be first approved by the judges. And so on, citing many more rules but no surprises.

Were there any questions? There were many, all duly answered and clarified. There were so many questions, in fact, that barely had the judge pronounced, "Then I officially declare this Great Game begun!" and clapped her hands, then Duke Stanwin, as host, asked if the nobles cared to adjourn for the noonday meal. But everyone was too excited to begin, so he simply pointed them to the groaning food tables. Veronica was the first to grab a plate.

Byron sidled to Rose. "Good morning! I'll bet you're glad to be free of the kitchens. You'd wear your legs to stumps plodding from the first to fourth floor toting trays and casks."

The girl stared coolly until Byron felt himself shrink like a mouse before a cat. "I am glad to be free of the kitchens, but not because I'm afraid of work. I can help the dukedom up here, unlike some people who can only fall out of bed and hit their empty heads."

Byron blushed as if the room were suddenly hot.

He'd offended her last night by mistaking her for Ingrid. But why should she care? Unless . . .

No, he thought. Women didn't find him attractive. Cerise wanted his magical knowledge. Ingrid lusted for his cards. Veronica wanted his soul. So Rose must want something, too.

But what, he hadn't a clue.

Cerise snagged his doublet and towed him to the duke's table. "Stop daydreaming about pronging my valet and get over here. We've work to do."

When play finally began, Byron stood close to Stanwin's table. There were cards. Stacks and stacks of them. Byron whistled. He'd never seen so many cards in his life.

The duke's safe table stood at the front wall between tall windows, squarely between the two noble houses at the far ends. Along with Cerise and Byron, there were some two dozen people clustered around, including Ingrid. The duke stood at their center, the chancellor at his right hand. The table was already littered with papers marked with lead and charcoal: strategies and plans and lists.

And cards in neat stacks. At a quick glance, Byron saw one deck represented the fiefdom's food supply: the cards were green-edged for orchards or golden-edged for grain. The top card showed a sheaf of wheat. Next to it was a green deck representing forest wealth: trees to be sold as masts to shipbuilders in Waterholm, maples to be tapped for syrup, horn-beams for treenails, cedars for shingles, and more. The next stack was water power: watermills, ponds of stocked fish, herring runs, bridges to be protected or destroyed as enemies advanced, dams that could flood lowlands, anticipated rainfall, and so on. One deck stood for livestock: goats, cattle, sheep, cheese, wool, hides. Another stack represented industry: iron foundries, fulling mills, jewelry shops, armories, glassblowers. In the first row, closest to the duke's brawny hands, lay his military might: infantry, rangers, scouts, knights, dragoons, musketeers, generals, and officers. At one end were cards for civilian aid: tanners, blacksmiths, wagoners, surgeons, cooks, tailors, and more. At the other end were crises and uncertainties the army might face: human and animal plagues, surprise attacks, bad weather, turncoat allies, shortages of gunpowder or arrows. And many more decks.

Thousands of cards, Byron guessed, representing almost every person and resource in the fiefdom— which only made sense. In war, everything a noble commanded had to be used and risked. Byron reflected that someone had worked months to fashion all these cards, then taken days just to sort and stack them.

And now the duke looked up from the vast array of cards to his other great resource: his cardmasters and cardsmiths.

There were, Byron counted, eleven, including himself and Cerise. There was only one other cardsmith, a bony strawberry-blonde woman with serious eyebrows. She wore black, like Byron, with silver filigree across the yoke and shoulders and black gloves with chasing down the backs: a cardsmith of some years' study. Unlike himself, who wore black like a crow without a silver stitch anywhere. But then, he'd still be an apprentice if his master hadn't conjured himself into an icicle.

Like Cerise, the other cardmasters were sporty as paintings or peacocks or pirates. Cloaks hung on silver chains from shoulders, hats were adorned with ostrich plumes, doublets were slashed along the sleeves to show a contrasting color underneath, silver pins and stamped buttons and good luck charms were flaunted until the sunlight's flashing made Byron squint.

It made sense to have so many cardmasters and so few smiths. The game required the skill and daring the swashbucklers cultivated, and besides, magic was disallowed at the tables. Byron must not even approach within arm's length of the gaming table, lest some judge think he was slipping in magic and so strip him of all the cards he carried—the only wealth he owned in the world.

There would be magic used during the game, but it would be strictly behind the scenes. He'd have to speak to the other cardsmith soon, to test her mettle and compare notes. When her gaze alighted on him, she nodded as if reading his mind. But she also noted the lack of silver threads in his clothing, and knew him to be the rankest amateur.

Byron stifled a mental sigh. With only a small fortune to sustain him in the world, and no clear goal, he hoped to carve something from the next few days that would give him hope and direction and purpose.

Any purpose.

One problem with being totally free, he thought, was you could venture anywhere at any time. But the reverse was, nothing tied you anywhere, no more than a boat that had slipped its mooring.

The duke picked up a piece of paper, had it taken away and another given him by the chancellor, cleared his throat, and pronounced, "Friends, let's begin. Cerise, you're from the steppelands. Plains? Close enough. We'll ask you to take the cavalry deck. Nanette and Byron, if you'll be so kind?"

The young cardsmith jerked out of his reverie. "What? Uh, sire? *Me?*"

Stanwin fingered a deck of cards from the military array. Cerise picked it up; it was five inches thick. Without even looking at the cards, she handed them to Nanette, the other cardsmith. The bony blonde nodded Byron to stand beside her. Wondering, he did so.

Without changing the order, the cardsmith flipped through the entire deck, taking time to run her thumb over each card. Watching, Byron understood. At one point she paused over a card, then continued on. Without a word, she handed Byron the deck.

The journeyman felt every eye on him as he took the deck. It was heavier than he expected, as if the iron sabers and bridles and horseshoes it represented had gotten into the stack. Not as expert as Nanette, he set the deck down in a clear spot and began to flip through the deck, feeling each. When he reached about the middle of the deck, he felt a slipperiness under his thumb. He plucked out the odd card. A green-clad knight with a yellow plume impaled a red dragon that twisted around him and his white mount. When Byron mashed the card to his nose, he could smell rust and snake musk and horse sweat. He handed the card to the duke. "This one is enchanted."

"What?" Stanwin hadn't paid attention. He snatched the offending card with a frown. "But that can't be right. They're all supposed to be common. If the judge—"

He stopped and everyone nodded. If Cerise had

started play with that deck, and a judge discovered the magic card, the entire deck would be hurled into the fire—crippling Thallandia's "cavalry." As Stanwin looked around the table, everyone thought the same thing: was it an oversight or deliberate sabotage? Had a rival slipped the magic card into the deck? Stanwin chose to mutter, "Probably an oversight. Thank you for finding it, Byron."

Byron was pleased at the compliment, and at being useful, but made sure to skim the rest of the deck for magic. There were no more offending cards, so he handed them to Cerise. She smirked at Nanette and raised an eyebrow.

The silver-chased cardsmith nodded. "He'll do."

Ah, thought Byron. A test. Nanette had deliberately left that card to see if he could spot magic. By skill and luck, he'd passed.

He congratulated himself until he was handed another deck. Then he realized. *All* these thousands of cards would have to be checked. And not just once, but many times, to see no one slipped in more magic cards. He stifled a mental groan.

Cerise thumbed the deck to see what she had. "I was right to bring you along, Byron. You'll earn your share of winnings."

Dazzled by the enormous work laid before him, Byron could only mutter, "If we win."

"We'll win."

More decks were divvied up and checked for magic. Other cardmasters took the heavy and light infantry, ranger, barbarian corps, and other battalion decks, the offensive factions of the army. Ingrid got lancers. In addition, one female cardmaster had a deck representing the field itself: weather, tree lines, soil type, wells, dykes, roads, natural defenses. Another cardmaster team assembled defensive decks to protect the duke's "castle," which had a deck of its own: engineers, sappers, lifeguards, cannoneers, and more. Then all of them swept to the gaming table to play war—for a very real dukedom.

Byron checked decks for night work: ward cards and spell cards, as well as codewords and passwords to protect against night beasts, vapors, assassins. Once everyone was engaged, he was released for the nonce. He was glad: tension in his back felt as if he'd run ten miles. He wandered over to see how Cerise fared.

All non-players were kept back from the tables behind a white line chalked on the floor. Spectators— friends and relations and minor, visiting nobles— toed this line to follow the play. Byron joined them. Rose crowded alongside, so close Byron could inhale her milk-and-honey scent. But he was careful not to glance over and antagonize her further.

Cardmasters perched on stools inside and outside the gaming table. The only ones allowed to circulate were judges. Since this was the first contest of the Great Game—scores of battles big and small would be waged before the final outcome—all the judges wandered and watched while the scorekeepers scribbled furiously.

Cerise sat on a high stool, weapons hanging from her hips, her dog sleeping under her feet, a full glass of wine and uneaten sandwich close at hand. Four other cardsmiths on her team faced Otto's military team across the table. Lady Lenda's troops, Byron noted, had yet to engage: they still argued strategy at the end of the room. Byron saw military cards arranged in complex rows and intersecting angles. Players added and subtracted to rows, calling each move. Deadly serious words crackled as cards were flicked, flipped, covered, discarded, withdrawn.

" . . . Heavy cavalry charges . . . Archers loose volley for three . . . Lancers move up, skirt cavalry to threaten archers, return three . . . Captain arrives, adds one . . ."

Byron found himself hooked: in his mind's eye he could picture the entire battle. Spectators murmured and waged bets. The judges asked for silence, please, and got it.

"Heavy cavalry strikes barbarians, loss of six . . . Barbarians retreat, no effect . . . Cavalry attacks infantry's right flank, adds five . . . Grass reveals bog, slows horses for loss of two . . . Sand fills bog, for two, no effect . . . Infantry makes orderly retreat to hilltop, gains six . . . And ruins add four to defensive posture . . . Weather threatens rain . . . Trumpeter blows dress on colors, adds . . ."

"I see no trumpeter," interrupted a judge.

The cardmaster, one of Otto's men, glanced hurriedly through his deck. Cerise pointed idly, and the man saw a trumpeter card played earlier far down the "field" away from the current action. The judge nodded to the scorekeeper. "Ten point loss to Otto. Resume."

The cardmaster swore in his thick black mustache as Cerise chuckled, "No trumpet signal, your line wavers. Field shows small slope, no effect. Heavy cavalry takes hill, breaks line here." Deftly she flicked a hand, shoved two decks apart. "Loss of twenty."

The cardmaster angrily turned to a judge. "She

can't do that, can she?" One judge looked to another, both nodded, and the play resumed.

"Archers fell captain, loss of two . . . Ruins stall retreat, loss of two . . . Musketeers move up, no effect yet. . . ."

The quarreler flicked a card showing a man with a soupbowl helmet and long axe. "*Veteran sergeant halts crumbling flank, adds—*"

"Afoot," Cerise interrupted, "sergeant is too slow, adds nothing. No trumpet for signals, either."

Ingrid flipped a card. "Lancers drive barbarians into infantry ranks, loss of four and two."

The mustached man demanded of his teammate, "Weather? Hurry, damn you!"

"Threatens rain but adds nothing," conceded a teammate.

"Trumpet peals are louder when the air is wet," Cerise jested. "But not loud enough."

The mustached man stabbed black glittering eyes at her. "Forget the trumpet! Chariots—"

"Bog on the line, remember? And sand adds nothing. You threw the card yourself." Cerise's grin infuriated the man. She flipped over a pair of cards close at hand. "Chariots at treeline add nothing. *No trumpet signal*, so my rangers rise and pepper charioteers with arrows. Unsupported infantry breaks. Loss of— aha!—*thirty-five!*"

"*Time out!*" bellowed the mustached man. He leapt to his feet, grabbed his sword pommel with a rattle, leaned over the table and cards. "Would you care to discuss my playing abilities *outside*?"

"Time out it is." Cerise kicked away from the table and hitched her jingling baldric. Alerted by danger, Magog scrambled up, thumped the table with her head, and trotted out to see. Cerise bowed. "At your service, good sir. You might bring a trumpeter to play music over your grave."

"I'll play music with my sword on your breastbone!"

Snarling, the two left the room trailed by Magog. Spectators and cardmasters followed, laying bets.

Byron didn't bet, he prayed. "Oh, Kabul and Muchi, please don't let Cerise be killed on the first day!"

Chapter 11

"Whom do I have the honor of duelling?"

"I am Joash of Nikus, called the Terrible."

The two swordsmasters glared past blades raised in salute. Byron and Rose and Ingrid and others encircled them well back. With the game suspended, Duke Stanwin had even come, with Veronica hovering unnoticed. Afternoon sun bronzed the duellists, pinned their shadows against the warm cobblestones of the castle courtyard.

"I am Cerise." The cardmaster swept her sword down in a sizzling arc and began to move sideways, flatfooted to prevent a stumble.

"That means 'cherry,'" Joash smirked. "You kept the name, but gave away your cherry long ago, no doubt. To whom, a muleskinner?"

"No, to a candydipper. She promised—"

Figuring he'd wait to hear the rest, the swordswoman

leaped. She feinted high and Joash parried. But Cerise had not pressed hard, and now struck low. Her blade tip sank a half-inch into the man's thigh, then she slid backwards out of range. She teased, "You're called the Terrible after your style of swordplay?"

Ignoring the wound, which leaked scarlet down his white breeches, the swordsman stamped forward without a word. He slashed sidearm for Cerise's head. *Clang*, she parried upwards. Joash hooked the blade around her wrist, riposted for her throat. *Cling*, she counter-parried, back-cut towards his face. But the man ducked low to stab at her groin. *Pang*, she countered the blade to the outside.

Cerise scuttled backwards, waited to see what her opponent would do. Her bosom heaved more from excitement than exertion, for the fight was only seconds old.

Joash hollered, a noise to frighten, lunged and stabbed for her middle, hoping to smash past her defense. True, he was far stronger than the woman, so she didn't fight toe to toe. To his three lunges she skipped back once, twice, then jumped sideways. Backcutting in a sizzling arc, she skinned his hip.

People chortled. It was obvious Cerise could have killed Joash, lanced his liver and lungs, yet had refrained.

Pinked in two places, the man whirled, stamped flatfooted. His eyes were red, Cerise noted. His bad humor was getting worse.

Hollering again, Joash drove for Cerise, feinted low, then flicked high to skewer her face. The frontierswoman coolly snapped her head to one side and held her sword straight.

Joash's lunge carried him onto her blade. He gasped as steel pierced his right shoulder and pricked out the far side. Spectators gasped with him, then some cheered and applauded Cerise. Magog barked.

The crippling blow would weaken Joash as the seconds ticked by. Without mockery, Cerise asked, "Yield?"

Growling, Joash spat. Grabbing at his belt, he withdrew a *main gauche*, a "left hand" dagger with down-swept hilt and a foot-long blade. People whistled. The man was either extremely confident or stupidly stubborn to fight with his sword arm punctured.

Cerise watched his eyes and blades as she pondered. With the stakes raised so high, she could withdraw without dishonoring herself. But Joash's temper was out of control: left alive now, he'd only plot revenge for later. The frontierswoman knew better than to turn her back on an enemy.

Coolly she drew her own dagger. The crowd hummed. Like all her battered equipment, this was no fancy matched dagger, just a blacksmith-forged blade with a wire-wrapped handle and simple curved crosspiece. She lifted the blade in silent acceptance—the duel would continue, and one would die.

Joash began to circle sideways, as did Cerise. He didn't rely on brute strength now, but studied his opponent for a weakness.

Cerise smiled at his late effort: she'd been studying him all day. Now she saw an opening. The man was always careful to slide his left foot but, probably owing to an old wound, consistently picked up his right foot, coming down heel and toe. Not a good idea on uneven flagstones.

His eyes flicked uneasily to her dagger. While he held his blade upright, like his sword, she held blade down, like a knifefighter. She knew he wondered where that downthrusting spike might end—

With a skip-step to the right, Joash leaped in, steel whirling.

Again using his strength, he beat at her, his blade low to knock hers high. At the same time, he jabbed for her belly.

Cerise relaxed her wrist, let her sword be knocked upwards, but protected her middle with the long knife. That would give Joash confidence, having two blades against one.

Almost forgetting his sword, blind with anger, Joash jabbed for her guts with his dagger. Her own dagger poised, Cerise easily hooked his blade and flicked it sideways, out of harm's way.

Engaged on hers, his sword blade hummed alongside her right ear. The edge was not sharp, so she didn't fear it. But any second he'd whip it back to slash her face. So—

Cerise stepped forward and left to crowd him.

Startled, his twin blades locked up, Joash faltered, started to jump back. Pushed, he could only step right on that bad leg. Hung for a split-second, he was unprotected.

Like a badger vaulting from a hole, the swordswoman struck. Her sword arm was tilted high by his upthrust, so her fist was high, too. Straight down, she hammered her fist and sword pommel into the man's face, aiming for an eye. He flinched in time, ducked, but the diamond-shaped pommel raked his scalp to the bone. His head snapped back, his hat tumbled off, he stumbled. Spectators hissed in agonized sympathy.

Taking advantage of a weakness, Cerise jerked her dagger blade free of Joash's sword, raked the tip across the throbbing thigh wound. Disengaging but leaning far forward, she bobbed on the balls of her feet, ready to strike from two directions, wary if—

Yes, he got his feet under him, bounced back. Desperate, Joash roared and tried her trick, crowding close to lock her blades.

Cerise slid to the side, out of his way. The hatless, bleeding swordsman lunged through the space where she'd stood. His boots clattered on flagstones as he fought to regain his balance.

The swordswoman didn't go far, watched carefully. She resisted leaping in to finish him. Let him expend his strength first. He was bullheaded, bull-strong, bull-unpredictable.

Foregoing any defense, Joash whirled to jump her, to grapple if possible, arms wide. Cerise was close enough to kiss. His dagger hand flailed, tangled her sword blade. Howling, Joash whipped his blade at her head. He didn't even try to back and cut with the last sharpened foot: he'd knock her senseless with the steel shaft.

Except he forgot he'd raised the stakes by introducing daggers.

Cerise's defense was automatic. Turning her wrist, she presented her dagger. Joash lunged right onto it. The wicked steel slid into his brisket clear to the hilt, piercing him through the liver, a killing blow. But one that meant days of slow internal bleeding and blood-poisoned infection.

Stupefied with horror, the man stared down at the wire hilt pressed to his belly. Still wary of his blades, Cerise whipped hers clear, the blade red, and danced backwards.

Joash watched her, arms still spread, unsure what to do.

Cerise knew. With a surgical stab and twist of her rapier, she severed his windpipe, jugular, spine.

The man gasped, gargled blood, tumbled forward. His head smacked the flagstones with a sickening crunch that made folks groan.

Still in defensive posture, Cerise stood panting, exultant. She was still alive. A robin piped overhead. The breeze was cool on her sweating brow. She smelled roses and manure in a castle garden. Wonderful scents, sights, sounds.

And people were applauding, another sweet sound.

Weak but trying not to show it, Cerise knelt, wiped her blades clean on Joash's cloak. Fishing in his shirt, she found his packet of cards, her booty. The pouch was on his right, away from the heart, where cardmasters traditionally carried them: not on the left, where a heart wound would bleed and spoil them for the victor. She sliced loose his money pouch, too, and liked its hefty feel. Another wonderful-to-be-alive sensation. Finally, she tugged off his baldric and sheathed his weapons. The blades were clean, with none of her blood on them.

People milled for the doorway and staircase. Ingrid left without a backward glance; briefly, Cerise recalled her promise they would cross swords some day. Now Ingrid had seen Cerise duel, learned her fighting style, while Cerise knew nothing of Ingrid's. Knowledge of an opponent was power. But she'd worry that out later.

Byron and Rose approached. With a grin, Cerise handed the baldric to her new valet. "Stow these in my room. They'll fetch a hundred crowns in the capital."

Byron grimaced at the dead man on the flagstones. Castle guards came to lug him away, having already cut cards for his boots. But Veronica held the guards up as she knelt to pray for the dead man's soul.

The cardsmith asked, "Is that a normal day's work?"

"No!" Cerise was grinning, happy to be victorious and not dead. "Most days aren't this profitable!"

"Gods on the loose, you killed a man!"

"Aye, not the first. So what?"

Byron rocked back. "Just how many people *have* you killed?"

Cerise laughed again. Nothing could spoil her good mood. "Do Shinyar count as people?"

"Um . . ." Byron was flummoxed by her calm discussion of human destruction. He looked at Rose, who was equally put out. "Fine. Why not?"

"Over . . . let's see, fifteen, I'd guess."

"You can't remember the exact number? That's like saying you can't remember the number of people you've made love to!"

Cerise laughed merrily and batted his shoulder. "That number I know! Shall we adjourn upstairs? We've a game to win!" And like a girl seeking meadow flowers, the stocky frontierswoman skipped up the stone steps after the spectators.

Shaking his head, Byron climbed. Rose hiked her skirts and stayed close by his side, asked, "How many people have *you* made love to?"

"What? Um, I can't remember." He looked at her sidelong. "How many have you?"

"None of your business!" the girl snipped. "And I know one man who *won't* be counted in that number for certain!" Skirts and petticoats flouncing, she skipped up the stairs.

"What did *I* do?" Byron asked the air.

"It's what you *didn't* do," answered a voice. Veronica, pattering behind him.

"All right, I give up! What *didn't* I do?"

The skinny priest rolled her eyes and hurried past. "Honestly, Byron. If you don't know, I'm not going to tell you."

Then he was alone on the stairs, muttering. "All women are mad. That's the answer. Or all men. . . ."

He arrived in time to see Cerise perch at the vast open table, slug her untasted wine, glance over the cards and huff, "Where were we? Oh, yes. Chariots in the treeline can't advance through bog, there's no trumpet signal for Otto's left flank, rangers rise from hiding and slay charioteers with arrows. Loss of thirty-five puts infantry to flight, Otto's left flank crumbles. Correct? Yes! Now to destroy the right flank!"

The game, everyone knew, would eventually be played day and night. But this first evening, Duke Stanwin offered to suspend the action until dawn tomorrow, and Countess Lenda and Earl Otto agreed. All sides wanted to discuss strategy, assessing the cards and cardmasters, how both could best be used.

Dinner was lavish but oddly quick. The main hall had been rearranged. The head table now sat nobles with two tables of cardmasters and -smiths flanking. At the foot tables were lesser hangers-on. The white-robed judges had left the castle to occupy the finest inn in town, guarded by a private force and isolated from bribes and influence.

Cerise and Byron and Ingrid plowed through plain but hearty food and too much wine and ale. They heard speeches about how well the game had begun. But after only a couple of hours, Lenda and Otto excused themselves. Duke Stanwin graciously let them go. Chancellor Clement announced a play being performed, then eased family and spectators and visitors out the huge double doors. With guards posted inside and out, the duke, his cardmasters, his military advisors, and a very few others put their heads together.

The duke complimented Cerise's team for routing half of Otto's army. He'd be handicapped when the game resumed, and they discussed how to exploit his weaknesses. They argued about why Lenda's army still stood off.

Stanwin explained, "While Otto's forces are conventional, made for field-fighting in lowlands, Lenda's land is hilly and her population small. I know she employs scouts or rangers and mountain troops, but she might surprise us with hired barbarians or crossbowmen. I suspect she'll fight defensively, make us advance into her territory to be picked off from ambush. But we don't know . . . If only I had my father's strategy!"

The last phrase burst from him, and people murmured. Cerise's eyes hardened and her fingers drummed the table. She whispered, "I was afraid of that! I *knew* we fought without a strategy!"

"What kind of strategy?" hissed Byron. "I thought—"

But the room had gone quiet, and Young Stanwin heard him. "A strategy," he explained for the benefit of all, "is a master plan for waging a Great Game. Even the simplest game needs a plan, even a peasant's

game of football, kicking a bladder around a field.
And I know that even before my father issued the
invitation, before he even mentioned the words 'Great
Game,' he was working on a strategy. Probably for
years, mulling it in his head. But when he . . . passed
on, the strategy was lost. It wouldn't be much, perhaps
only five or six pages of parchment, but we can't
find it. Clement here—"

Incredibly, Clement interrupted his master, showing
the depth of his despair. "We searched from cellar
to cupola, sire! We turned this castle upside down!
Ask the servants! We tore it apart! I had your father's
bed dismantled and rebuilt! We turned over all the
furniture, we hunted behind every tapestry! We all
but plucked the mortar from between the stones!
But nowhere did we find a hint. . . ."

"I know, I know," the duke consoled. "My father
was a clever man. He'd have hidden it somewhere
safe."

"Oh, had he only told us *where!*" Clement smoothed
his curls with fat fingers as if to scrub himself bald.
"But he never let *anyone* see his plan! He sent out
scouts and spies, half the time not telling *them* what
to search for! He called in the steward of the grounds,
and farmers from the far reaches of the dukedom,
even a shepherdess to ask about caves in the hillsides!
He'd take their reports, then lock himself in the
tower to fashion his plan! It must be the finest strategy
since the gods sat down to fashion the world!"

"And it's as lost as that plan," Stanwin sighed.
"We can blunder along a while, stack the decks as
best we can, but without all that knowledge of the
enemy . . . Well, we'll just muddle through and do
our best. That's all we can do, in the end."

The players took heart at his youthful optimism, but Cerise shook her head. Shortly thereafter, the meeting broke up. Cerise towed Byron and Rose towards the stairs.

"Come on!" she hissed. "We're going to find that strategy! Without it, we'll fight blind as that fool I skewered this afternoon!"

Though muzzy-headed from wine and lack of sleep, Byron recalled the man who'd bled to death in the afternoon sun. He didn't argue.

They hunted for hours and found nothing.

Relying on Rose's knowledge and Magog's nose, Cerise and Byron poked and prodded and padded through the servants' passage, the duke's chambers, the stairwells, the cellars, even the tower room where Old Stanwin had worked alone on his strategy. Magog sniffed everywhere and only spooked a mouse. Having gamed all day, the three stumbled along, their eyes baggy and red in the wobbling light of two lanterns.

Finally, even plucky Rose sighed, "I'm sorry, Cerise, but we *did* this already! Clement made the servants search every inch of the castle, in pairs so we wouldn't overlook anything. He consulted a map of the castle floors, even compared an antique map from before the back walls were built. He bade the engineers pry up flagstones, had us girls stick needles through the tapestries in case false panels were sown inside, had the huntsman fetch in the hounds even. We found some things, an old shoe, a toy sword Stanwin once dropped down a stairwell, even some hidden love letters, but *no* strategy. And I'm so *tired*!" She sank against the wall in a flurry of skirts.

They'd returned to where they started, the third

floor passage behind the old duke's chambers. Refusing to give up, Cerise peppered Rose with questions. Was there a hunting lodge in the hills where the duke might have hidden the plan? Could he have buried it in the gardens inside a chest? Stashed it under the eaves in the privy? Under the straw in the henhouse or mews? The girl just shook her head. The castle had indeed been torn apart. Always-efficient Clement had used the opportunity to give it a good cleaning and repainting too, so the new duke could assume his title in a gorgeous and spotless castle.

While Magog lay her great shaggy head on one boot, the swordswoman rubbed her chin with a rough brown glove, clearly stumped. Byron felt stumped too. His natural curiosity prodded him to search longer, but he lacked any new place to hunt.

Except . . .

He aimed a lantern along the rough rear wall. "You said there are caves throughout the mountain?"

"Yes." Rose clambered to her feet and brushed dust off her gown, perking up at Byron's attention. "But they're sealed off. There're two or three spots where rubble fills gaps, but those are emergency boltholes. If the castle were overrun—not likely—sappers could tumble the walls quickly with sledgehammers."

"Where do the caves go?"

"Go? Oh, out cracks in the mountain that overlook the fields and the pass. I haven't seen them, but the lifeguards did."

"Show me these temporary walls, please."

Game, the girl carried a candle down the passage, trailed her hand along the whitewashed walls. "Let's see . . . Here's one."

Byron squatted, squinted, leaned to trace where

blocks jammed a craggy portal. A black trickle between two stones caught his attention, and he touched it, examined his stained finger. "This is soot. Why here?"

Rose explained, "Clement checked these boltholes, too. Matching his old map, he bade the lifeguards circle the mountain, crawl through the caves, and find the opposite side. They held up red and green lanterns on their side and we held candles on ours. We shouted for hours sometimes. Finally we'd spot their colored lights and Clement would mark his map. Some of these boltholes he ordered torn down and restacked: the stones are only two or three feet thick. It didn't do any good. We found nothing."

"Someone . . ." Byron snuffled his nose to the crack, felt a breeze from the other side, "should have looked . . . harder. . . ."

Exhausted, Rose's temper flared. "I *told* you! There *are* no more places to look! Do you think I shirk my duties?"

"No, no, of course not! I know you're clever and hard-working . . . Cerise, may I borrow your dagger, please?"

Curious but patient, the swordswoman handed it over. Fishing with the blade, Byron impaled something shrivelled and brown like a cockroach. The women asked in unison, "What's that?"

"It's a puffball shell." He unfolded a crumpled brown sphere. "The assassin who poisoned the duke probably did it slowly, over many nights, to look like a natural disease. They probably threw the shells down a garderobe, but they must have panicked once and stuffed it in this crack. Maybe they saw a servant or guard coming. Later, they couldn't retrieve it, or forgot it."

"But how did *you* find it?" Cerise asked.

"I smelled it, but I knew what to hunt for. This whole passage is musty, so one more musty odor goes unnoticed. There's no reason Rose and the rest should have found it." The chambermaid smiled at his gallant excuse.

"But we're no closer to the murderer." Cerise idly scratched her dog's shaggy head. "We have no proof, for instance, that Lady Lenda or Earl Otto are behind the duke's murder."

"True," Byron agreed. "And those two have the most to gain: look how their chances of winning the Great Game and becoming High Duke improve if the old duke dies and his strategy stays lost. But someone *in* the castle could have poisoned him, too."

"Poppycock!" bleated Rose. "None of us would do that! We all loved Duke Stanwin! He was a kind, sweet man! And no one else has died—oh, wait . . ."

"Wait?" piped Byron. "Wait for what?"

"Well," breathed the girl, "those two cardsmiths died, too . . ."

"I guess we forgot them in the hurly-burly after the duke's death."

The three adventurers again perched on Byron's wide bed and whispered by candlelight. Magog climbed aboard and flomped down to hunt phantom rabbits in her dreams.

Rose explained. "Two cardsmiths wintered here. Duke Stanwin hired them to answer questions about his strategy, I guess. One fell down the stairs and broke his neck. Drunk, they said. The other was a woman who choked to death on a chicken bone in her chambers. She'd been meeting someone in a private dinner. We don't know who."

"When was that?" Byron asked. "And was Nanette, the strawberry-blonde cardsmith, here?"

"Umm . . . It was after winter solstice when they died. The ground was frozen and they couldn't be buried, so they were laid in a crypt till spring. And no. Nanette only arrived a little before you did. I made up her room."

Byron huffed. "It's no great calamity for two people to die in a castle within a year. Anyone can fall down the stairs: I've almost done it myself a few times. And there must be scores of people living here . . ."

"Sixty-something," Rose supplied. "Mostly the servants' families and old friends of the duke's with nowhere else to go."

"Accidents happen," Cerise put in, "but to the only two cardsmiths in the castle? Those are long odds."

"And now we know the old duke was *murdered*."

"*Three* murders?" asked Rose.

"Could be," sighed Byron.

"I'm glad I'm not a cardsmith. The local air makes them sickly." Cerise yawned, whapped Magog off the bed. "I'd say you need protecting, Byron."

"Protecting?"

"Night and day." Cerise slid off the bed. "Constant companionship to keep you safe. I'll assign my valet the job. Come, Magog!"

Byron watched the jingling swordmaster swing off with her trotting hound. The door closed with a loud click.

Still dazed by the prospect of murder, Byron didn't feel the hand on his collar until it tugged him backwards. His head thumped on the bed.

Rose leaned over his face until her dark hair shut out the light. In new darkness, she whispered, "So, I'm to protect you." Her hands began to wander over his body, stroking his chest and belly.

"Is that what you call this?" Byron gasped.

She gripped him by the crotch. "Your miserable worthless *life* is in my hands."

"Miserable?" chirped the cardsmith.

"Do you really think I'm clever?" the girl asked.

"Hunh? Did I say that?" Why did women always change the subject? To deliberately keep men off-balance? Byron tried to sit up, but Rose mashed her forehead on his, pressed him back down, giggled. "Uh, yes, I do," he stuttered. "I think you're very clever."

"Do you like clever girls?" She nibbled the end of his nose. "Or do you prefer them dumb and helpless?"

"Uh, no, I like them smart." Byron's hands settled on the curve of her waist, began to stroke her back. "I can't stand women who prattle. I like—thinkers."

"Like me?"

"Oh, yes."

"Blonde thinkers or brunette thinkers? Or snippy brunettes with empty skulls and ratty blonde streaks that make them look like they stuck their pinched faces against a fresh-painted fence?"

Byron stroked her soft hair. "I like this kind."

"And me?"

"Yes . . ."

"A lot?"

"Ummm. . . . yes."

"So there aren't any other girls in the world?"

"Girls? What other girls?" He felt the curve of her hips, caressed her soft bottom under layers of petticoat. "I've never seen any other girls! Not pretty as you."

"Good!" She flopped on him, her modest bosom pillowed on his chest, her hips grinding his groin, her mouth mashing his.

"I like the way you protect me," he mumbled mushily.

"Shut up and kiss me."

He did.

By and by, Byron fell asleep with his head pillowed on Rose's lap. He had no nightmares.

Chapter 12

A demon with breath like death slobbered in Byron's face.

Hairy and whiskered, the demon tried to rip out his tongue with white-hot pliers. Byron screamed and the demon stuck a long red hand down his throat. He twisted, pushed, but the drooling monster stabbed for his heart with four daggers while clubbing his chest—

Byron gasped awake, struck blindly.

A dog yelped.

Magog stood on Byron's chest and groin with heavy paws and pointed toenails, licking his face furiously with a red lolling tongue.

Spluttering, shoving, swearing, Byron shoved the dog off and rolled over, panting. Magog hopped off the bed, making it toss like a ship at sea.

Someone was laughing. Cerise, in the doorway,

hips tilted and hung with weapons. "A kiss from a
beautiful maiden to wake the sleeping prince! Come
on, time to rise! We've got a dukedom to win and I
need you to make some cards. Though I see you've
made something else the night long. No wonder
you're hard to rouse." She stooped and picked up a
white petticoat.

Byron scrubbed his mouth with a bedsheet. He
was groggy, unsure if he'd dreamt of demons or not.
"Where's Rose?"

"She's washing her face. You don't need to. Magog's
seen to that. So get up!"

Grabbing hold, the swordswoman whisked the
covers off the bed and Byron. He squawked and
covered his skinny white nakedness with his hands.

Cerise laughed and turned for the door. "Poor
Rose. She'll be black and blue from wrestling those
knobby bones. Come, Magog!"

Jingling, the cardmaster sauntered out the door,
the dog trotting happily after. She left the blankets
on the floor and the door wide open, so Byron had
to crab off the far side of the bed. Hunkered, he
searched for his clothes, strewn everywhere.

Then he halted. What had Cerise said? He'd make
cards? What kind of cards?

Despite the early hour, with the sun barely risen,
the War Room was full. Byron looked for Rose but
didn't see her. Followers of Stanwin, Lenda, and
Otto crowded their respective tables, arguing and
gesturing. At the gaming table, a contest raged among
three cardmasters using blue-edged cards. They
squabbled about dam and weir levels, traditional
salmon runs, canals that diverted rivers, flooded

fields, access and tow paths, yearly rainfall, and more. Byron assumed this dawn battle over water rights preceded a larger contest, such as troop movements or food production. Otto's army had "retired" yesterday when its flank disintegrated. The earl was licking his wounds and weighing his chances. Countess Lenda had yet to field a single "soldier."

Along one windowed wall lay a sumptuous breakfast feast: ham and sausage, blood puddings, deviled eggs, cheeses, breads, raisins and winter apples and pears, pitchers of mead and cider and herb tea. While Byron folded a sausage into black bread and grabbed a mug of mead, someone at his elbow loaded a plate so full she covered her thumb.

"Veronica," he teased, "if you keep eating like that, you'll look like one of your big-bellied bishops."

"Isn't it won'erful?" The girl's mouth was full. "Try one'a'ese strawberr' tarts! They're divine!"

"Poor Stanwin," Byron teased. "He'll go broke feeding a wife who eats this hearty."

"S'all right," she gulped. "I asked Chancellor Clement. Stan has an eye for milkmaids and farm girls, girls with heft. But they're already proposing him brides. Now that he's duke, marriage offers from princesses and duchesses and countesses flood in. He'll have his pick of beautiful noblewomen." As she watched Stanwin across the room, her blue eyes filled with tears.

"Well, none of them would be as nice as you." Sorry for her heartsickness, Byron ceased his teasing. "Just stay close. He'll notice you eventually."

Turning from the table, he hooked tankards with Edric, Stanwin's cousin. "Terribly sorry, old man, my fault. Just getting breakfast, you know. I'm useless without it." The wastrel poured a mug of mead, sprinkled in chopped eggs, added a dollop of pepper sauce and brandy, then chugged it while Byron and Veronica gagged.

Munching soggy eggs, Edric exclaimed, "Well, must be off! I've got border duty with my little deck! Most important! So good to have you both with us!" Bending low, he kissed Veronica's hand and tottered off.

"A likeable drunk, anyway." The priest wiped the back of her hand on a napkin.

"And happy and untroubled on an undisputed border. Well, I'm off, too. Good day." Byron steered through the breakfast crowd for Stanwin's table.

The young duke looked haggard, as if he hadn't slept, his face lined with worry. Yet his clothes were crisp and he was the courteous host. "Welcome, Byron. You'll enjoy that mead. It's brewed by a family on our Calabar River. They've used a secret recipe for thirteen generations now. When you have a moment, would you be so kind as to review this deck for me? You aided us greatly yesterday with your keen vision."

Flattered by the compliments and attention, Byron was glad to set down his food and check cards. Momentarily, he reflected that the duke had true nobility: pride in his country and people, grace under strain, kindness for his lowest helpers and commoners. Such a man, he thought, deserved to be High Duke, would do his damnedest to protect the kingdom from invaders. And if he could sacrifice and give his all, then Byron could, too. This contest, he remembered, was about preserving their life and liberty. With that in mind, he paid extra-careful attention to his work.

As he'd guessed, the deck represented food
production. There were cards for grains—rye, wheat,
spelt, barley, malt—as well as livestock such as pigs,
cows, and chickens. There were cards for farmers
and barns and grainmills and good harvest weather,
even cards for earthworms and manure. Byron scanned
each card carefully, found them all common.

He reported such to Stanwin, but added, "If you
please, I'd like Nanette to review them, too—just
to be sure."

Stanwin rubbed his eyes at a new complication.
"You aren't sure they're not enchanted?"

Byron started to shrug, but resisted. Stanwin's
good manners were rubbing off. "Nothing in magic
is sure, sire. There are ways of cloaking cards an
amateur like myself might miss."

Nodding, Stanwin bid a page to fetch Nanette.
"I'm glad you recognize potential weaknesses in yourself
and seek to correct them. Someone who realizes
they make mistakes is ten times more valuable than
someone who thinks they're infallible. I hope you'll
be quick to point out my errors. T'would do our
fair land no service to let me proceed with a blunder."

Byron nodded soberly, admiring this noble more
and more. In his limited knowledge, a lord who'd
admit to human mistakes was rare, and therefore
treasured.

Otto's cardmasters and Lenda's flocked to the table
for the day's contest, but Stanwin begged a delay
for double-checking. In the lull, Chancellor Clement
raised a list of issues. Stanwin rubbed his eyes and
attended patiently.

"First, there was a raid on our second outpost in
the pass. I've sent a lieutenant to inspect it. Sacked

and burned flat, possibly by Shinyar, perhaps by bandits. Fourteen men and women dead or missing. Your orders?"

Stanwin held his head as if it throbbed. "Uh . . . That's on a high spur with a good view. We must maintain a post there. Rouse the engineers to replace it. Send old Inigo: he's fought the Shinyar and can recognize their handiwork. Choose one or two soldiers from each of our garrisons for the new post, so they'll gain experience, then fill their numbers with new volunteers. See their horses are the fleetest in case they must flee. Raid my own stable if necessary. I don't want our people cut off."

"Very good, sire." Clement made a note. "Now as to guest quarters. Otto's sister, Lady Solita, dislikes the sun waking her in the morning, so perhaps a move around the corner . . ."

Byron gulped breakfast and felt sorry for Stanwin. That list of troubles looked endless.

Cerise caught his arm and towed him aside to a quiet corner. Magog nibbled for his sausage sandwich. The swordswoman said, "I mentioned I want you to fashion a card. Here's why. Yesterday, just before we suspended play, I detected someone pawing through my mind. It was magic for sure. Do you know any spells that could do that? And can you counter it?"

Munching and sipping, Byron frowned and thought. To skirt the ban on magic cards at the table, someone was triggering cards elsewhere and then sitting down: bringing magic to the table in their head. Not strictly against the rules, and all was fair in love and war. And cardplaying. For in spite of polite smiles and urbane quarrels, this Great Game was a substitute for war.

"Um . . . a Forethought spell lets someone read whatever's in the forefront of your mind. But usually they must touch you. Did anyone?"

Cerise shook her head. "I wouldn't let anyone touch me during a game. Not even nudge my boot under the table. That's why I station Magog under me."

"Good idea. Uh . . . Thoughts are slippery things, like fish in a pond, rising to the surface then sinking again, Rayner used to say. Probably the spellcaster waited until the end of the day when you were tired: it's harder to concentrate then, easier to plunder your thinking. You need something to cloud your thoughts but not your thinking. Tricky . . . A Secret Garden builds a wall around your thoughts so you can think privately, but makes it hard to get your attention. Oh, wait! A Jingle spell, or Jangle spell, creates a maddening little ditty that swirls around in your mind forever. Oh, and you'll like this!"

He hushed to an excited whisper. "It has a fun side effect. You've got this maddening ditty rattling in your head. When someone reads it, it sticks in *their* head! *They* might slip and whistle or sing it, then *you'd* learn who poked at your brain!"

"Wonderful!" Cerise laughed and clapped his shoulder. "Go make one quick as you can!"

"Oh." Byron blinked. "Um, surely. If I can figure out how . . ."

"You'll figure it out. Ah, here's your friend."

Cerise accepted a war deck from Stanwin. Byron turned to find himself nose-to-nose with Rose.

She didn't kiss him, as new lovers might, but her dark eyes sparkled. As Cerise's valet, she could eschew green: she wore a wine-red gown and bodice with a yellow chemise flower-embroidered at the cuffs. Mock-formal, she cooed, "Good morning, Master Cardsmith. I trust you slept well under our blankets of Thallandian wool?"

Byron sparkled back, but kept his wits. Obviously she wanted their liaison kept secret. "Ah, yes, miss, thank'ee. I might have slept better, but there were bedbugs, or one overlarge bug romping under my sheets last night, kept me tossing and turning."

"Bedbugs," she pouted. "Well, we'll take care of those. I'll give you a club tonight, and if anyone's jumping around, you can whack them with it."

"Actually," Byron put his nose in the air, "I always take a club to bed with me. A large white one I carry everywhere."

"I've seen that club," Rose teased. "It's no larger than a writing quill. You couldn't stun even a bedbug with that puny thing."

Stumped, Byron gaped. The girl laughed at his slack jaw, then sashayed off to the breakfast table. He liked the way she walked, as much side-to-side as forward—

Visions of Rose were blocked by someone with dark and light hair who reeked of orchid perfume.

Dazzling Ingrid the cardmaster wore her embroidered leather jacket slung around her shoulders, blue silk breeches that clung to thighs and lush hips, and a yellow shirt cut to her ribs; Byron stared at heavy breasts more outside than inside the shirt. Ingrid let him look, then shifted her hips so her baldric and weapons chimed. She glanced back, saw Rose glaring.

"So, Byron," she purred, "sampling the local produce?"

"Uh . . ." Byron was hypnotized by stunning cat-eyed

beauty and mounded flesh. "Um . . . No, we're not . . ."

"Tut, tut," she interrupted. "It's all right. Just remember she's an appetizer, but I'm a full meal."

Actually, Byron rankled, if Ingrid craved his body that bad, she'd had plenty of opportunities to sneak into his bedroll or bedroom. So far, she'd resisted. Girls who talk about it never do it, ran an old pub saying.

Ingrid smiled—laughing at him?—and hooked the front of his doublet. She dragged him close to kiss, but Byron craned his head back. He was nobody's toy. The cardmaster pursed red lips. "By-ron! You shouldn't—*Awk!*"

Ingrid leaped two feet as a tremendous splash of mulled wine burst around her head and shoulders. Sticky redness slopped in her hair, ran down her neck and bosom, soaked her fancy jacket and breeches. The cardmaster hissed at both the surprise and the sting, for the wine had been mulled over a firepot.

Behind Ingrid, Rose had "stumbled" to her knees. "Oh, ma'am! I'm so sorry! I was only fetching the punchbowl to the other end of the table!" The girl fluttered her hands, wide-eyed and innocent. The food table was twenty feet away. "I'm *so* clumsy! Please forgive me!"

"You—you—" Ingrid stood with arms wide, hands clawed like a harpy. Stringy red-dyed hair flapped around her face. Her silk blouse was ruined, her breeches stained. But hurt worst was her pride, for many in the room chuckled or laughed outright. "You—filthy—little—tight-assed—bitch! I'll gouge your eyes out!"

Before she could take a step, Cerise interposed. In mock horror, she piped, "Oh, Ingrid! How awful!

You've ruined your best clothes! Why, they must have cost you three crowns at least! But it's my fault! I told the girl to move the bowl. Rose, dear, run to the kitchen and fetch another, will you? And Byron, would you get busy with our little project? Thanks awfully. Oh, and look, I'm needed at the table. Well, ta ta!"

Rose had vanished, Cerise trotted away. Amazed at the calm serenity and capability of women, Byron backed towards the door. Ingrid was left standing in a red pool, swearing furiously to herself.

Alone in his room, with the door bolted, Byron sat on the floor, a borrowed harp across his lap and a crayon in one hand.

He stared at a blank card, stared until sweat ran down his forehead, until his hands shook, until his body chilled to the marrow.

Jingle, he thought. Just a simple jingle!

The card stayed blank.

Magic was too hard, he thought bitterly. He was too inexperienced, and the card wasn't properly prepared. It had been steeped in Rayner's "magic brew," but the old cardsmith had usually augmented blanks further, often without telling his apprentices. A Crumble card was sprinkled in brick dust, a Charm Beast buried in dog hair, a Lust card soaked in perfume. Byron had borrowed the harp from a musician, strummed it idly for musical notes, but nothing helped the magic bind. Damn it, magicmaking had too many questions and too few answers!

Entranced, staring, shivering despite a fire in the hearth, Byron felt alone and afraid. As if he'd tumbled into a deep well, splashed hip-deep in nigh-freezing water while his life force slowly drained away. As if he were trapped and dying of chills.

It should be simple. Music to rattle in one's head. He heard a tune distantly, far above the mouth of the imaginary well. But the magic wouldn't take. The magical essence, the mana, billowed and broke around him like foggy breath on a winter's morning, real but intangible.

He should quit. But Cerise needed this spell. She'd helped him, befriended him, saved his life. He wanted to help her back. So he stared, sank deeper into the trance, spiralled deeper into the well.

The cold grew stronger, made his fingers ache, his skull throb. It bit into his bones and wrapped ice around his heart.

This was bad, he thought vaguely. The living shouldn't submerge this deep into magic. If he went too far, he'd pass a veil of darkness—

Then it happened. Crushed by freezing walls, his soul shrivelled in his body, tore free of his flesh. Like a balloon, his spirit bubbled up, kicked free, fled to escape the suffocating cold and leave behind Byron's hollow shell.

Too far, the cardsmith jolted. He'd gone too far.

His soul fluttered like a dying butterfly over the chilly water of the well. A butterfly too weak to climb out. Soon it would fall into freezing water. And he'd never get out.

Cerise and Rose and Veronica, his friends, would find him frozen dead like Rayner.

Panicked, abandoning the card and the magic, Byron clawed for sunlight. His fingernails ripped on stones lining the well, his feet stuck in mud and wouldn't suck free. Up above, ghostly, he saw his spirit hovering, abandoning him. He'd never been this alone, for even his soul had deserted him.

He whimpered, shouted for help, grabbed at a rock jutting overhead. Touched by sun, it looked warm, but was sheathed in ice. His fingers clawed, slid off. He couldn't grip the stones. Soon he'd plunge into blackness.

Then the walls of the well crumbled—

From all sides, rocks broke away, landed with a thunderous splash in the well water. Faces that were twisted, bat-eared, and fanged leered from behind cascading rocks.

The demons had found him again. They hunched in holes around the well like gargoyles on a cathedral roof, hooting and gibbering.

Hairy gnarled hands grabbed his arms, his doublet, his legs. The fiends yanked in every direction, laughed when Byron shrieked.

This was it, then. He'd died, gone too far, hurled himself straight to the netherworld. The demons would ferry him down. Unfreezing, his left-behind body would rot while his soul was steeped in hellfire, bandied around, a plaything for monsters forever.

But the fiends pulled him, not down, but up. From below, one boosted his rump. Others yanked his arms upwards. Claws and warty hands and tentacles, some colder than well water, some hotter than scorching rocks, latched on and tugged. Grabbed in a hundred places, blinded by scabby fingers, Byron was shunted up the well like a centipede with a thousand legs.

He popped into light like a flower breaking the earth.

Onto the floor of his bedchamber.

Groggy, chilled, manhandled, the cardsmith crawled in an aimless circle, careful not to fall down the hole again. But the hole was gone. The floor was solid. The harp and crayon and blank card lay on blue flagstones.

Why had the demons rescued him? Why return him to life? Why not drag him off to hell? Wasn't that their job?

He crawled to the bed and dragged the counterpane and blankets around himself, crawled to the fireplace until cloth smouldered. Shivering, he tried to get warm. His hands were tender and skinned, his fingernails ripped. His doublet and breeches showed ragged slashes as from demon claws. He was wet all over.

Were the demons real or not? Had demons clawed him, or had he clawed himself? Had he wrecked his hands on flagstones? Was this sweat or well water?

It must be imagination. He wouldn't believe the demons were real. Because if so, the netherworld and this world were drawing together—with Byron trapped in the middle.

Hours later, near sunset, Byron stumbled into the War Room. Still clutching a blanket around his shoulders, he looked shabby but didn't care. Better that than freezing. His blood felt like slush straight off a snowpeaked mountain.

Some cardmasters gamed, but Cerise supped from the buffet. Rose was beside her, sipping soup. She bleated when she saw him. "Darling, what happened? Your door was bolted so I left you alone! But I thought you were napping."

"Lately, yes." Magog yipped at Byron, and the

cardsmith patted the huge shaggy head. It felt warm as a stove to his palsied hands.

Cerise looked at the blanket, bloody hands, torn shirt, then handed him a flagon of mulled wine. Gratefully, Byron drank it all. The cardmaster said, "You look like you've been to hell and back."

"Don't say that!" Byron gulped.

"Did you make the card?"

"No. I failed." Byron thought to explain about the demons, but refrained. No one could keep them at bay, so no need to tell the world he was haunted.

Seeing his distress, the swordswoman didn't condemn. "No matter, I suppose. No one's been probing my mind: maybe they found it held little. We're muddling along, blocking each threat as it comes. Sticking our heads inch by inch into a noose, one of the generals thinks, but there's nothing for it until we find Old Stanwin's strategy. We've survived another day."

"So have I," Byron let slip.

Pouting with worry, Rose hitched the woolly blanket higher on his shoulders. Cerise fished in a belt pouch, put silver coins in the girl's hand. "There's nothing much doing this evening. Some cardmasters quibble over timber harvesting, whether war machines can be built, what should pull them. They're digging fortifications, and that will take all night. Someone's leading a scouting party to harass pickets and stir up superstition, steal horses if possible. Small stuff. Take those coins and go to the fair."

A weight of fatigue made Byron's knees stagger. "I don't want—"

"Go," Cerise insisted. "Otherwise, you'll just crawl back to bed. Get outside and move around, get the ice out of your spine. Drag him along, Rose. Fetch him back by midnight. But mend his shirt first. What do you have, fleas, that you scratch so hard?"

Byron managed a wry grin. "No, Mother, and thank you." He let Rose take his hand, though she hissed at his touch, chill and clammy as a corpse.

"To a fair for fun, eh?" He grinned lopsidedly.

"Just you and me alone," the girl nodded. "And if that fat-assed Ingrid shows her painted face, I'm going to ram it in the nearest pigsty."

"That promise," wheezed Byron, "makes the trip worthwhile."

The fair was as lively at night as by day. Birchbark torches were stuck atop poles, and most booths had lanterns with yellow or red glass. The fair's "streets" meandered past corrals of prize-winning animals, rickety stages where jugglers and acrobats capered, booths selling food or geegaws, tents where fortune-telling and other secrets lurked, and much more. Nobles and commoners and animals rubbed elbows. The air was warm and heady with the scent of roasted chestnuts and hazel nuts, maple syrup on popcorn, braised chicken and lamb, mulled cider and switchel. Smells of pigs and leather and armor polish and privies and perfume and incense mingled into an aroma that began to thaw Byron's guts. Before long, he folded the blanket over his shoulder and strolled along hand-in-hand with Rose, who smiled to see him happy.

"Oh, Byron, isn't it grand?"

Byron laughed at her delight. He'd been to several carnivals in Waterholm, but this was Rose's first big affair. She jinked the coins in her hand, determined to spend them all. In an hour, she'd bought herself a peacock feather for her hair, admitted them to a tent to see a two-headed calf, had their fortune told by a dark woman with stars sewn on her shawl, lost bets on a wrestling bout, gobbled sweetcakes. Rose towed Byron eagerly, hurrying to see all the sights at once.

But turning one crowded corner, the girl jerked short. Byron had run square into a broadchested cardmaster hung with a glittering sword and dagger.

Actually, the man had run into him. He chopped down on Byron's hand to free it from the girl's. The cardsmith stepped back, puzzled. The man was one of Lady Lenda's, whose team had done nothing much so far. Sporting flowing red hair and a red chin beard and mustache, he was dressed wildly in a purple shirt with trailing dagged sleeves and crisscrosses of silver, and pants of white doeskin over flop-top boots. A hussar's jacket edged with ermine hung from one shoulder on a silver chain. Obviously proud of his glorious hair, he disdained a hat. Two more cardmasters bracketed him.

"You're Byron, aren't you?" the man demanded. "Of Waterholm?"

"Yes," replied the smith. Stalling for time, he asked, "And you?"

"Deklan of Tregeagle. I see you're intimate with Ingrid, she of the brassy tackle."

"Intimate?" Byron's voice squeaked on the word. He had to look up at the man, he was so tall. At this busy corner, squished amidst booths and kiosks, many folks stopped to see the show: a fight in the making. "No, we're not intimate."

"I say you are!" Deklan snarled. "I saw you kissing her this forenoon!"

Rose piffed. "She didn't get the chance!"

Byron wondered at this assault. What did the man want? Was this real outrage or more plotting? Trying to placate him, and think things through, Byron conceded, "Uh, it was more she tried to kiss me. But we needn't fight. You can have her—"

"*What?*" A gloved finger big as a roll of coins thumped into his chest, rocking him. "I can have your *castoffs?* Your *leftovers?* The *garbage* you're done with? Is that what you're calling Sweet Ingrid?"

"Sweet?" Byron bleated. Backpedalling, wishing Cerise here, he stammered, "No! I mean yes! Uh— if you wish to—court her—"

"*Court her?*" the man roared. Another jab pushed Byron stumbling against a tent rope. "You'd *dick* her, wouldn't you? Is that how you treat a lady?"

Rose made to help Byron, but a female cardmaster hip-bumped her aside. The cardsmith found his feet, held his tongue. Anything he said—

A leather glove batted his head half-around. Still weak from his magic casting, he sprawled over the tent rope. He opted to stay down, but a hammy hand grabbed his mended doublet and yanked him up.

"Well? Say it!" Deklan demanded. "Do I have to slap you again, coward?"

The man turned as a small fist thumped his shoulder. Rose had shoved past her opponent. "Let go, you bully! He's not a fighter like you! Or a coward like you, to pick on someone smaller!"

"Say it!" Deklan shouted into Byron's face, shook him. "Say it, you gutless snot! You puke!"

Byron's head wobbled. Say *what?*

"Keep quiet, Byron!" Rose shrilled. "Don't challenge him! He'll get choice of weapons!"

Deklan growled and shoved Rose back, angry his strategy had failed. He slapped Byron again. "All right, then! I'll call *you* out! I challenge you to a *duel*! What do you say, coward?"

Byron's eyes jiggled in their sockets, but through swirling lights he saw Rose nod vigorously. He drooled, "I accept!"

But what the hell was the girl *thinking*? He'd get *killed*!

Chapter 13

"*Here?*" asked both Byron and Deklan.

"Right here," replied Rose.

The duellists looked around. They were not far from the main courtyard where Cerise had killed Joash the Terrible. Except they stood around the corner behind a head-high wall.

The kitchen dooryard sported a well with twin buckets at one side, a clothesline hung with wet chemises and breeches and diapers, and a corner sty where pigs rooted for garbage. Flagstones were wet from dishwater hurled out the door; from the door wafted aromas of fresh-baked bread and cinnamon rolls. Clunks and slaps of washing and kneading mingled with men's and women's voices. Dawn spilled over the gray white-striped mountains to draw long shadows.

Deklan had two seconds, his swordbearing valet

and the cardmaster in peacock blue. Byron had Rose and Veronica: all three looked small and pitifully unarmed.

The cardmaster sniffed at the idea of duelling in a dooryard. "But t'will be convenient for the sculleries to scrub away your blood."

Byron shrank at the words, but Rose and Veronica patted his shoulder. He wished Cerise were here to dispatch this brute, but she'd mysteriously declined. Rose had met secretly with Deklan's seconds last night to set the time and place for the duel. Now she surprised him again.

"There won't be any blood in this duel," Rose pronounced. "As the challenged, Byron has choice of weapons. We'll use what he's accustomed to, and he's no swordsman."

Frowning, Deklan turned to his seconds. The female cardmaster just spread her hands: rules are rules. The redbeard snarled, "Right then, fetch your weapons. I fight on an empty stomach and want breakfast quick."

Byron gulped. He had an empty stomach too: otherwise, he'd vomit from frazzled nerves. Despite Rose's vague assurances, he hadn't slept a wink.

Rose and Veronica squeezed past a white-clad crowd of cooks and helpers who'd paused for the fight. Byron heard bets being offered, but no one would take his side. He couldn't blame them.

The cooks laughed as Rose and Veronica waddled out of the kitchen with buckets slopping-full of soapy water in one hand and mops in the other. Byron blinked, Deklan frowned.

With a salute, Rose presented a mop to Deklan, then Byron, then plunked the two buckets ten feet apart in the middle of the courtyard. She waved the men forward.

"The duel," she proclaimed, "will be with wet mops. Byron's used one many times cleaning up his master's workshop." (*I never said that*, the cardsmith thought.) "Deklan seems master of many weapons, so shouldn't have any trouble."

The cardmaster ground his teeth, shook the mop as menacingly as possible. "What are the terms?"

"You fight until one falls on his back," said Rose.

Byron sighed with relief. He could simply fall down and lose and be done. But he sighed too loud.

Deklan sneered, "Whoever falls on his back *after ten minutes!*"

Rose and Veronica nodded to Deklan's seconds, who nodded back. Byron had no say.

"Fine." Deklan laughed nastily. Tossing his mane of red hair, he shrugged off his ermine-edged jacket, baldric of weapons, and fine tunic. Stripped to a white silk shirt and breeches, he looked even bigger and broader. He dunked the floppy mop in suds. "I've wielded a mop, too, aboard his majesty's ships. Once in a battle, I was surrounded on the forecastle and lost my cutlass overside. So I beat three pirates to death with a mop handle. It took less than ten minutes."

The girls blinked. Byron groaned. At Rose's urging, he soaked his mophead, his arms trembling so badly he slopped on his shoes. Then the men were ready, so Rose could only say, "Begin!"

Roaring so loud his white teeth showed, Deklan hoisted the mop and charged Byron with the dripping head. *"Yahhhhhhh!!!!"*

Lurching backwards, the cardsmith tried to remember

the gist of Veronica's quarterstaff lessons. But he couldn't think of a thing, so just closed his eyes and stuck out his mop.

A hot soapy mass of suds and water slammed in his face.

Knocked flying, Byron half-rolled to protect his head and crashed on his shoulder. He got his eyes open—they stung like fury from the soap—just in time to see Deklan raise his mop like a sea god hoisting a trident. Byron threw himself sideways and the mop head flobbed onto the flagstones where his head had been. Cooks and helpers cheered.

Rolling, Byron scrambled to his feet, found himself on the other side of the wash line. As Deklan charged anew, Byron raised his mop and tangled it in someone's knee-patched breeches. Hollering like a sailor in a hurricane, Deklan stabbed with his dirty mop for Byron's midriff.

The young cardsmith flailed his weapon furiously and ripped down the whole line of fresh wash. Deklan's mop swished past him and slammed the wall, spraying Byron with suds. But the falling clothes tangled the cardmaster's shank. As he yanked down a basket's worth of washing, Byron ran around the end of the clothesline.

Stopping near Rose, he panted, "How much time?"

"Has passed? About thirty seconds!"

"*Is that all?*"

Deklan ripped at the washing on his mop, cursing like a madman. Byron ran.

Panicked, he didn't look where he was going, and boxed himself in the corner blocked by the pigsty. Startled by the shouting, three pigs milled and shrilled. Byron glanced back, saw Deklan charging and howling.

The cardsmith scaled the fence. The back wall of the dooryard wasn't high: maybe he could scramble over to safety. The rasping of his breath was louder than pigs' squeals.

How did Cerise stay so calm in a swordfight? Perched atop the wobbly fence, looking down at pigs and muck, he tried to remember how he'd gotten here. This was Ingrid's fault, he remembered bleakly. Which made it his fault, sort of. Which meant—

Teetering along a narrow fence in soapy squishy shoes, he slipped and fell.

He crashed in mud and muck that stank abominably. As he scrambled to get up, a mop swished over his head like a comet. It would have decapitated him if he hadn't slipped again. On elbows and butt he crabbed across the sty for the corner.

Deklan leaned on the fence, swinging his mop just out of reach. "Come out and fight, you coward!"

"No!" Byron felt almost safe as he skittered spiderlike into the corner. Still, Deklan might hurl the mop like a spear. "You'll kill me!"

"Damn right! Come out so I can bust you! It won't hurt!"

"Not on your life! My life! Hey, watch—"

Creaking under Deklan's wild stabs and lunges, the rickety gate shattered. With an oath, the cardmaster crashed on his face in filth. Terrified pigs trampled over him to escape the mad ranting. Byron thought that wise, too. Stepping square on Deklan's back, Byron bolted.

As he passed Rose, she yelled, "A minute and a half!" Only eight and half minutes left in which to be killed, Byron thought.

The only way out of the dooryard was blocked

by castle guards come to see the duel. Jammed in the entrance, they wouldn't let Byron pass and spoil the fun. Besides, many were bent over, helpless with laughter.

Seeking any shelter, Byron ran for the well. He wanted to slide behind, but the belt-high stone met the wall.

Shedding muck and straw, screaming like a banshee, blind with anger, Deklan ran swinging his mop at the end of his arms to bat Byron's head off. The cardsmith ducked. The mop slammed the end post of the well and sprayed him with more suds. If he were killed, Byron thought inanely, at least they wouldn't have to wash his corpse. Deklan raised his mop to smash down, as if Byron were a rat cornered in the kitchen.

Like a rat, Byron scampered straight between the cardmaster's legs. The mophead crashed on the wall and the shaft snapped.

People howled with glee as Byron galloped on three limbs, the mop clutched across his chest. Rose called, "Hit him, for pity's sake!" Byron tried. Swinging wild, he whapped the cardmaster across the broad seat of his white silk breeches with the mop.

Deklan whirled as if lashed with a whip. His mop handle, ash broken at a slant, had become a makeshift spear. Deklan charged. Byron quailed, backed, tripped over a bucket and fell. Soapy water cascaded around him.

Enraged, Deklan couldn't stop. Stumbling over Byron, he slammed face-down and slid along soap-slick stones on his belly.

Byron tried to jump up, lost his footing, crashed on his rump. Even Rose and Veronica laughed now.

From the corner of his eye, Byron saw cooks and guards hold each other and doorframes, crippled with laughter. Object of all this rage, the cardsmith didn't find it funny.

Deklan clambered to his feet. Water and suds and grit streamed from his proud red beard and hair. His face was also red as a sunset.

He'd lost his mop handle. Hollering, Deklan grabbed the remaining bucket, hoisted it high. But he forgot it was full of water, and slops poured over his head like a waterfall. Still, the bucket was made of heavy oak slats, and Deklan charged again, aiming to break it on Byron's head.

Scooting backwards on his bottom, desperate, Byron hoisted his mop but fumbled the slick shaft. The end of the mop plopped between two flagstones.

It turned out to be his best defense. Deklan ran his belly square onto the end of the fixed mop, slammed to a halt, grunted every ounce of air from his lungs. The bucket flew from his hands and clattered against the well.

The redbearded cardmaster toppled, slowly, off the mop and onto Byron. The skinny cardsmith grunted as the man's weight flattened him.

Byron was too spent to move, and just lay wheezing. Atop him, like a beached white whale, lay Deklan, also wheezing. But after a while, Byron heard stuttering. That changed to sobs, and finally he recognized the sound. It was chuckling.

Laughing, gasping, the redbearded master crawled off Byron, held his stomach and laughed and laughed. He laughed so hard tears ran from his eyes. And finally Byron was laughing along with everyone else in the dooryard.

"I never—I never—oh, my guts are burst!" Deklan sobbed. "I never—saw—such a *stupid fight*—in all my life!"

Helpless, he lay alongside Byron, who giggled until he thought he'd pass out.

Helped by their seconds, the combatants hobbled into the warm kitchen and plunked on stools. Towels were wrapped around their shoulders, and Rose dried Byron's hair. The men still gasped from laughter and exertion. The kitchen fell back to work, the guards back to their posts.

"I swear," Deklan wheezed, "if my old shipmates—could have seen that—they'd have dressed me in petticoats and marooned me on the Shoals of Whales! Oh, my stomach!"

They handed their clothes to cooks' helpers, who hung them by chimneys to dry. Sitting in their drawers, Byron skinny as a plucked chicken, Deklan hairy as a red bear, the two talked.

"That was my first duel," Byron grinned. "And I hope my last."

"You did well, considering," Deklan chuckled. "You drew blood across my arse and ran me through the brisket with your polearm. Maybe we should introduce mop brigades to the Great Game."

"T'would count for a lot of points, setting the enemy howling with laughter!" Byron joked.

"Aye! Platoons of chambermaids in clogs and pinafores, with mops on their shoulders and buckets for shields! Oh, it hurts! Oh, that bitch Ingrid, I'll skin her alive!"

Rose paused in drying Byron's hair. The cardsmith suddenly remembered why the duel had been fought.

"Uh . . . weren't you defending Ingrid's honor or something?"

Deklan blew the head off a jack of ale handed to him. "That slut probably gave her 'honor' to a gooseboy when she was thirteen. No, she egged me into it. Offered me a night's frolic if I'd pound you. Not kill, just pummel. That was bluff about killing you, mostly. But tumbling her couldn't be half as fun as brawling like that. Oh, my jaw aches from laughing."

Byron didn't know what to say. Why would Ingrid arrange to harm him? Because he'd spurned her, sort of? Or was it part of the larger conspiracy, whatever *that* was? Rose seethed and inadvertently yanked Byron's hair while asking Deklan a dozen questions. But the cardmaster knew nothing of Ingrid's thoughts or plots. In the end, still chuckling, he pulled on his dry clothes and weapons. "I must return to the game. Lady Lenda's moving her troops up today. See you there!"

Punching Byron on the shoulder hard enough to rock him, the big man strode out. Byron pulled on his clothes, saw the sculleries had mopped up the mess outside, so thanked them. Veronica went elsewhere while Byron and Rose aimed for the War Room.

Skirts in hand, Rose stamped up the stairs. "That hussy! I'll peel her painted face from her skull! I'll shove her down a garderobe! I'll kick her fat arse up and down every stairwell in the castle! I'll— Never, *never* trust *anyone* with dyed hair!"

Byron thought her fussing and cussing cute, but refrained from telling her so. He wondered how furious Cerise would be, and what she would say . . .

❖   ❖   ❖

Cerise's calm reply was unexpected. "I'm not surprised."

The Great Game hummed, with fifteen or more cardmasters spotted around the table, Ingrid among them. They had breakfasted, for Byron was famished, then watched the game and waited for a break. It took hours, and then just a pause for tea and watered wine and a bite to eat.

Cerise ate standing up, slathering corn bread with honey for energy. "The game's running hot and against us. All that pioneering and scouting and troop movement was for real, as were the assaults on the food sources. Otto introduced cards for locusts, arson fires, wheat rust and black beetles. Nasty. He's cutting roads and driving through the forest highlands around our backside, heading for Lenda's lands, but we don't know what she'll do if he gets there: unite with him, or drive him back. She's introduced odd factors: rumors of death mists to frighten our troops, hornworms to infest her own orchards. Plague cards even, but it's not clear if they're for cattle or horses. I never thought we'd need so many horse doctors. And Otto's pulled back his barbarians and engineers for mining, though no one's sure what they mine for—those cards are staying face down. And there's lots more we don't know: a library's worth of clues must be tucked into the old duke's strategy. We've played over three hundred cards so far, and most of it's reactive, just countering their assaults. We barely have time to take any offensive actions. That's hardly a battle plan."

Rose nodded her freckled nose at the table. "How's Ingrid's play?"

"Indifferent." Cerise shrugged, slugged wine. "She's good in a fight, keeps a cool head, but she's frivolous, no sticktoitiveness. Stanwin had her balancing the crop and fertilizer cards, but she got bored and lost a pile. So he pulled her off there and gave her a ranger party to fell trees across the high roads and cut supply lines. I got the corn and cowshit cards."

"I'd find those boring myself," Byron admitted.

Another shrug. "This Great Game simulates three entire fiefs, not just battle among three armies. Someone's got to mind the food stores. A hungry army won't take orders, they'll splinter to forage. Hungry peasants will hoard supplies, so the soldiers will attack and loot them. Then your populace turns against you and stops supporting the war. Some upstart general decides it's time to depose you, and while the officers are infighting, you lose the war and the dukedom. So a famine can be the trigger that fires the gun that kills you, as can a hundred other factors. Cardmastering's a job, and every job has boring parts. If you avoid them, you're a shirker."

Byron admitted that was true. It was the same with cardsmithing. Everyone thought it a glamorous occupation, but he'd spent hours cutting pasteboard and soaking it in vile concoctions timed to an hourglass. And there were always pots to scrub.

Rose asked, "But why are you not surprised at Ingrid's treachery? Isn't trying to kill someone on your own side treason?"

Cerise half-closed heavy-lidded eyes. "I'm not sure it's treachery. She asked a man to thump Byron, presumably for revenge. After all, he scorned her majesty to sleep with a poppet of a chambermaid."

Rose blushed, freckles on her nose prominent. Byron scratched his head, suddenly interested in his shoes.

"It's a school-girl prank, making your old boyfriend jealous," Cerise went on. "It means nothing except she's venal, and I knew that from watching her play. Anyone who attacks her cards, for whatever reason, wins an enemy for life. She seeks revenge for imagined insults and costs us points. She's a flibbertigibbet. Unless . . ."

"Unless what?"

"Unless she's partaking in some larger conspiracy, say the attacks on you by the bishop's guards in Waterholm, or the turncoat bodyguard attacking Stan. How do you juggle the clues? Did Ingrid join our party by coincidence or conniving? Did she save Byron and Veronica for kindness or conspiracy? That's the problem with intrigue: you never know what's connected or from which side you'll get stabbed. Or who seems to be on your side but is really on another side."

"If you suspect her, why not boot her from the game?" Byron asked.

"Or challenge her to a duel and puncture her fat tits?" added Rose.

"Think," Cerise chided. "I can't torture people at random for information. And it's not my place to boot her. Duke Stanwin invited her, plays her where she's strong, keeps her away from secrets. And we need extra hands at the table, even clumsy ones. If I whittle anyone, it should be from Otto's or Lenda's team."

She scritched Magog's head. "But there's intrigue under the table, too. I've been approached a dozen times to switch sides. The shares they offer keep rising."

Byron frowned. The cardmaster's eventual pay,

he knew, depended on points. The two losers must match with gold the points lost. Winners split the loot. Losers got nothing but experience, wild stories, and free meals.

If, for example, Stanwin's team won by six hundred points, Lenda and Otto would each pay three hundred gold crowns to the winning team. Split among six players, Cerise would receive a hundred gold crowns: what a master cardsmith might make in a year. And if the winners took six *thousand* points . . . On top of that, cardmasters were notorious for betting both in-hand booty and prospective shares on anything: their personal scores, the final point spread, number of cards lost. Sometimes they doubled or tripled their wages. Sometimes they blew it all.

And the game meant more to Byron than plain arithmetic. For his help, Cerise had promised him a goodly portion of her winnings. If she had any . . .

Someone called and Cerise set down her glass. "I have to get back. Otto's troops lost ground when they lost Joash—the one I skewered—but he's swarming across the border again, cocky as a rooster at laying time. We can't figure why. Without a strategy . . . But never mind. Take some time off, but check back before dinner. Go see the jousts." She gave them a handful of silver.

"Wait." Now that he'd fought his own duel and survived, Byron had a question prodding him. "Didn't it bother you to kill that man?"

"No." Cerise tucked away her purse. "He was a fool who would have been killed sooner or later. I just held the sword. I only feel bad when innocents die, people who work hard and mind their own business yet are slaughtered for pure malice." She tapped

Magog under the table and dragged up her stool.

"What did that mean?" Rose asked as they descended the stairs.

"Oh." Byron found her close enough to kiss, and did so where none could see. She giggled, but he sobered. "You don't know about her family? Her lost family?"

The girl shook her head.

Byron sighed for delivering bad news. "Come on to the fair. I'll tell you on the way."

Despite a slow rain, Byron and Rose huddled under his cloak to watch muddy jousts.

Clad in bucket helmets, chain or leather-studded mail, and bright flowing gypons, the knights entered the far ends of the long list, saluted, had their names and houses announced along with any terms of the duel, had lances inspected to assure they were tipped with wood and not steel. A drum thundered, and the men and some women charged and clashed, lances on shields and sometimes torsos. If both riders could remount, they did, until one was unhorsed and could not rise.

It was thrilling and satisfying to watch, to join the crowd leaning on the ropes, to cheer or boo or groan, to savor grudge matches bitterly fought.

Yet Byron was reminded again of how the Great Game represented an entire fiefdom with all its intrigues, for even here were mysteries to ponder.

The talk of the fair was the "House of Bronessa": twenty or so male and female knights and numerous retainers wearing brown tunics painted with a yellow sun. This gang hung back, vying little, oddly detached. They fought singly or in pairs, but neither hard nor long, and never in melee, the mock battles. If unseated once, they conceded defeat and left the field. If victorious, they collected small purses, avoided the crowd, and retired to their brown tents far down the field.

"They're a queer lot," an old man wheezed. "They fight as if they're bored, with nothing better to do."

"They're biding their time," his wife guessed, "but no one can figure for what."

A woman with a baby on her hip offered, "Some say they wait for their champion to lead them in melee on the last day of the tournament, and surprise everyone with some wild plan."

"He or she will have come a long way, from wherever Bronessa is. No one's ever heard of it."

"They're just stalling until everyone else is injured," said a man in passing. "It's knavish to hold back, borderline cheating, but not against the rules."

"Makes it hard to bet when no one can guess their strategy," the old man groused.

"Strategy . . ." Byron mused.

The rain fell harder. The marshals pronounced the field too muddy. Jousting was over for the day. Moaning, the crowd melted away.

"We should get back," Rose said. "I've mending for Cerise and chambers to clean before dinner."

"And I need to check more cards . . . You know, it's funny they should mention strategy. We're supposed to be hunting Old Duke Stanwin's strategy for the Great Game, but we're no closer."

"We're further from finding it, if you ask me." Rose took Byron's arm and held her skirts high as they plocked through mud. "We've run out of places to search. It's probably lost forever, stolen or thrown out accidentally in the confusion when the duke died. A servant probably used it to light a fire. It was wintertime."

"I hope it's not lost," Byron said. "Cerise needs it to win."

"She'll need to count on luck."

Byron checked cards, ate a meager supper and, with Rose away, collapsed on his bed. He hated to sleep alone, for that meant dreams of demons, but he was exhausted. Practicing magic and tracking the game, missing sleep and duelling had him shaky with fatigue. Maybe he'd be too exhausted to dream.

But the demons had plans for him.

Whirling, spinning, Byron fell and crashed amidst monsters.

Weak, weary unto death, he floundered to gain his feet, but he tumbled and rollicked down a slope of shale ridged like razors. Gibbering, screeching, pus-leaking, vomit-reeking fiends capered and gamboled all around.

The sky was pewter, the landscape more steep hills. Briar and thorn bushes clung in tufts among cracked rocks and ledges like broken glass. The cardsmith stabbed out a hand to stop his skidding, slashed himself on sharp flints that stung in the wound. Rolling faster, he grabbed for a branch but pricked his fingers on thorns and had to let go. Barely able to tell up from down, he couldn't twist his feet under him.

Perhaps he shouldn't. Scores of mad monsters pursued like dogs after a duck. Leaping, hopping, skittering and sliding, they, too, cut themselves on briars or stones while grabbing for Byron.

Skittering, he slammed to a halt against a silver-speckled boulder. Wracked in every bone, he had no chance to run or break free. He was too tired anyway.

He was snagged by forty or fifty demons, each different in its own horrible way. They flexed claws on his legs and arms and clothes, clashed long uneven teeth. He was almost smothered in hot slimy demon flesh, with only his head free.

They'd been chasing him in nightmares forever, it seemed. Now that they'd caught him, what would they do to him?

From the filthy pressing throng, a demon with a fat stomach hanging to warty knees leaned close over the captive cardsmith. A thumb big as a cucumber, with a black broken nail like a half a shingle, aimed for his face.

They'd blind him.

Byron screamed, kicked, struggled, pleaded. But entrapped a hundred ways, he could only twitch and whimper. He watched, horrified, as the demon's nail jabbed his forehead, shrieked as, like a burning brand, the knotty thumb sank into his skull. And twisted.

His brain felt afire. Pain shot through his bones until he thought he'd explode. Blood gushed over his face and into his eyes. But he still saw what came next.

Above him, the fat demon rammed fingers in his own face, twisted, and ripped loose an eye. Blood welled from the shorn socket, but the demon ignored it. One-eyed, he craned over and jammed the bloody eye into the hole in Byron's forehead.

The other demons, hunkering, limping, jiggling,

fell silent to watch. As if weeping at Byron's plight, tears spilled from their myriad eyes.

The new eye planted in Byron's forehead itched and burned. New nerves sent thrills to his brain, as if a spider or octopus had invaded his skull. The cardsmith wobbled his head, trying to dislodge it. Magic or not, he didn't want any part of a demon. He didn't want to be like them, didn't want to share their power.

Then the twitching eye opened.

Byron shrieked once—

—and sat bolt upright in bed.

"I see! I see!"

Chapter 14

Bounding out of bed, Byron fumbled a candle alight, dug under the mattress and dragged out his velvet pouch. With shaking hands, he spilled cards across the blankets. Charm Against Plague, Two Grumpy Men, Crumble, Mist, Bitten Apple—

"Ha!" A single big smeary eye stared back. Laughing, he kissed the card, shuffled the cards back in the pouch, threw on his clothes, and ran up the torchlit stairwell to find Cerise.

Even in the dead of night, the game plowed on. Twenty cardsmiths pored over cards laying in long rows and odd angles and heaps of discards. Ingrid snarled at a man at her elbow. Two women pointed cards and shouted as two weary judges listened patiently. By his safe table, black-bearded Otto growled commands to the cardmaster Deklan. Lady Lenda, pale and tired, reclined on a couch near her table but also issued orders. Stanwin dozed with head pillowed on arms like a child. A hollow-eyed Chancellor Clement stacked decks, sorting and resorting. The air was thick from warm bodies, sour wine, damp wool, and murky smoke from the fireplaces. Someone had lit incense to mask the fug.

Weapons atilt, Cerise argued with a cardmaster in a rose-colored tunic, jabbing a blunt finger. "It's a damned swamp, I tell you! See the card? You're not hauling wagons through there, so forget it! The judges'll back me! Find another route! You've lost ninety points already delaying the game!"

The cardmaster stormed off to Lenda's table. Cerise rattled orders to her team: unwrap more arrows, call up the militia, withdraw civilians to the strongholds, poison wells in the north. Then, with Magog trotting at her heels, she strode to her safe table to collect superstition cards: Fear of Dark, Fear of Damnation, Ghostly Presence, Refusal to Violate a Graveyard. Seeing Byron, she thrust them in his hands. "Check these and quick!"

"Cerise, I've discovered—"

"First things first! The game goes poorly! Check!"

Absently, Byron riffled the cards, handed them back. "Look, Cerise, I've—wait!"

Jumping, he snatched the deck back, felt again, laid each card against his cheek. He held up the Refusal to Violate a Graveyard. "This is enchanted."

"What?" The cardmaster took the card. It portrayed a small cemetery with a locked iron gate. The border was black, but the background gold for purity. "It can't be!"

"Smell it," Byron instructed, but she flipped a

hand, unable to sense magic. "Sorry. It smells of incense because it's a religious belief. But it's a different incense than they burn in these censers." He pointed to the blue smoke that trickled upwards in spirals.

Chancellor Clement clasped his curly head. "Nanette checked these an hour ago!" Sighing, he tottered off to fetch a drink.

"I don't understand!" Cerise ranted. "How the *hell* did it get in the stack? Who's tripping us up? You're *sure*? Shit!"

Whirling, she blundered into Magog, almost kicked her dog from underfoot, stamped over and hurled the card into a fireplace. Returning, she groused, "We needed that damned card! Lenda's mountaineers won't move through the pass if there's a cemetery in sight! But now—now I don't know what to do."

"Are we losing?" Byron had momentarily forgotten his own discovery.

"We might be. Our troops are spread too thin, and Otto and Lenda have infiltrated the roads and paths to intercept messengers. And half our soldiers are on short rations!" She waved at the table, and Byron saw lines of cards indicating their infantry were indeed blocked by cavalry and mountaineer cards. "Otto and Lenda have united too, just as we feared, and they've combined strategies to cover their errors—"

"Strategy! That's what I came for!" He caught her brawny arm and towed her to the windows for privacy. "Look what I found!"

Cerise looked at the smeary card. "An eyeball. What is it? Cure for hangover?"

"No, it's True-Seeing!"

Heavy-lidded, Cerise squinted. "How do you know

that all of a sudden? You toted that card around for weeks! Or have you lied to me?"

"No, of course not! I—"

"How do you know?"

"All right," Byron sighed, "the knowledge came in a dream. But I know it's right! I even know the token!"

"True-Seeing . . ." Cerise fingered her chin. She had trouble thinking clearly, Byron could tell. She'd been gaming intensely for twenty hours or more. "How do we use it?"

Byron told her, added, "I need your help to hold my hand."

The frontierswoman studied the big table. "The game can lurch along without me for a while. And your magic will only work for five minutes, right?"

"I'm not sure." Byron caught her hand and headed for the stairs. "Let's find out!"

They skipped down the stairs, Magog galumphing behind, to the second floor and Byron's room. They surprised Rose shucking off her gown and bodice. "Oh! Byron, I wondered where you were! Hello, Cerise." She patted Magog's shaggy drooling head. Her good shoes were wet from the jousts, so she wore peasant clogs. The wooden shoes clumped and clunked with a tremendous racket whenever she moved.

Byron gave his lady-love a quick kiss, then grabbed a candlestick and lit one for Cerise. He told Rose, "Get dressed and come upstairs! We'll need you!"

"For what?"

But cardsmith and cardmaster and dog slipped behind the tapestry to the servants' passage. They mounted the stone stairs, passed the wall behind the duke's room, continued until Byron said, "We'll start here."

Cerise held up the candle to look around, saw nothing new. "It's your magic show."

On the rough back wall was the sooty crevice where Byron had discovered the spent puffball: it marked a gap Rose explained led to caves but was now blocked with rubble. Magog snuffled the floor idly, then Byron's ear as he dropped to one knee. Setting down his candlestick, he bent over the eye-drawn card and rubbed his own eyes hard.

"What are you doing?" Cerise asked.

"In my dream, a fat demon gouged a hole in my forehead and stuck in a demon eye; a 'third eye' like witches and wizards try to win. Because it's invisible you can see into the spirit world."

As he mashed his eyes with his fingers, Cerise snapped, "There's an invisible eye stuck in your forehead? Sure you didn't fall and bang your head on a chest of drawers?"

"No. I mean, yes. I mean no, I don't have a third eye. The dream is an allegory, a way of ordering your thoughts. The knowledge was locked in my mind, but I couldn't get to it. That's what dreams do: free your thoughts. In wondering how to find Stanwin's strategy, I mulled possibilities, things I already knew, fashioned a dream of the third eye to remember the eyeball card. The demons aren't real, you see."

I hope, he added silently. His bruises and tattered clothes spoke otherwise, but he ignored them for now.

"Glad to hear it," Cerise sighed caustically. "I don't

know about hidden knowledge, but I believe your brain has holes in it."

Rubbing his eyes made tears run down Byron's nose. When one splashed on the card, he immediately clapped it to his forehead. He sensed a cloud puff from the card, shuddered at clammy fog filtering into his brain. "Tears are the token. Something from your eye, and what else is there? Once I knew the true purpose of the card, it was easy to guess. Ahh!"

Quiet as a shadow, Cerise jerked her sword from her scabbard. "What?"

"Your leather jacket is sheephide," said Byron in a strange voice. "Your baldric is oxhide, originally yellow then stained brown with acorn dye. Magog's got a deer tick over her left eyebrow . . ."

"Hunh?" Sheathing her sword, Cerise fingered her dog's scalp. "I'll be. Hold still, darling."

Byron peered around like a child seeing for the first time. The passage was washed in a blue-white glow, as if the roof had dissolved to admit moonlight. Everything he looked at, he understood intimately.

Cerise's sword cup was steel, the handle wrapped with copper wire tarnished by her sweating palm. The tunnel floor was no longer dull gray, but a patchwork of colors from mouse fur, garden loam, flecks of horse manure, granite dust, drops of candle wax, pine and oak splinters. Looking at his hands, he saw burn scars and smudges of mercury, sulfur, pine pitch, fennel green, though the stains were ground deep into his pores, actually below the skin.

And on the wall against the mountain . . .

"Look at the cracks! They're everywhere!"

"So what?"

"Give me a crayon! Quick!"

"I don't have one!"

"Anything! Your dagger!"

Wondering, the cardmaster handed it over. Ruining the fine-sharpened tip, Byron traced, scratching the whitewash. "See here? *There's* the rubble, but over *here* are fitted blocks! See them?"

Cerise peered with the candle. "No. I only see plain wall. The whitewash covers everything." Magog made a noise, curious at her mistress's tone.

"Yes, of course, you can't see it. Good. The magic is working." Picking with the knife tip, Byron moved down the wall. "Somewhere down here— Whoa!"

With hypervision, he saw clearly a demon face that peeked from inside the wall. It was the fat, warty demon, one eye socket still weeping blood. Crooked teeth grinned at him.

Byron reared back. "Get away!"

"Why?" asked Cerise.

"Not you! You!" Byron waved the knife, but his weird vision couldn't gauge exactly where the face lay. "Go, scat!"

"Who are you talking to?" demanded his partner.

Quick as it had come, the ravaged face pulled into the wall and disappeared. Frantic, Byron wondered: Why was he imagining them here? Making demons check on his work? Was using magic hastening some encroaching madness?

"I said," Cerise grated, "who—"

"Never mind. It's gone. It was never here anyway." Ignoring her exasperated sigh, Byron scratched more lines, tracing the edges of irregular blocks. "This isn't original cave wall! This entire wall was constructed from blocks long ago! But the construction was masked to look natural!"

Following with the candle, Cerise squinted but saw nothing. Byron shut up. Describing true-sight was like trying to explain color to a blind man. He hurried, for the magic wouldn't last long.

Six feet from the sooty crevice, he stopped. "A door!"

"What?" Cerise bent close. "Where?"

"Here!" Byron traced a crooked line up, across the top, down the other side. "There must be a latch . . . Unless it only opens from the inside . . . Gods, yes! Quickly, lead me downstairs, back to my room!"

"Why? Can't you see?" But Cerise took his hand and towed him towards the stone stairs. Magog bumped their knees, eager to join the fun.

"No, I see *too* well!" Byron reached for the wall, missed, lurched. There was too much to look at: he was "blinded" by super-vision. Every speck of dust, every dimple in the floor, every niche shouted for attention. The smooth floor looked cratered as the moon, and he stumbled because his feet couldn't understand it was safe. The stairs were worse, a ragged mountain chain, but with Cerise's help, they gained the second floor.

New sights burst upon Byron as if he'd discovered a whole continent. It was the same dust and hair and whitewash, but all mystically enchanted. He forced himself to hunt only for continuous cracks.

As if from a distance, he heard Cerise mumble, "What's keeping Rose? We should hear her a mile off with those clunky clogs."

"Stop here!" Plying the dulled dagger, Byron traced another uneven door not far from his room—with a ragged slot along one edge. Inserting the knife, he fiddled, felt a clunk, and lifted.

Silently, a stone door swung towards them. Magog barked and Cerise grabbed her muzzle with a gloved hand.

"A secret staircase!" she blurted. "A secret passage *inside* a 'secret passage' that everyone knows about!"

Head spinning, blinking, Byron leaned on Cerise's broad back. Slowly the blue moon-glow faded. The corridor was black except for Cerise's rosy circle of candlelight. He rubbed his eyes, irritated and bloodshot as if he'd stared into a desert wind. "There! Normal again! Whew!"

"Good work, Byron! You're the handiest companion I *ever* travelled with!" She gave him the candlestick and drew her sword. "My turn! Let's see what's inside *this* secret passage!"

Not a lot, they soon discovered. But enough.

The secret stairwell was tiny, steep, and narrow-shouldered. A mouth of darkness gaped above and below. A misstep would send them tumbling to the cellars with many broken bones.

"Smells musty," Cerise whispered. "No windows in this one, no fresh air." Pointing her sword upward, she shooed Magog ahead, then climbed after. Byron trailed.

At the third floor, a landing no bigger than a coffin held an old table. More stairs turned and ascended, and Magog snorfed up those.

At the left hand was an oiled latch that only worked from inside. Lifting it, Byron peeked into the servants' hall, saw his candle flickering six feet away. He retrieved it and closed the stone door.

Cerise leaned over the table. Spindles on the legs were sloped with dust, but the top was clean. Stacked atop were cards: four decks down the left side and four down the right. The lefthand decks were bound with red ribbon, the right with black.

"They match," breathed Cerise, "except for the ribbons." The opposing decks showed the same cards: two Sacred Sanctuaries, two Rye cards, two Siege Towers, two Bloodhounds. "Check for magic. But don't move them."

Carefully, Byron touched the first red-ribboned card—slick and warm under his finger. "Enchanted." He felt the black-ribboned card—grainy with paint, cool. "Common."

"Identical cards, one magic, one not. I never saw such a thing. But it explains a lot."

"Such as," Byron whispered, "how do those pesky magic cards keep slipping into Stanwin's decks even though Nanette and I check them regularly? Someone's using 'magic,' and I don't mean thaumaturgy."

"No," Cerise grumbled, also whispering. "Plain old cardsharping and sleight-of-hand. Someone sabotages our decks by sliding magic cards out of one sleeve and squirreling away the commons."

"And they must plan more mischief with all these reserves. But who could it be?"

"Someone who knows the castle, obviously. Not Otto or Lenda."

Byron had a wild thought. "Could it be Edric? Drunks do weird things. Or could his drunkenness be an act?"

"I know drunks. That's no act."

Stumped, Byron looked around the tiny niche. The stairs turned at this landing and ascended. "What's up there?"

Cerise frowned. "Nothing, everyone says. The

servants' stairs don't extend behind the War Room."

"But these do." Raising her sword and candle, Cerise climbed.

The stairwell ended in a round chamber that was warm. A square recess in the wall faced the War Room. Magog filled the space and scrabbled at the floor. Byron crouched past the burly dog, fumbled in the dark for the recessed wall, then snatched his hand back. "Ouch! There's another latch, but it's hot. I know! It's the back of a fireplace! She smells the food out there." Cerise only grunted.

Holding his candle, Byron surveyed the chamber. It was chiseled from the mountain, round-roofed like a bread oven, contained only the recess to the fireplace and descending stairwell. But something niggled at the back of Byron's mind: something was missing from this room, it seemed. But what—

"Come on," Cerise padded down the stairs. "We've got more to investigate."

Whatever Byron missed would stay missing, he guessed. He followed her descent to the third floor.

"I don't understand," Byron mused. "Clement consulted old maps of the tunnels, made the soldiers and servants hunt like rabbits in a warren to hoist lanterns and shout through cracks. How could he miss this secret stairwell?"

"Because it's not on the maps. No schemer would commit them to paper." Cerise held the candle to peer under the table. "And all the latches are on the inside except for one floor and maybe the cellar. It's too risky to put an entrance near Duke Stanwin's chambers: the lifeguards were sure to find it."

"But all those servants searching for days. . . . Hey, where's Rose?"

"Hey, what's this?" Cerise tugged open a drawer in the front of the table, gasped and drew out five large sheets of yellow, crinkly parchment. The pages were curled and smeary, scraped clean and redrawn often, a maze of crabbed handwriting and diagrams and plans and simple maps. "The strategy! The plan Old Stanwin slaved over to save the kingdom!"

"We found it!" Byron hissed.

"Congratulations!" boomed a cold voice. "Now hand it over!"

Parchment crinkled as the two whirled.

On the stairwell, aiming a double-barreled horse pistol, stood Ingrid.

The blonde-streaked cardmaster waggled gloved fingers. "Give me."

Slowly Cerise turned towards the twin candles burning on the table. "These papers are old and fragile. One touch of flame and they're smoke."

"One touch of this trigger and you're bloody gobbets." Ingrid's hand didn't waver.

Byron watched the two cardmasters gamble their lives. He tried to think of something to do, anything useful, but his mind was a blank. The gun barrels looked like twin cannon.

"That pistol won't fire," Cerise stalled. "You've got gray Eunom flints. Cheap and unreliable. Like yourself."

"Shall I test by aiming at your fat thighs? I can hardly miss. Hand me the strategy."

With a sigh of defeat, Cerise stuck the sheaf straight out.

Don't do it! Byron wanted to scream. Once the papers are safe, she'll fire!

Ingrid snatched the strategy, but Cerise clung on. Far above, Byron heard Magog's toenails click on stone. The dog gurgled at her master's strained tone. The armed woman snarled, "Don't toy with me—"

Whipping her free hand backwards, Cerise knocked the candles flying. They bounced off the walls and extinguished.

Plunged into darkness, Byron heard parchment tear. Then a flint struck. He glimpsed a spark, heard gunpowder in the pan fizz. Someone's hard hand slammed him against the wall—then the world exploded in flame.

The concussion in the tiny room boxed his ears like armored fists. Buckshot spattering off stone nicked his ear like a whiplash, peppered his neck, stung his thigh. Flinching, he stumbled into the stairwell and pitched headlong. Bouncing, rolling in total darkness, Byron caught himself on the stone risers by skinning both palms.

Cerise shouted, faint as a mosquito buzz in Byron's ringing ears. "Get after her! Go! I can't see!" Magog barked and drowned her out.

Jammed headfirst down the black stairwell, not wishing to rise into the line of fire, Byron slithered like a snake down rough cold stones. At the second floor, he wriggled sideways out the door into the servant's hall.

Crawling saved his life, for a swordblade stabbed the darkness above him.

Looming, silhouetted by light from his open bedroom door, stood Ingrid. Her face was twisted with anger, and blonde wisps swirled. In one hand, she clutched the torn strategy; in the other, her brass-hilted rapier. Hot to kill pursuers, she'd stabbed blindly. Byron recalled Cerise saying her judgement was rash.

But he was half-curled in a doorway and Ingrid had all the time in the world. She drew back her arm to stab him through the guts—

—Byron saw something green and white flicker behind her—

—then the white thing crashed alongside Ingrid's head and exploded into fragments.

The traitor's eyes rolled up white, and she collapsed onto Byron. Her sharp blade clattered alongside his ear.

Standing in the tunnel was Rose, bosom heaving, hair disheveled, curled crockery in her fist: the handle of a chamberpot.

"That bitch shoved me from behind into the wardrobe, then wedged a stool in the frame so I couldn't get out! I had to kick the back panel out and tip the whole wardrobe over!"

"I'm glad you wore clogs," Byron grinned.

Clunking, Rose stooped and kissed him hard enough to ignite his hair.

Twenty minutes later, all four were gathered in Byron's room. Cerise's eyes were swollen, flaming red and running tears. After knocking Byron to one side, she'd leapt low after Ingrid. Lead balls and buckshot had missed, but the muzzle flash had peppered her face with burning powder. Byron wore strips of bandage around his thigh and neck and skinned palms. Ingrid was lashed to the bed's footboard with curtain ties. A lump on her skull puffed her hair.

Her glittering weapons and the strategy lay on the big bed.

Cerise dashed a ewer of water in Ingrid's face, half-choking her, then slapped her awake. "We'll make this fast! Who do you work for?"

Ingrid shook her head, spat, said nothing.

Quick as an adder, Cerise snatched out a dagger. Yanking back Ingrid's hair, the frontierswoman laid the still-sharp edge alongside her ear. Ingrid grunted at the hairpulling but sneered, "Do your worst."

"Oh, I will."

With one stroke, Cerise sliced through Ingrid's ear and down her cheek.

Chapter 15

For a second, Ingrid—and Rose and Byron—could only gape in shock. Then blood welled in rivers down Ingrid's neck. She opened her mouth to scream, but Cerise slapped her as if to snap her neck, then wrenched Ingrid's hair to expose the right cheek.

"Scream and I'll make both sides match!" Her hiss was deadly as a snake's. "I'll slice your pointed nose off! I'll peel your painted face from your skull! You stupid conniving tramp! This is no longer a game! We've played Lenda and Otto long enough to know one's a fool and the other a fop! Duke Stanwin *must* win, because he's the only lord strong enough to keep the Shinyar from overrunning civilization! Now talk! Who do you work for? Did the bishop send you?"

"No, no!" Despite the hairpulling, Ingrid shook her head and made blood fly. "It was old Horacio!

I went to him for cards the next day, after you escaped! He was sore enough to tell me Byron had cards! I just tagged along and caught up to you!"

"You're lying!" With her dagger, Cerise sawed away Ingrid's bleached strands and threw them on the floor. Magog barked in excitement, and Cerise told her to shut up. "There's more to this conspiracy than one stupid slut's greed! Tell me!"

"Gods have mercy! I'm *bleeding* to death!" Blood spilled from Ingrid's shorn cheek like red rain and soaked her bosom. Rose ran out the door holding her mouth. "Please believe me! I just cozied up to Byron to steal what I could!"

"You were damned slow about it!" Cerise slapped her face, smearing her hand with red. Magog barked ferociously. "You could have slit his gullet any night and taken the lot! You're *still* lying!"

"No! I was after the strategy then, following you! To sell it!"

"*Sell it?*" As Cerise's fury mounted, she tugged Ingrid's right ear until Byron thought it would snap off. His frontier friend was as savage as the Shinyar she loathed, he thought in wonder.

"Only our *enemies* could *use* that strategy! Otto or Lenda! You'd murder us and sell out the game, the whole goddamned kingdom, for a handful of *silver*? You lousy—opportunist! You're a cheaper whore than I thought! What's the rest of it?"

"There's nothing else! I swear!"

Scoffing, Cerise punched the blunt dagger through Ingrid's right ear. The woman shrilled like a pig at slaughter. Cerise braced to flick her wrist.

"*What's this about?*" boomed the voice of authority. Filling the doorway, hands on hips, cloak framing wide shoulders, stood a frowning Duke Stanwin, every inch a lord. Behind him crowded half a dozen guards. "Cerise, explain why you're torturing this woman and be quick about it!"

"Sire!" Cerise snapped erect but didn't quail. "Byron and I located the lost strategy in a secret passage— an unknown one! This *assassin* tried to steal it and blast us in the bargain! She almost blinded me! She's an enemy of everyone in this dukedom, sire, and we need her information! I'm going to scalp her if necessary—"

A swipe of Stanwin's hand cut her off. Stalking to the bleeding weeping Ingrid, he demanded, "Is this true?"

"No, sire, no! *They've* betrayed you! *I* found the strategy, but these assassins *stole* it—"

"That's a bald-faced *lie!*" Cerise bellowed. Byron shrank back: he'd never seen anyone so furious. "She's too twisted to tell the truth to the gods' own faces! You need to rack her and crank on thumbscrews—"

"*That's enough!*" The duke's temper matched Cerise's, but his was under control. "There's never been a torture chamber in this castle and there never will be! You, tell me what happened!"

Byron jumped as the duke whirled on him. Stammering, the cardsmith confirmed the attack, pointing to the strategy and double-barrelled horse pistol on the bed. Stanwin ordered Rose dragged in. White-faced, rubbing her mouth repeatedly, the chambermaid added what she knew of the story.

Frowning, the duke shook his head at Ingrid. "That's three reliable witnesses against one of dubious honor. Good enough. Guards! You, you, you!" Three women

with halberds stamped forward. "Fetch whips from
the stables. Strip this traitor to the waist, shove her
out the gates, and flog her from the dukedom! Don't
stop until you reach the border! If she falls, let her
rise, but lay on hard as you can! Go!"

Sobbing, shrieking, Ingrid was cut loose and
manhandled out the door. Bright drops of her blood
sparkled in the candlelight.

The duke pointed at Cerise. "And *you* remember
who rules and who metes out justice! Or I'll have
you whipped through the Eagle's Road to the frontier
whence you came! Now hand over this fabled strategy."

Meekly, Cerise gave him the five-page plan. Stanwin
called for candles to read by.

"It's my father's handwriting, to be sure . . . 'Otto
is weakest of triad, can't forget insult. Offer personal
combat on the field.' Beard of Hales, yes, that might
work! And look here! 'Lenda loves orchards. Tear
down Long Grote dam as threat to flood trees.'
Damnation! he's right! We *reinforced* the dam as
an emergency bridge!" He turned the parchment
sideways, pieced together the tear. " 'Death mists
are sham discovered by Angor on crusade,' that's
Lenda's father, 'actually nightshade poisoning left
behind in wells.' So we mustn't drink the water!
Oh, and here, it's *coal* reserves that Otto's mining!
So he doesn't need wood at all! Ye gods! Finally,
victory is in our grasp!"

Smoothing the strategy, he bid Cerise, "Come. I
need you to stall the game while we study this!"

The duke and guards clattered out the door. Cerise
lingered long enough to hiss, "Go loot Ingrid's room
before her baggage disappears!"

In the abrupt quiet, Byron breathed, "Lords of

the Air! Has little Stanwin learned to take charge or what?"

"My stomach hurts," Rose whimpered. Byron kissed her cheek.

Then their strength gave out, and they flopped back on the bed.

After sunup and a few hours' sleep, the two lovers trekked to the top floor.

The Great Game hummed like a hive of bees. Or three hives: two battered by a storm, one hunkered down and buzzing happily.

All of Duke Stanwin's cardmasters crammed the big round table and slapped down cards from thick decks. There were five separate attacks, and Lady Lenda's and Earl Otto's cardmasters were stunned by intersecting rows and cascading triangles and heaps of cards like autumn leaves. Some slouched in their chairs, stumped, while others made excuses to fetch wine while shaking their heads.

Cerise battled three other cardmasters alone. As fast as they laid cards down, she shuffled her deck and blocked their actions. One cardmaster quit, scooping up her cards and scurrying for Lenda's safe haven. The other two pleaded time, and Cerise agreed, and they ran to consult Otto.

The cardmaster joined the cardsmith and chambermaid at the breakfast table. Despite powderburns and red-rimmed eyes, she grinned as she crumbled a hardboiled egg into a pocket of bread and dashed in red pepper sauce, slugging it down with chilled sumac tea.

"We've got them on the run! The new strategy threw them for a loop, upset all the lords' plans!

We've broken through their defenses and severed their supply and communication lines in a dozen places! Their best troops are cut off in the forests or in the open. We waylaid a gold shipment, the troops' pay, because Old Duke Stanwin showed what to look for, so they've got mutiny in the ranks and mercenaries quitting. It's gotten so bad both lords connive to abandon the alliance, but both worry about collecting a knife in the back. They don't know which way to piss without wetting themselves! But we do!" She banged down her goblet and skipped to the table. Earl Otto's cardmasters had stormed up with new plans and fresh decks.

Famished from a long night's work, Byron and Rose wolfed smoked salmon on barley bread, honeycakes, boiled eggs, and mead. Then they split with a kiss; Rose to attend chores, Byron to check cards.

The cardsmith shuffled for two hours and found no enchanted cards. That made sense, for Duke Stanwin had personally inspected the secret stairwell, confiscated all the matched magic and common cards and locked them away. The young lord now resumed his place at the table, directing his cardmasters' attacks and answering a thousand questions. All around Byron buzzed rumors and legends and whispers and plots, as players and nonplayers alike discussed the news.

But the big question, the identity of the cardsharp and strategy-thief remained a mystery. Byron wondered if they'd ever know who it was, if the person or persons hadn't already fled the castle and dukedom. He hoped so, and that their troubles were over. They'd suffered enough.

Nanette arrived, grinned at Byron. "Our job will be easier now, thanks to you!"

Embarrassed, Byron waved a hand. "Oh, I did nothing. It was Cerise and Rose who saved the day. Can you take over guarding the decks until Chancellor Clement arrives?"

Watching the game, the bony blonde shook her head. "Yes, I can watch. But Clement won't be back for a while. There was another Shinyar raid in the pass last night, another guard post wiped out. Clement rode out to inspect the damage personally."

"Oh, yes, the Shinyar." Once again Byron was reminded why this Great Game was being waged. But the thought of savage hordes spurred another idea. Striving to sound casual, he asked, "Nanette, do you ever suffer from—nightmares—after you've been cardsmithing?"

The woman blinked. "Nightmares? No. Fashioning magic fags me out so much I sleep like a baby, round the clock sometimes. Why do you ask?"

"Just curious. My, uh, old master used to dream of demons."

A shrug of black and silver shoulders. "Perhaps your master bargained away his soul."

"Oh. Perhaps." That was a new and frightening idea. "Uh, I think I'll hie to the fair."

"Have fun."

Murky, muddled thoughts rattling in his head, Byron hunted Rose, found her mending Cerise's shirt, and dragged her away to the fair. She didn't argue.

The two lovers waded through crowds to the jousting lists. But they'd barely touched the ropes before Byron became a celebrity when the crowd spotted his black clothes.

"Been to the War Room this mornin'? How goes the game? Heard someone found a secret plan last night, knocked Lenda's and Otto's plans into a cocked hat. True? Who are the odds favorin'? Duke by two to one, last we heard. What's your opinion?"

Byron held up his hands, begged for peace, and related how Stanwin was pressing a new and successful attack. Thrilled, many bettors ran off to post new odds on the game's outcome.

Rose and Byron watched the bouts, cheered and booed. But, at one point, the cardsmith's curiosity stirred. Something far down the field looked odd. Amidst the jammed tents of knights and their retainers was a new clear space of trampled grass.

He asked a neighbor at the ropes, "Who's gone from there?"

"Eh?" A young man with bright clothes and a girl on his arm calculated odds on a slate. "Oh. House of Bronessa disappeared in the night."

"Really? Why?"

"No one knows." A shrug of shoulders made little bells jingle. "Lousy trick, too. Here's the second-to-last day of jousting, and everyone swapping bets and expecting House of Bronessa to pull some trick out of their sleeve, but they're gone back wherever they come from, the bastards. Hey, have you seen the secret passage in the castle? The new one?"

"Yes . . ." Byron hesitated. "But who told you about it?"

"Everybody. Some cardmaster stumbled against a brick in the floor and a secret door popped open. She found the strategy and tried to blackmail the duke. Stanny Boy took it and had her flogged out the gates clear to the border. There were bets she'd collapse and die, but she was strong, made it over the Lord's Lookout. Finding that strategy's thrown everything into a cocked hat. Hey, you want to bet Lenda withdraws by sunset? I'm giving ten to one."

Byron declined, so the oddsmaker encircled his girl and pushed off through the crowd.

The bouts broke for the midday meal. Rose caught Byron's hand to thread the fair. Under lowering skies, they were surrounded by bright colors and wild sights: dancing bears, fire-eaters, belly-dancers, harp players, tumbling dwarves. Smells of roast corn and chestnuts and spiced wine enfolded them. Shouts and growls and laughters and song batted their ears. Yet the cardsmith's feet dragged, and twice he bumped into people and had to apologize.

Finally Rose steered him to the corrals and plunked him down on a bale of hay. Pungent smells of feed and manure and horsesweat mingled. The girl planted hands on her hips. "Byron, what's on your mind?"

Byron stared past her shoulder at a distant cloud. "Too much. Much too much. . . . Funny how everyone knows about that secret passage all of a sudden. We only found it, what, six hours ago."

Rose shrugged. "Gossip blows through a castle quicker than a winter wind."

"I know. Everyone in a castle knows everyone else's business, you said. So only two or three people at most could have known about that passage."

" 'Three can keep a secret if two are dead,' is another old saying."

"Right again. So the schemer is likely just one person. Even Stanwin didn't know of the passage, and he explored every inch of the castle as a boy."

"So? His father must have known. Perhaps he

waited until the boy was old enough to keep a secret."

"No. . . ." Byron closed one eye, thinking. "We don't know that Old Duke Stanwin knew of the secret passage."

"Of course we do. The strategy was in the old table."

"True, but anybody could have put it there." Byron plucked a straw from between his knees, chewed furiously. "There's so much to think about, it's like juggling pitchforks. . . . What do we know? I found a puffball shell in a crack in the wall near the secret door. The assassin put the shell there. So, probably the assassin knew of the secret passage and used it, slipping inside to hide from guards and servants. And what did we find *inside*? The strategy, which the assassin probably stole when the duke died. *And* we found the trick cards, the ones someone slipped into Stanwin's decks to sabotage the game. So, the assassin is probably also the saboteur. Which makes sense, because we think this whole plot—whatever it is—is planned by one person. That person had been working hard a long time: they spent half the winter poisoning the duke and were still sneaking enchanted cards into the deck last night. I found one and showed it to Cerise. Gee, I wish we had her to help us think, but she's busy saving the game. . . ."

"The more we learn, the more explanations become clear, anyway," the girl mused. "I remember those two cardmasters spent weeks stacking the decks for the game. After they died, poor things, Chancellor Clement and the cardmasters spent three weeks checking their work. Probably, the decks were sabotaged with magic even then."

"They could have bollixed it worse. Only a cardsmith

can detect magic." Byron slid over on the bale as Rose smoothed her skirts and perched alongside him. He spat flecks of straw. "Cardmasters and the chancellor could eat those cards and never know they were charged."

"You're forgetting the judges. They can detect magic."

"Not all judges can detect magic, no matter what they say. I think one judge can spot a magic card, and the others fake it. Remember, only one person in ten thousand can feel enchantment."

Rose took his hand and smiled. "And you're one."

Byron grinned self-consciously. "Yes, but I can't take credit. It's an inborn ability, like wiggling one's ears."

"Still," the girl insisted with a smile, "I'm proud of you." She kissed him, and he kissed back. Back of the corral fence, a mule curled its lip and blew derisively. They both laughed, but then Byron's brow clouded again.

"I wonder how the troublemaker slipped in those enchanted cards once the game started. The decks are watched day and night. The secret passage reaches to the War Room; we found out, but only through the fireplace, and they've kept a fire burning ever since the Game started. It'd be one tough assassin to crawl over burning logs."

Rose matched Byron's daydreaming. "You know . . . it's very odd we never found that secret stairway. I heard the lifeguards shouting from the caves, and I was standing there when Clement put his eye to the crack and spotted the red and green lanterns. I saw him mark the map, and it looked complete to me."

Concentrating, Byron chewed timothy. "Cerise explained that. A truly secret passage wouldn't be marked on maps."

"But still." The girl spread her arms. "You were inside! It's wide as your shoulders with two thick walls on each side! Six feet wide or more! You'd think—what, Byron?"

The cardsmith stared at a mule so hard the animal hoicked its teeth off the rickety fence and plodded to another corner. "Clement looked and listened at the cracks . . ."

"Yes. So?"

"And the rubble is only supposed to be two or three feet thick, so the sappers can tear it down for an evacuation . . ."

"The chancellor did order a few walls torn down and rebuilt. So?"

"But he never noticed the discrepancy of six-foot thick walls . . ."

"Well, it was usually dark and—"

"Yet he held the map in his hands all the time."

"Yes, he did. But—oh. Oh!"

Lost in thought, excited by a new idea, Byron grabbed the girl's arm so hard she squeaked. "What if—what if—what *if* Clement *knew all along* the staircase were there? Then, with the map in hand, he could steer the guards *away* from the secret passage?"

"True!" Rose nodded, eyes wide. "Clement directed the search! He insisted on marking the map himself, in case the marks got confused, he said!"

"By the gods!" Byron shot to his feet. "If Clement is the true master of the castle, the man who runs it top to bottom, who oversees everything from the wine in the cellars to the dovecotes on the roof,

then he'd be the *perfect* one to know its secrets!
Even more than lords and ladies who spend their
days ministering justice or hunting hawks or, like
Young Stanwin, riding the far reaches of the dukedom
tending the flocks! By the gods!"

Rose tugged Byron's wrist like a bellrope. "And
Clement stacked the cards! I just said that! If the
bogus cards were hidden in the staircase, and Clement
knew of them, *he* could slip the enchanted ones
into the decks! Oh, yes! He insisted on overseeing
the deck-stacking in person! But—that means he'd
want to sabotage the game! Why would he do that?"

Dizzy with new thoughts, Byron clutched the corral
rail. "Wait, wait. He may not be sabotaging the game,
only delaying it. If Clement stole the strategy—and
by the brow of Ophir, who knows better where the
Old Duke hid something than his faithful chancellor?—
then Clement could 'find' it one morning, stuck between
the leaves of a book, say. Any story would work . . ."

"But *why*? Why sabotage *or* delay?"

"Why . . . to control the game the same way he
controls the fief? It's as Cerise said, courts always
have intrigue. Could Clement have stuck a bargain
with Lenda or Otto? Let one of *them* become High
Duke so he can be *their* chancellor? But what does
that gain him? He's in control now . . . We need
Cerise to think about this."

"But," Rose put in, "we don't *know* Clement's a
traitor! We're just guessing! And besides—Clement
is so *nice*! He's a charming man, fat and jolly! He's
always got a 'Good morning' and a joke for the kitchen
help and us chambermaids! He pats children on
the head and sees the dogs get meat scraps! He
throws crumbs to the birds in the courtyard!"

"You needn't be cruel to be a schemer or traitor. A villain doesn't need piggy eyes and a long jaw and bad teeth, like a play-actor on a stage. A plotter can be jolly, especially if he stands to gain control of—"

"Of what?"

"Edric!"

"Edric?" Rose looked around for the duke's drunken cousin. "What about him?"

"Not Stanwin as High Duke!" Byron was almost shouting, and people near the corrals looked in curiosity. "Edric! He's next in line to inherit the throne, since Stanwin's not married and has no siblings! If Clement could install Edric on the throne, he could work him like a puppet! Clement would be the *real* High Duke!"

"But," Rose objected, "how could he get Stanwin out of the way? Oh, my, he wouldn't—"

"Yes he would," Byron nodded grimly. "The saboteur is the assassin, remember? Stanwin must die for Edric to assume the throne. Accidents happen. Two cardsmiths died because they would have detected magic cards in the stacked decks: one choked on a chicken bone while having dinner with a stranger, the other fell down the stairs. Old Stanwin got poison spores puffed into his lungs. Whoa! Clement's *already* tried to kill Stanwin! The chancellor oversees the lifeguards, doesn't he? He could have bribed that clean-shaven Ferdinand to become a bandit and murder Stanwin on the highway!"

"By the rime on the mountains!" Rose breathed. "It all fits! Clement *must* be the murderer! A viper at the duke's bosom! And no one ever knew!"

"Aye, no one—"

Stunned by a new thought, Byron wrenched out his purse of cards, shuffled frantically. He found the two grumpy men staring at one another.

"*Now* I know this card! It's Reveal Traitor! I'd only heard of one, never seen it! Old Duke Stanwin must have written to Rayner and asked him to fashion the card. Oh, of *course*! Old Stanwin couldn't ask his *local* cardsmiths to fashion it if he feared a *local* traitor! That's why he sent all the way to Waterholm!"

"Enough talk!" In a flurry of hay, Rose yanked him clean around. "We must warn Duke Stanwin!"

Together they raced through the fair, bumping spectators aside, skirting piles of vegetables and cordwood, vaulting guide ropes, dodging warhorses and capering bears. Finally they broke clear of the fair and pelted down the streets of the town. It seemed to Byron the distance had increased ten-fold since he'd last walked this way. Some townsfolk watched them run past, called questions. Others pointed to the castle and queried their neighbors.

"What—" Rose panted. "Oh, no, it's started!"

For the first time, there were no guards at the gate of the high castle curtain. The only thing moving was the portcullis, the heavy lattice of wood and iron, dropping into place. They pattered up just as it thudded on the granite threshold like great iron teeth.

"Don't look!" Byron cautioned. But it was too late.

Through the portcullis, they saw castle guards littering the courtyard. Eight lay unmoving, their proud green tabards slashed and soaked red. Blood dripped from above the gate, so Byron knew guards were dead on the ramparts, too. Rose began to cry, for many had been friends. "Oh! Who would do such a horrid—"

"Ahh!" Byron yelled as if in pain.

At the top of the ramp, the entrance to the main hall, a green-clad guard stumbled backwards out the wide double doors. Bloody and belabored, the woman was riven with a pike and pitched off the ramp to crash in the courtyard like a bag of laundry.

Her killers whirled back inside the castle: knights in brown tunics painted with blazing yellow suns. As the two watched helplessly, six more vandals ran around a corner to mount the ramp, bearing swords and shields and polearms.

"The House of Bronessa! The mercenaries!" Rose panted. "No wonder they hung back from fighting hard! They *were* biding their time, just as everyone suspected!"

"Yes." Byron's voice was bitter as he grabbed the impassable portcullis. "Their time has come. They disappeared last night, and Clement disappeared this morning, no doubt to trigger this plot. Now they've taken the castle. And with it, the dukedom."

"Then we're too late!" Rose cried.

"Aye," Byron spat. "Too slow and too late."

Chapter 16

Screams and shouts made them whirl.

Past the town streets, palls of white-gray smoke roiled from the fair in three, then four, columns. The fire spread panic. A spooked donkey hitched to a cart bolted and spilled cordwood. A drover wrestled with yoked oxen who milled dangerously. A father yanked his children from the path of a stampeding bear. Squealing pigs shot underfoot as people juggled bundles and baskets as they spilled from the twisted maze of the fairgrounds. A tent collapsed as someone tripped its ropes. Curious townsfolk ran that way and added to the chaos.

"Four fires?" asked Rose.

"Arson," Byron guessed. "That smoke, gray and wet like that, is from hay fires. More of Clement's scheming, probably; Bronessans setting fires to rout folks to panic. They'll be too busy to note the goings-on in the castle."

He coughed. The muggy day threatened rain, so the smoke crawled along the ground like monstrous serpents. It oozed from the fairgrounds towards the castle, for once pushed by lowland winds stronger than the eternal shriek from the Eagle's Road. Byron had to squint to see Rose's anxious face.

She murmured, "An east wind. That's rare. A bad omen."

"Is it?" Byron asked. "Perhaps not . . . It gives me an idea—"

Cardsmith and chambermaid were shouldered aside by frantic guards in green. Armed with spears and halberds, they'd been patrolling the fair. Now they were locked out. They howled when they saw their dead companions. One woman dropped her polearm to scale the portcullis, but a sergeant yanked her back to earth, pointed to the down-jutting spikes that ringed the battlements to hinder climbers. Bawling and cursing, the sergeant split them three-and-three to try other gates.

Byron and Rose backed against the tall stone curtain and cast about. Townsfolk and transients, sensing the unrest in the castle, gathered to gawk in the eye-watering mist. A lost child wailed. Dogs barked and snapped. Hooves thrummed in the short town street as a pair of knights in blue and yellow squared off. One lifted his visor and shouted through smoke like a hedgerow. A challenge was accepted, for the knights lowered their visors, couched lances in armpits, and charged the smoke and each other. Byron and Rose heard a fearful crash but saw nothing.

"What's that all about?" Byron wondered. "Whom

are they attacking? Are there Bronessans out here?"

"There must be!" Rose guessed. "But who knows? Maybe someone's accused someone else of treachery, or they're just settling a grudge! Wild rumors get wilder in times of trouble!"

"The whole world's mad," Byron groused. He pressed back against the wall as castle guards ran past the other way. "There's no way in. Clement will have sealed all the dooryard gates and such, and the bridge across the garrison. And the kitchen help or anyone who might help us is probably locked up. Or dead. How many Bronessans are there, do you know?"

She shook her dark hair. "Not sure. We saw twenty knights or more jousting. But they had these burly sergeants and pages old as we are, and all their women went armed. Gods, there might be sixty or more to wield swords!"

Byron held his temples, trying to think. "And how many lifeguards are there?"

"Forty-some, but someone's always sick. And we know there are—eight dead. Or more."

"And a handful locked out here. There are fewer than thirty cardmasters, maybe five retainers for each lord. Bad odds, and the assassins have surprise. Clement must have attacked the War Room by now."

Instinctively, they looked over their shoulders, but could only see the tall curtain wall. Byron pointed across the arch of the Eagle's Road to the garrison castle, where the soldiers of cooperating fiefs barracked to defend the pass. "What about the garrison guards? There's five hundred of them!"

Rose shrugged. "They answer to General Tugg, but he's with Duke Stanwin. And I know they can't

meddle with internal disputes: by law, they're
forbidden even to enter the castle grounds. They're
no use." Indeed, men and women from all over
the kingdom, including some of Waterholm's soldiers
in red emblazoned with a waterfall, milled and
gaped at the castle while their commanders argued.

Chaos and confusion worsened. The bawling sergeant
and three soldiers lugged a tall ladder they'd com-
mandeered from a barn in town. Thallandian townsfolk
helped them lever it against the curtain wall. But
it was too short, lacked six feet to the top. The sergeant
yelled for a cart to stand it in. Someone shouted
and pointed. High up, two green-clad guards teetered
across the roof ridge of the arch connecting the
castles. Thallandians cheered, then groaned as the
two soldiers were struck by crossbow quarrels from
within the castle. Mortally wounded, they tumbled
down the roof slates and crashed to earth. A captain
of cavalry thundered up on a roan horse and called
all the able fighters of Thallandia to fetch weapons.

But resistance inside the castle was stiffening.
Byron saw a handful of knights spill from the front
doors of the castle. These were not Bronessans, but
independent knights marked by their own heraldic
devices: a fist clutching lightning, a white horsehead,
a bishop's miter. Unsure who they were, the milling
throng of townsfolk watched as the knights mounted
the stairs and ladders to the wallwalk. Any hope
they were friends was extinguished when a green-
clad body was rolled off to thump in the courtyard.

"Oh, no!" Rose breathed. "There's more of them!
Clement or the Bronessans must have recruited them
to aid in the coup!" To punctuate the observation,
they heard steel clashing; some wounded Thallandian

being dispatched, no doubt. From within the smoke shrouding the town and fair rang more swordfighting.

Byron ground his teeth. "This is impossible! All of Thallandia's hamstrung! We've got to get in there!"

Rose just spread her hands, asking how.

"The wind is right . . ." The cardsmith dug in his shirt, pulled out his purse, shuffled cards, then sighed in disgust. "I knew I didn't have any birds. Those sell fast. I'll have to improvise. Find me a feather!"

"A feather?" But not wasting time with questions, the chambermaid tucked her green skirts into her waistband and charged into the smoke. Byron stuffed his cards away, keeping a blank and a clay crayon.

Unnoticed in the madness, he hunkered against the curtain wall, slid onto his heels. He was concentrating on the blank card when Rose returned, triumphantly held up a small curled brown feather. "Ta da!"

Byron glanced up, back at the card. "That's a chicken feather! Find something else!"

"*What* something else? I had to catch the damned chicken to get this!" No one could hear them for shouting.

"Chickens don't fly! Try a pigeon or a hawk!"

"Where will I find—you're going to *fly*?"

"*We're* going to fly." He stared at the blank card. "I hope. Levitate, actually. Simpler than flying, but you can't control the direction. Like a paper balloon. If the wind stays right. But find a feather from a flying bird. Look for a swallow's nest in the rafters of a barn."

"Fly . . ." The girl grabbed skirts and dashed off again. She was back in minutes, having plucked a tail feather from a peacock crushed in the road. But she bleated when she saw Byron.

The cardsmith was hunched with the card against his knees, the dark crayon clutched in twisted fingers. His face had gone white, his hands trembled, and he rocked like an idiot.

Entranced.

Byron's mind was a turmoil of cold wind.

He stared down a tornado from above like some sky god. Whipped in the wind below him, swirling in dark clouds, soared birds, hundreds of them. Barely able to stay aloft, they flapped wings frantically to ride out the spinning storm. Squinting against the cold gale blowing in his face, the cardsmith recognized sooty seagulls, wide-winged albatrosses, tiny black-masked terns, long-necked cormorants, fat pelicans: birds built for gliding great distances, that could cross vast oceans without weakening and dying. Their wide wings full of broad strong feathers could give Byron and Rose lift. The salvation of Thallandia, perhaps.

Reaching down a god-like hand, Byron snatched for a whirling bird. Any bird. But his clumsy fingers couldn't catch them. The canny birds banked, wheeled, dipped and dived to elude him, skittered away from the fat stiff digits like autumn leaves in a dust devil.

Straining to breathe, Byron reached deeper into the storm. (Hadn't he almost lost his soul descending a well at the last conjuring? Why had he now conjured the image of a storm? Because of the smoke? Because a storm was pending? Because a man-made storm of violence swirled within the castle walls? There was so much magic to learn!) He grunted with effort, his arm almost pulled from the socket as the tornado ripped him. All his muscles ached. His stomach was constricted, pressed tight against itself. Down he reached, until gulls and albatrosses and other seabirds spun around his wrist, thick as a mast. But he could grasp nothing.

Then the demons arrived.

Laughing, giggling, keening, gobbling, they bounded into the hurricane and spun around the eye of the hurricane as if out on a lark, like ugly children sharing a swing. Byron cursed. What would they do this time? Bite his hand? Jab under his fingernails? Drive the birds away?

No. Amazed, the cardsmith watched the demons herd the birds. Graceful gulls and twittery terns squawked as warty lumpy demons leaped after them like demented frogs. With clawed hands and crooked feet, they chased the birds, knocked them flying and flapping, all the while gobbling like mad things.

Confused, Byron watched feathers pinwheel as real demons and imaginary birds (or the other way around?) tussled and dodged. Before, back in Waterholm, the demons had always thwarted him, interfered with his magic-making. Lately, more confusing, they helped him. Which notion was scarier? Why help him? What would they demand in final payment? Nothing was free, Rayner had intoned time and again, especially magic.

With a frenzied bumbling cooperation, the demons drove a dozen flapping, bating, kicking, biting birds into a milling mass of feathers and beaks. Held them just long enough. Craning, leaning way too far, in danger of toppling into the void (And what lay at the bottom of this tornado well?), Byron strained fingers big as cannon to pluck up an albatross that buzzed in his hand like a fly.

Gently, he cradled the hysterical animal. Give me, he pleaded of the bird, lend me your power of flight. I need it. Duke Stanwin needs it. All the kingdom needs it.

In the shrieking maelstrom of wind, cutting and freezing cold, Byron struggled to concentrate, to capture the bird's flight. The ungainly bird, a tiny body and long skinny wings, squawked its protest. Demons capered across Byron's knuckles as he strained to read the essence of the bird's frightened mind, to feel into its brain and muscle, to make its heartbeat match his own.

All at once, he felt a tingling in his giant fingers. And a scrawling at his knee as clumsy hands hashed a drawing.

He'd caught the power. With a gasp, he let the bird go. All the birds, and the storm as well.

The tornado funnel split, fractured, blew into a thousand tiny puffs. Sunshine splashed over a flat sea. Birds wheeled in every direction, squawking with joy at their freedom. Unsupported, the demons fell howling into the water.

Thank you, Byron called. But they'd sunk back to their lost plane of nothingness.

Dark brown eyes peered into Byron's. Long silky lashes above a serious pout. Successful, he felt like kissing the pout. "Rose!"

"Are you all right?" The girl squatted on her heels, skirts drawing a circle around her, and held his shoulders. "You're soaked with sweat but cold as an icicle! You've got a fever or chills or something!"

"No, it's just magic." The cardsmith tried to stand, instead fell flat on his bottom. Both hands were cramped as an old man's, but he unpried his fingers. The clay crayon was broken, the point smashed. His fingers were filthy. But on the card was scrawled a blobby shape with wings. "Here. A bird."

The girl wrinkled her nose. "That's a bird?"

For some reason, this mild criticism annoyed Byron. Cardsmiths risked their lives and sanity and souls to fashion cards, and people sneered as if at a bleary watercolor of the canal. "Yes, a bird! But don't thank me! Thank the demons and that albatross instead!"

Rose looked at the smoky sky. "What alba—did you say *demons*?"

"No! Never mind. It's magic. I don't understand it myself." He tottered to his feet, she helping.

"If that's making magic, I'll stick to making beds. Gods, your hands are freezing! Can you walk?"

"Barely." He tottered to the portcullis. The crowd had grown bigger, but a restless quiet pervaded both the gateyard and the courtyard. Inside looked deserted except for the dead. The big studded doors to the main hall stood half open, an oddly frightening image, as if Duke Stanwin's reign had been cast aside. "But I don't need to walk. We're going to fly. Levitate, anyway."

"Fly? Really?" Rose stepped back. Townsfolk nearby goggled as they listened. "Uh, maybe that's not such a good idea. What happens if we get up there and—"

Byron locked his arm around her waist and hobbled back from the castle curtain, shooing the crowd. Four knights in Clement's pay peered from atop the wall curiously. In Byron's left hand was the new Levitate card. "Got that feather?"

"H-here." Hand trembling, she held up the long peacock feather with the golden eye.

Byron waved the card. "Touch it to this."

"N-now?"

"Now."

The tip of the feather waggled as the girl brought it close to the card. And touched.

Suddenly, they had no weight.

Byron's tired feeling of heaviness, of being tied to the earth, drained away like a dream at dawn. Rose shrieked as their feet left the ground.

The girl paddled her toes madly, trying to get down to safety, but Byron held her tight and cooed reassuringly. They rose alongside the castle wall, watching fitted stones drop past as if the wall were sinking. The white card with dark scrawls had puffed and gone limp as goose down. When Byron tried to toss it away, it clung to his fingers like lint.

The crowd around the gate first gasped, then grunted, then cheered as at a fireworks display. Some applauded the magic. The villainous knights occupying the wallwalk shouted for their appointed captain.

Near the top, Byron snagged a downthrust spike imbedded in the wall. They stopped ascending, bobbed in place. Byron held Rose hard against him, the feel of her soft hips and thighs making his cold legs tingle. "All right?"

"What happens when you let go?" she squeaked.

"We drift higher."

Rose turned a white face towards the sky. "How high? We won't go over the mountains, will we?"

"No!" Byron actually laughed. Having fashioned a proper spell, flying for the first time, holding a beautiful girl, receiving the approval of a crowd, he felt strong and capable and smart. "The spell's only good for three minutes or so."

"Then hurry!" She cast a glance downward and pinned her skirts flat. Coarse laughter floated up. "Those bastards can see up my dress!"

Byron chuckled. "Aren't you wearing drawers? With the white lace and the flowers around the band?"

"Just fly us, damn you—look out!"

Like a rabbit from a hole, a knight popped out between two ramparts and thrust a spear at them. Another crawled over the wide stone to slash at them with a sword. Their captain had evidently ordered them killed.

With a grace that surprised him, Byron let go the iron spike and kicked away from the wall.

"Byyyyyyy-ronnnnnnn!"

Relentlessly as a bubble in water, cardsmith and chambermaid floated both upwards and back in a stomach-lurching half-circle. Then the smoky wind took control and shoved them towards the wall again. The five knights, unused to flying opponents, only stared open-mouthed. By the time they slashed the air with polearms and swords, their quarry had risen out of reach, though Byron pulled his toes up. Thallandians locked outside their own castle yelled and cheered encouragement. Rose bleated as a hurled spear lanced her skirts between her legs, then dropped away.

Wafting over the blood-stained courtyard, Byron could see for miles. Far behind, the smoke in the fairgrounds had diminished, volunteers having beaten it out or stolen its fuel. The town street was packed with commoners armed with polearms and hayrakes and brushhooks. The cavalry captain shrilled at the hastily-mustered force. With the fighting and fires under control, throngs of people, thousands, were converging on the castle for news. Byron wished there were some way to use their might: perhaps he should have exploded open the portcullis with a card instead. But Explode was a weak and dodgey spell, as apt to fizzle as kill the wielder. And perhaps he could have—

But the die was cast, he admonished himself. He and Rose proceeded as best they could towards Stanwin and Cerise. He just hoped they could arrive in time, and help when they did—if.

Past the castle, still and solemn and cold, rose the gray skyline of the White Bone Mountains with their streaks of wind-blown snow. Compared to that world of stone, Byron felt tiny as an ant. Those frowning crags didn't care what happened at their feet, who ruled or who succeeded or who died. They'd been here forever and would be forever.

Interrupting his thoughts, Rose gasped, "Am I floating, too? Or are you carrying me?" Twenty feet high, they were still rising.

"What? Oh, no, you're afloat, like thistledown." Close, the girl's dark hair whipped in the breeze and tickled his nose and mouth. Byron recalled something a cardmaster had told him: floating, your hair and hems blew around at first, but once you matched the speed of the wind, everything hung still. "If I let go, you'd drift—"

"*Don't let go!*"

On this day of miracles and madness and mixed emotions, Byron laughed again. Practicing magic was usually a dangerous and dirty affair, but drifting on the breeze, with the low cloudy sky almost close enough to touch, he enjoyed magic's rewards—actual flying. A barn swallow with nesting straw in its beak flickered by, circled, decided they were no threat, and darted with forked tail dipping.

"We're part of the air," Byron murmured.

"Marvelous," Rose gasped through clenched teeth. "H-how do we get down?"

Some people weren't meant to fly, Byron thought with a sigh. "Once we strike the wall—"

"*Strike?*"

"Touch, touch. We'll duck into the War Room. Won't take a minute."

The girl clung to his shoulder with workworn hands that bruised flesh. "We don't *have* a minute, do we? You said it would only last three minutes—"

"Uh, oh! Look!"

Down below, a knight had bolted across the courtyard for the castle. At the castle doors, a brown-clad woman gaped up at them. She whirled inside. "That's bad news. She'll blab."

"Byron!"

Rose covered her face with a hand as they drifted towards the stone wall of the castle. With one foot, Byron nudged them to a gentle stop. Practicing magic for years had prepared him for oddities. "We're weightless, remember? Like a boat drifting against a dock. Now hang on."

"I'm hanging!"

"Good." Holding Rose like a rag doll with limp legs, Byron cat-footed up the wall while the breeze at their backs pinned them in place. They reached the third story and Rose squealed as Byron vaulted an open window. Despite a thrill at this new activity— "Wallwalking" would make a fine card, fetch a fine price—Byron listened at the bedroom window for signs of fighting. He heard muffled shouts but no clash of steel, and saw no one.

He craned his head up. Time was running out. The spell might quit without warning, and they'd plummet like shot geese, break legs or worse. Sticking a toe in a crack, he steered for a large window on the top floor—the War Room.

"Coming up," Byron warned. "Be ready to dive for cover if need be. They might be fighting."

"I—I don't hear anything." Rose stared at the distant cobblestones with the fascinated horror of a rabbit watching a snake. "Maybe a buzzing like bees?"

Strange, Byron thought, since the castle was under siege. Keeping time mentally, the cardsmith caught a windowsill above him. Relaxing his wrist, they fell *up* and he could peek inside.

Cardmasters crowded the three safe tables: Duke Stanwin's, Earl Otto's, and Countess Lenda's. The three lords issued orders hard and fast, but in low tones Byron couldn't catch. Cerise stood with Stanwin, gloved hands on her sword belt, listening and nodding. A mixed contingent of cardmasters and castle guards blocked the doors, weapons unsheathed. With their plumed hats and embroidered jackets and flashy pants, the cardplayers were a sharp contrast to the six guards in plain green and gold. They attended some activity on the other side of the double doors. Byron raised Rose to eye-level. "We're in luck. The room is still secure—"

His words were lost as the doors exploded inwards.

In a flash, Byron saw cardmasters and guards blown aside, limp and shredded as rag dolls.

He barely had time to duck, cradling Rose's head and face from the blast, before something slammed into the windowsill.

It was a dead cardmaster. She'd been hurled half out the window, her back snapped against the stone frame, her red hair whiplashed across the sill. Oddly, her face was peaceful, eyes closed, only a trickle of blood spilling from a nostril down her cheek.

Byron struggled to retain his grip on the windowsill, his hand trembling. Rose began to cry. "Oh, the poor thing. Oh, Byron, Duke Stanwin's in there—" Her words were drowned out by a crashing in the room. Fighting.

They both yelped as the dead woman snapped open both eyes. Stunned, helpless, she gurgled, gasped, then lay still. A single ruby drop of blood fell onto Rose's skirts.

Rattled, unthinking, Byron let go the windowsill.

Free, the two bobbed into the air, past the window. The room was a tumult of shouting and rushing. A wave of brown-clad warriors with painted yellow suns charged in. They wore leather coats studded with copper rivets, and pointed helmets painted brown with yellow stripes streaming from the crown. Knights carried tall kite shields and broadswords. A second wave of sergeants and pages and other retainers bore long wicked spears or heavy maces with iron studs. The Bronessan mercenaries rushed like a raging river of muddy water to engulf green-clad guards and flower-bright cardmasters.

All this they glimpsed, replaced by stone as they soared past the window. Ever-practical Rose shrilled, "Byron, grab something!" She snatched at the roof.

One arm full of girl, Byron did likewise. But the

edge of the roof was a simple cornice round as a loaf of bread. No handholds. Byron went cold. If they rose too high, they'd crash on the roof when the spell wore off—in a minute, or seconds. The cardsmith flailed at the cornice, but grabbing only pushed him away.

"Wait! I—" Rose sagged in Byron's arm, as if she were gaining weight, kicked out with her sturdy wooden clogs. They stopped rising. "Got it!"

Feet floating out behind him, Byron craned to see. Rose had hooked her pointed toe on the upper edge of the windowsill. Just below, the dead redhead stared at the sky. "Good girl! But, honey, you're—"

"What? *Ulp!*"

Now Rose felt it. Byron kept an arm around her back, hand hooked in her armpit, but she dragged him down. Like a weight. "I'm sinking!"

Byron resisted cursing, for that would cost time. Magic being imperfect, the spell was wearing off Rose first, perhaps because Byron had held the card. So what now?

With her foot crooked inside the window, Rose bent in the middle, her shapely rump hanging over the courtyard. Byron thought furiously. "Reach inside and grab something! As I lose weight and sink—"

Both squeaked as the dead cardmaster below them jerked again. A grunt sounded inside, then the redhead was manhandled up and tipped over the windowsill. She made a crunching thump on cobblestones four stories below.

We'll splat like that in a second, thought Byron. But who . . . ?

Then he recalled. A Bronessan at the castle door had spotted them drifting across the courtyard, had run to tell her officers.

"Oh, *balls*! Rose! The villains know we're out here!" Rose shrilled.

Spear in hand, a Bronessan craned out the window, identified the fliers, and stabbed straight at the chambermaid.

Chapter 17

Rather than hold Rose to be stabbed, Byron let go.

With half her weight regained, Rose dropped, screaming, skirts flaring, knocking the spear askew and plumping in the Bronessan's arms.

Byron shot upwards like a balloon with its string cut.

The Bronessan thug swore and tried to shove Rose off. Hanging half out the window, the girl clung to the man's tunic with strong calloused hands. But now the two of them were pitching out.

Sailing upwards, Byron grabbed for the rounded cornice, found nothing, grabbed for the back side, still found nothing, kicked with his toes and bounced off the edge, bobbed high enough to see the rooftop—

—and felt the spell wear off.

Byron crashed on the Bronessan's back. The man

wheezed as his chest was crushed against the windowsill. Hanging in space by his collar, Rose windmilled her legs and hollered for help. Cobblestones yawned four stories below.

Teetering, skidding down the Bronessan's back, Byron snagged a toe on the man's helmet and tore it loose. It clonked off Rose's head. She yelped, screamed anew as all three people tilted farther into space.

Not graceful by nature, Byron made do with mad hysteria. He clawed at the window frame, hooked his hands inside, arrested their tilting. But the Bronessan struggled to heave his gut off the sill while Rose hung like a monkey to a vine, still screaming.

The War Room was madness. Armored Bronessans lumbered like elephants to chase unarmored cardmasters who flitted away like bees. Brute strength and broadswords were pitted against finesse and rapiers. As long as the cardmasters could maneuver, they danced around the Bronessans, pinking here, stabbing there, finding chinks in armor and drawing blood. But pinned against furniture or trapped in a corner, they were rammed with shields and hacked down.

Byron saw it happen not twenty feet away: a cardmaster skipped backwards but misjudged a table, rapped his butt on the corner, stumbled briefly. Immediately the Bronessan swung his shield to fold the cardmaster over the table's edge. A solid blow from his war axe below the shield chopped the cardmaster's thigh to the bone. A higher chop spilled guts, and the Bronessan disengaged to kill someone else while the cardmaster fell.

The great gaming table was upset, and hundreds of colorful cards spilled like autumn leaves into pools of blood. Fights surged back and forth, punctuated by screams and shouts, as cards and men and women were trampled underfoot.

Cardplaying was done, Byron's mind flashed. The battle for the dukedom had spilled over into real life. And real death.

He scrambled to get his feet on the floor but, to Byron's dismay, two Bronessan knights, a man and woman, saw their comrade's plight and charged to his rescue from two sides.

No place to go except out the window, Byron thought. This was it.

Then a furred giant streaked in and bowled over the male Bronessan. Ferocious growls sounded as white teeth closed on the man's throat below his helmet strap. He howled and flailed his sword sideways in awkward defense.

The woman ruthlessly ignored her companion to stab Byron. Framed in the window atop the Bronessan's back, he flinched backwards, ready to fall out or be jabbed out, tried desperately to think what to do. But there was nothing—

Silver glinted, a flint sparked, and a gun crashed not two feet from Byron's head. The female Bronessan was blown sideways, half her face shot away by buckshot and ball.

"Cerise!" Byron chirped.

With no time to holster, the frontierswoman shoved her smoking wheellock into her broad belt. Her rapier blade was bright with blood. Her black cloak swung by its chain over her left shoulder as a partial shield.

She grabbed Byron's hand and yanked him into the chaotic room to crash on his knees. Then she grabbed the Bronessan by a boot to pitch him out. "Where's Rose?"

"No!" Byron snatched at her arm, missed and crashed again. "Out there! Hanging on!" Scooting, Byron latched onto the Bronessan's legs as the man was steadily dragged out. "Down there! On him!"

"What? Oh!" Nothing surprised Cerise. She lunged over the suffocating soldier, latched onto Rose's hands, and dragged the girl in to flump atop Byron in a flurry of skirts and petticoats. Cerise caught the mercenary's leg and flipped him over the sill, yelled, "Thank you!"

Then she whirled, barked at her beast, "Magog, back!" As the dog tore loose of the bleeding Bronessan, she planted her point in the man's throat, stepped back to avoid the frothy red spray.

Byron helped Rose rise, made to thank Cerise, but she hopped in front of both. "Look out!"

A pair of Bronessans with spears rushed them. Magog hopped nimbly aside and bit the shaft of one spear. Cerise feinted right, then back, sidestepped a lunge, then grabbed a shaft and stabbed. Her rapier split the brown tunic and the leather coat between copper plates, then the man's liver. As the dying man gasped, Cerise twisted her wrist to free the blade and worsen the wound. The man dropped.

The woman whose spear was clamped in Magog's jaws was strong. She swung a boot and kicked the dog's throat, wrenched her spear loose, slashed sideways at Cerise. The blade ripped the swordswoman's thick cape. But Cerise had loosed her wicked dagger, now hooked the spear shaft to the outside with her rapier blade. The dagger sliced the woman's throat and she fell spouting blood.

Another Bronessan ran in behind Cerise. Rose bleated, grabbed an upset stool, threw it at the man's face. Dodging, he slipped in a puddle of blood. The chambermaid caught her twisted skirts in both hands and kicked. But her sturdy clogs had fallen into the courtyard long ago, and she sprained her toes on the man's helmet. Frantic, Byron grabbed a shield, shouldered the hopping Rose aside, and pounded the assassin flat as a snake.

Byron wiped his forehead with shaking hands and cast about. The room was a pitching maelstrom of bodies, more brown than colorful. All around the long room, knots of cardmasters defended here and there in rings of steel and upset furniture, but many were mowed down by broadswords like wildflowers by a scythe. And more Bronessans, freed from securing the castle, ran in the door.

"We must get out of here!" Byron yelled. "We're losing!"

Puffing, Cerise shook hair and sweat from her brow, watched for the next attack while she hastily reloaded her pistol and rammed the charge home. She whistled for Magog. The dog bled from the mouth and a sliced ear, but enjoyed the tussles. Cerise pointed to Duke Stanwin and his defenders backed against a fireplace. "Grab a weapon!"

Rose retrieved the stool and a long knife from someone dead. Byron picked up a spear, found it slippery with blood. Holding it awkwardly, he tried to recall what Veronica had taught him about staff fighting. At the moment he couldn't think of a thing. Stanwin's party looked to be a hundred miles off.

"Here we go!" Shrieking a frontier battle cry, Cerise slashed a storm of steel as they tore across the room. Magog barked and yipped and skipped while Byron and Rose ran to keep up. The swordswoman steered for open spots between donnybrooks. A woman turned to engage with her broadsword, but too slow, and Cerise slammed her head with the barrel of her heavy pistol. A man lunging from the floor had his wrist slashed with a sword tip. Rose clobbered someone with a stool, and Byron fended off a wounded man with the butt end of his spear—flustered, he'd spun it around and almost sliced Rose.

Somehow they reached the besieged party, now had to breach the solid wall of brown attacking it. Slashing, stabbing, Cerise fired her pistol point-blank into a woman's back, then trampled over her. Duke Stanwin and Veronica leaped apart to admit the newcomers as they vaulted the upturned table: the duke's "safe table" become exactly that.

Flipping erect like a cat, Cerise spun back to battle. Rose looked for a slot to fill. Feeling useless and foolish, the only one not fighting, Byron tried to think of how to help. Perhaps twenty defenders, remnants of Stanwin's and Lenda's and Otto's teams, were besieged by too many Bronessans. As he watched, four more trotted into the room to join the fight.

Or slaughter. The duke's party was the last standing, and trapped against this wall.

And fireplace.

"Cerise," Byron called. "Give me your cards!"

"What? Down my blouse!"

Grimacing as Cerise spun rapier and dagger, Byron stretched over her shoulder, past hard muscle and soft breasts—she clucked at his cold hands—and plucked out her purse of cards.

"Get to work," Cerise shouted. "Whatever you're planning!"

"I need your money purse, too!" But she was busy fending off a pair of spearmen, so Byron just reached around her broad hips and tore loose her small purse of coins.

Then he ducked into the fireplace.

As always, a fire blazed in the hearth, though no one had fed it recently. Frantic, he kicked charcoal and ash aside, burning holes in his black hose and shins, then crouched amidst the hot embers to ply his trade.

Squatting, soles of his feet burning, face running sweat from hot chimney walls, Byron juggled cards and money. With his teeth, he tore open Cerise's card purse and quickly thumbed through the pasteboards, found what he wanted.

A severed hand floated on a pale blue background. He'd assessed the card for Cerise long ago in Waterholm, guessed the token. Now he prayed he was right.

Fumbling with strings, he shook coins into his sweaty palm. Coppers, silver, pieces of gold coins. Pocket change. He hoped the token wasn't bronze or some gemstone.

Carefully, he held the card in his right hand and striped a gold coin across it. Nothing happened. He tried silver, stroking slowly.

The hand image vanished from the card, leaving a hand-shaped gap outlined in blue.

Byron felt something enwrap his right hand. Cold and clammy, like a wet glove of thick wool. But invisible.

An Invisible Hand spell, triggered by silver. Designed for work at a distance: to grab a cat out of a tree, or strangle someone, or slip a love note through a shutter high up.

Or to trip a secret latch on the other side of a wall.

Having guessed correctly, he wanted to shout with joy. Instead, he went to work.

Facing the hot back of the fireplace, he wiggled his thick-clad fingers, felt something respond at a distance. Somewhere outside his reach, perhaps two feet, *another* hand matched his movements.

He closed his eyes to better "see" the task. But that made him aware of noise. Cerise shouted, Magog barked, Rose bleated. They'd all be killed soon if he failed.

Concentrating, his right hand writhed in the air as his magic one felt the rough stone of the secret passage. Inching phantom fingers, he felt more stone, then a crack, the outline of the hidden door. Like a spider, he magically traced until he found iron. Small, square. The head of a bolt. A hinge pintel.

"Hellfire!" He had the wrong side of the door. Damning his faulty memory, crunching ashes, he scooted around, whisked his invisible member along the door, found the opposite crack, explored, heard a jingle, felt a curl of steel. Resisting a war whoop, he caught the latch with his phantom hand, lifted, pulled.

Not a budge.

Cursing, Byron tugged with his magical hand. Remembering he had another real hand, he leaned on the hot fireplace wall and pushed. The secret door was ancient, gummed by creosote and ashes. But it had to give—

—a crunch sounded as something let go. Byron tumbled into a cool dark niche. Exultant, he bobbed upright like a turtle, yelled back through the fireplace. "I've done it! This way!"

He was almost crushed in the stampede.

Duke Stanwin, slashing back and forth with his sword, framed by Yves and Molly trying to keep him alive, yelled to Countess Lenda and Earl Otto to get through the passage. Lady Lenda wasted no time. Hiking her skirts above smoldering embers, she darted past Byron's face into the passage. He backed out of the niche. Soot and dust trickled from overhead, tickled his nose. Behind Lady Lenda crowded her escort, then Earl Otto's men, all big like the lord, whose wide shoulders sent soot cascading. People shouted questions and orders and advice, a cacophony echoed by the clashing in the War Room. Byron hoped Cerise and Rose and the rest could disengage without getting lanced through their backs.

Meanwhile, he had more work. As he remembered, this secret chamber was round as a bread oven and not much bigger. It was pitch black and he had no candle so, using his only non-card spell, he snapped his fingers alight.

There was the descending stairwell off to his left. He had to block it before the refugees pitched down it and broke their necks. Once down the stairs, the lords' parties could escape to the third floor servant's hall or the cellars, if need be. Once free and clear, the fighters could take command.

But as Byron reached the stairwell, it lit from below.

Crouching on the first step, shushing those pushing behind him, Byron blew out the flame on his fingers. The square stairs stayed lit by a small yellow glow.

A rustle of clothes and leather sounded in the stairwell. A candle flickered. Someone was coming up the stairs, shielding the light with their hands, trying to be silent. Many someones.

"Oh, balls!"

Behind him pressed many panting bodies, Lady Lenda the closest. "Young man, can you lead us down? It's getting crowded in here."

"It's about to get more crowded, milady."

One flight down, Byron saw faces peer up. They wore helmets streaked with yellow and carried shining swords. Seeing they were discovered, the mercenaries gave a shout and rushed up the stairs like wolves after sheep.

"Bronessans!" shrilled Lady Lenda. "Below us!"

"And behind us!" someone echoed with a curse. Well, thought Byron, how could magic help now?

Byron reared back from the Bronessans' charge. There'd be slaughter in this room in seconds, and he was useless again. Then someone bowled him aside, an elbow rapping his ribs, a long shaggy form banging his knee.

"*Hyaah!*" Cerise jumped to the top stair, rapier flashing, screaming and stabbing. Magog dropped both paws on the stairs and barked like a cannon crash. Cerise jabbed a knight in the face, piercing his cheek and penetrating his brain. The man slid off her sword blade without a sound. She pricked another woman in the neck, severing her windpipe. The bodies slumped and tumbled onto their oncoming comrades.

But the mercenaries below caught the bodies and shoved them upwards, shielding themselves with their dead. Cerise had to back up one step, then another, as did her snarling snapping dog.

The frontierswoman swore. Having the high ground was a priceless advantage, because it forced her opponents to strike upwards in a narrow staircase at an awkward angle, while she had freedom to place her jabs and the weight of gravity to help. But the knights drove on like a steel-and-leather battering ram.

A blade pinked Cerise's knee, stinging like fury. Another sliced along her calf and made the leg weak, trembling. Ducking, she lanced the arm of a knight propping a body. Then the candle below extinguished, either fumbled or snuffed deliberately. Absolute blackness enfolded them.

With no light, Cerise could only stab blind. Magog had the advantage here and she growled as she savaged her foes with long white teeth. Two cardmasters or castle guards joined Cerise, but they had to grope to find her and then aim at sounds. Likely they'd stab her accidentally. And any second a spear might find her guts. Once the defenders lost the top stair, the Bronessans would flood the chamber, and everyone inside would be hacked to pieces.

Squashed against the sloping wall of the chamber, Byron knew death was only minutes away. As people butted him with elbows and shoulders and knees, he wondered desperately how to help. Mentally he shuffled his deck of magic cards, came up blank. If only there were some *other* way out—

But perhaps there was.

In a flash, he realized what had bothered him about this round-roofed chamber. When they'd first explored it, they reasoned the secret stairwell ran from the cellars to the War Room and opened on two floors. But something had niggled at Byron, something missing. He'd lost the thread at the time. But now he got it.

What was missing was an exit to the caves inside the mountain.

Now it seemed obvious: even a rabbit was clever enough to dig two or three boltholes. Caves honeycombed the mountain, but were sealed and checked regularly. Yet it seemed a gross oversight that this stairwell, a warren for assassins and traitors, could only enter the castle, not the caves and the freedom of the entire valley.

Or could it? Cerise had been in a hurry, and Byron hadn't had time to investigate. Now he hoped it wasn't too late.

Squashing by milling bodies, he turned to the back wall, the side facing the mountain. Snapping his fingers alight, he squinted at the stone wall.

And there they were. Mortar or plaster and soot and dust-covered they were but, knowing what to look for, Byron saw blocks had been stacked to fill a hole.

And where there was mortar, he could trigger a spell.

Crouching, fishing in his shirt, he pulled out his cards and hurriedly shuffled one-handed with black fingers. A card showed a castle toppling, and the cardsmith blessed the name of the dead Rayner for manufacturing it.

The room was a windstorm of noise. Fighting raged in two places, through the fireplace and on the stairs. A roar of triumph welled from below: the Bronessans had shoved Cerise and the guards aside and gained the top stair. Byron prayed she was still alive as he wedged the card in a crack.

Clayton Emery

His flaming fingers burned agonizingly and he smelled skin scorching, but he couldn't snuff the light. Lacking a knife, he ripped a knee buckle from his breeches and scratched at mortar. (He never had finished collecting the tokens for the cards he knew. A stupid mistake, possibly fatal.) Scraping, he heard more than saw a crumbly trickle patter on the card.

Pushing back against the surging crowd, he snuffed his finger-fire and shouted, "Stand clear!" No one heard.

A flash almost burned off his eyebrows. Magic rippled through hidden mortar like cracks in glass, instantly dissolving the bonds between them. Crackling, snapping, and popping pinged around him. Mortar dust spat on the cardsmith's face and chest.

Mashed by the throng, Byron had the awful thought the stone blocks might topple onto him. He had to prevent that. Grimacing, he laid hands against the shifting wall and shoved.

The ancient wall crumbled like week-old bread.

Rough-cut stones big as breadboxes growled and crunched and fell away. Byron only snatched his hands back a second before a cascading stone smashed down. Dust and mold kicked up in gusts, blinding his eyes, making him sneeze.

But as he ungummed his eyes, people shouted and shoved him anew.

Before him gaped a block-lined hole. And dusty sunlight and freedom.

The hole was chest-high and an armspan wide. Cool air scented with grass blew into Byron's face. Idly, he recalled rain had threatened at the fair.

That was little more than a hour ago, but it seemed years.

Someone shoved him from behind as they saw light and smelled safety. Stumbling over tumbled blocks, wiping gritty gummy eyes with sooty hands, Byron ducked through. Strange, he thought wryly, that a cardsmith led the rescue. Or stampede.

A tunnel had been hacked through stone for six feet. Trotting, Byron found it entered a cavern the size of a meeting hall with rough and craggy walls. Gray filtered through a man-high cleft above arm's reach. Rain trickled through, for they were near the top of the small mountain framing the castle.

"Byron, you're brilliant!" Rose grabbed his hand, kissed his dirty cheek.

"Rose! Are you all right?" She was grimy as him, speckled with her own or others' blood. Other people crowded around, swords or rapiers or broken spears in hand.

"We'll have to form a human ladder to squeeze through that opening." Rose glanced over her shoulder. "But that'll be hard with Bronessans hacking at us."

Cerise limped up, clothes slashed and bloody. Magog bore red on her muzzle and gouges in her flanks. "The Bronessans are holding back. As if they're waiting for something."

"Make way! Make way for the duke!"

Duke Stanwin pressed through the crowd, hatless, clothes torn, bloody longsword in hand. Molly and Yves clung close as shadows, as did Veronica, unnoticed.

The young lord cast about, panted, "I know this place. As boys we climbed down through that cave from outside. But it was never so infernally neat.

Someone's knocked down stalactites and levelled this floor."

"But who?" Rose asked. "And why?"

"Where does that lead?" Byron dropped the girl's hand and tiptoed to where the cavern dipped and turned. With gray light above, Byron saw only blackness down the stone throat.

"Nowhere," the duke answered. "It's a dead end."

But returning, his eyes adjusting, Byron discerned irregular shapes along a dark wall. Creeping, he touched cold iron and wood: spades, crowbars, mattoxes, sledge hammers. "Look at these. Someone's been digging and prying."

"Aye, and here they stood." Cerise dropped to one knee. Red earth had been dumped in a hole and flattened by many footprints with short fat toes. "Bare feet. It can't be. . . ."

"Gods of the Sky!" interrupted Duke Stanwin. "Look!"

From deep within the inky tunnel, like a mole, peeped Chancellor Clement, the long-missing traitor. Roly-poly, pop-eyed, still wearing his long official vest, he seemed the jolly fat servant he'd always been. Until one noticed his face was etched with worry and fear, the rewards of treachery.

Duke Stanwin's followers hissed when they saw the quisling, shouted for his blood. Two guards dashed past Duke Stanwin to get Clement. More joined the rush. The pudgy ex-chancellor whirled and jogged into the darkness.

Byron was confused. Wasn't that a dead end? Why was Clement in these caves? Where had he last been seen? Nanette said he'd ridden into the pass to inspect the damage of a Shinyar raid. But he must have been in the castle to begin the coup this morning, mustn't he? Then his thoughts were cut off as Cerise shrilled beside him.

"Run far, villain! It won't be far enough!"

"Hush!" The duke swore an oath, the first Byron had heard him use. "There flees the betrayer of our dukedom and murderer of my father! But let the coward go! We must hie to safety! You two, climb up to that hole! Molly, Yves, we'll form the rear guard! You two, escort Lenda and Otto—"

Garbled shouts drowned out his orders.

From the tunnel, from deep in the mountain, came a pattering of bare feet. Then battle cries in a foreign tongue.

Then a hairy screaming horde.

Byron goggled at the strange folk, unlike any he'd ever seen. Male and female warriors with tawny skin wore only a hank of leather or cloth twisted around their loins. Their black hair was pulled into flopping topknots. Barbaric jewelry adorned their ears and eyebrows and nipples. All carried wicked curved swords and leather shields, and a few bore clumsy musketoons.

Their fierce appearance and unearthly screaming froze Stanwin's followers.

All but Cerise, who barked a single angry word. *"Shinyar!"*

Chapter 18

There had been times in this adventure, Byron thought, when he'd been frightened, terrified, panicked. Those times were nothing compared to the horror he felt now.

The Shinyar were tough and savage nomads of the steppes and plains, folk who killed all they met, who tortured captives for fun and ate what was left. Rabid tigers and wolves would have been jolly company compared to this insane mob.

Fifty or more barbarians rushed from the dark tunnel. With Bronessans surging behind, Duke Stanwin's defenders, perhaps twenty, were trapped.

And that was the rest of the plot, Byron realized. Clement had not only hired the Bronessans to seize the castle, he'd even bargained with the kingdom's mortal enemies, the Shinyar, on his excursions into the pass, or else through more turncoat bodyguards.

Somehow, he'd shown the Shinyar where to cut and widen caves to reach the back of the castle.

So the duke would be crushed between hammer and anvil.

But while the cardsmith wished he were home, Duke Stanwin thundered orders and encouragement like the battle-hardened ruler he'd become. "Cardmasters to the rear, opposing the Bronessans! Soldiers to the front! Form on my left and right! Yves, watch our back! Molly, my left! We'll form a living wall and walk away from this yet!"

Then, disaster. Four Shinyar leading the charge jerked to a halt and raised bell-mouthed musketoons. Aiming for the duke, they loosed a blatting hailstorm. Lead balls and iron nails pinged and rocketed off stone walls. Molly cursed as a nail lodged in her forearm. Slammed by a ricocheting ball, Rose was hurled against Byron. Magog yelped as her ribs were skinned.

Duke Stanwin was bowled over as a lead ball creased his skull, the only missile to strike him. For while the enemy raised their weapons, tiny Veronica had pushed past Molly and jumped in front of the young lord. Clumsy in her blue robes, the girl with the tonsured head nevertheless saved his life. Lead and iron peppered her body and blew her like bloody rags against the downed Stanwin.

In that instant, the defenders' hopes for survival died. Some soldiers, thinking Stanwin dead, burst into tears while others hurled weapons at the Shinyar. Cardmasters guarding the rear faltered as the Bronessans crept forward, shields up and spears levelled. People turned to the other lords for orders, but

Earl Otto and Countess Lenda only bickered over whose fault this disaster was.

Cerise took command, whapping her sword left and right, slapping guards and cardmasters into lines. "Up halberds! Get your swords up! We've got to—"

Too late.

Howling Shinyar hit their line like an avalanche.

A male warrior with hair across his shoulders like a werewolf leaped high, waving his curved sword. A guard caught the fiend in the guts, but the dying barbarian slid down the pike shaft and split the guard's head with his blade. A female barbarian hacked at Cerise and caught a sword point in the eye. Another chopped two-handed at Magog, but the dog was quicker, and bounding into the man's chest, crushed his throat in powerful jaws. Earl Otto stabbed out a gloved hand, grabbed a woman by the topknot, and smashed her skull with a mace. From behind him, Lady Lenda poked at arms and legs with twin silver-hilted daggers plucked from her belt. Even Rose picked up a fallen sword and stabbed across Magog's scant protection. But a roar from the rear announced the Bronessans were closing with broadswords and shields. The massacre would be over in minutes.

No fighter, Byron hunched behind the battle line and shuffled madly through cards. He had precious few left that he understood and the choices made him despair. Test Gold, Charm Beast, Ship Protection, Garden Pests Begone, Charm Against Plague.

Serpent Staff came to hand. Although broken and dropped spears lay scattered about, he didn't know the token. Mist might help, or would it make the battle more chaotic? Same with Explode: what to blow up? And he didn't know its token. A half-bitten Apple. Two mountains split by water. He howled in desperation, "I don't know the damned cards, let alone the damned tokens!"

A flying sword brushed his shoulder, knocked from someone's hand. A guard toppled across his shoulders and died gargling blood. Magog yelped as a Shinyar sliced her withers. Cerise's wheellock crashed to her fierce battle cry. Of all the battlers here, only Cerise had a personal reason for hating the Shinyar.

Byron reached the bottom of the deck, the blank cards, and almost cried. He could do *nothing* while others fought and died!

Unless . . .

Hunched, frowning, he stared at a blank. Could he improvise something, a spell to drive the attackers back? What? Nothing came to mind, yet anything would help, he gasped in frustration. Even a Devil's Fart would halt them back for a moment. But how to save everyone?

Vanish, he thought desperately. He'd heard Rayner mention it, though he'd never fashioned one or seen one. Turn everyone into phantoms, say, for just a minute, long enough to escape out the cave mouth to the green fields below. Just that little would suffice. It wouldn't take much, he lied to himself. (Untrue. Changing tons of flesh to spirits and back was an *enormous* task.) But he had to try or die, like everyone else around him.

Staring at the white pasteboard, clutching a clay crayon, he struggled to concentrate amidst turmoil and terror. He'd already improvised one difficult card today, Levitate. To make another so soon was to risk—well, the final fate of Rayner. But he had to try.

The whiteness of the card filled his vision, like a fogbank sweeping in, like an iceberg looming over a ship. Its vast blank menace threatened to engulf him, run him under, crush him like a cockroach. He stared deeper into the card, gradually shut out the noise around him. He willed an image to appear, a vision of vanishing. But what? A sunbeam winking out? A candle snuffing? He didn't know: he'd have to see what appeared, trust to luck. He brought the card closer to his nose, concentrating, losing himself—

Something fluttered against his nose. The card.

His hand trembled violently. Then his whole arm.

Cold. He gasped, but couldn't draw breath, cold throughout his body. Shivering, he tried to unclench his hand, move his arm, but couldn't, though they shuddered uncontrollably.

Something was happening to the card, some magic working, but he couldn't see it clearly. His eyeballs were riming with ice.

Vanish, he thought in wonder. He was making his spirit vanish.

He was losing his life force, his vital energy. He'd started a chain reaction he couldn't stop. His soul was being sucked into the card.

He'd freeze and die, like Rayner.

The cardsmith opened his mouth to cry out, to alert Cerise, to beg for help if she could grant it, if she were still alive. But his tongue was frozen, too.

His vision faded. Blackness crept from the outer

edges, oncoming storm clouds of darkness, until he saw only a pinpoint of white light, the road back to life, steadily shrinking.

His brain was freezing, dying. He fought to touch the light, to move, to breathe, to scream.

No good.

The light snuffed like a candle flame, like a sunbeam winking out. Eternal night crashed in.

Byron screamed soundlessly as he fell for miles.

The demons were waiting.

They caught the falling cardsmith with a howl of triumph like a banging of gongs, the crashing of barrels of nails, like glass breaking. Byron landed in upraised scaly warty hands, helpless as a rag doll. Then, like a giant centipede, the macabre parade of fiends rattled off across a vast plain with their prize aloft.

Byron tried to move, to wiggle, to turn over in the grasp of many clawed mitts. But he was still frozen, more tired than if he'd run fifty miles. He could only lay and let them carry him away.

And why struggle, he thought? By now all his friends were dead. Cerise and Magog cut down by Shinyar swords, Veronica shot to bloody ribbons, Duke Stanwin butchered. And Rose . . . What would happen to her? Would she be tortured, flayed or burned alive, then eaten by cannibals? Or would she be killed in the fighting? He hoped for that least-cruel fate. And she wouldn't have to see him, the man she loved, he guessed, hunched over and frozen like an icicle, and just as useless.

Byron hadn't appreciated his friends. He'd enjoyed their company, but had not understood how much until now it was too late. He wished he could see them again, tell them he loved them.

And vaguely, he wondered about himself. His body was frozen in a mountain cave. His soul was lost in a neighborhood of hell. If his life were over, what came next?

And why did all his visions of hell differ? This place was a cracked and blistered plain of gray rock with a gray sky but no sun overhead. There was nothing to see but a single low mountain in the distance and a passel of obscenely ugly demons.

Perhaps, Byron thought for the first time, he'd eventually become a demon himself, cursed to howl and gibber and bear his ugliness, to suffer by thinking of better times and lost opportunities. An eternity of self-pity and loathing. *That* was a fate to make him cringe.

So he lay in a hammock of warty dripping hands, crushed with sadness and regret, joggled and jiggled and jostled, ferried towards the mountain.

Or was it a mountain?

Byron told himself he didn't care. But his curiosity—his damnation—made him crane and look again.

And gasp.

At the foot of the mountain, the demons eased him down, propped him upright. Too weak to stand, Byron was clutched by his arms and clothes. The stink of demons was frightful, like the worst odors of sewers and sickness and rot. And they were loathsome in their startling, individual ugliness. One demon had a split face, so Byron saw brains through the forehead and broken teeth behind a hairlip. Another had earlobes so long they flopped around its shoulders, which were plated in facets like a turtle shell. Another had thorns protruding from its flesh and blood leaking from every puncture.

But as the monsters clustered around, their touch was not unkind. Why had he ever feared them? Perhaps, in time, Byron would accept them, recognize their good points, if they had any. Then he truly would be one of them.

But for now . . .

Leaving the demons behind, he shuffled on trembling knees and awkward frozen feet.

And stopped, and stared.

It was a mountain of cards.

Millions of cards.

They were all shapes and sizes, some big as bibles, some small as tinderboxes. Some were plain, showing only a faint squiggle. Others were detailed as a master painting, with scenes that receded forever deep into the cards. Some were of dark wood curlicued at the edges. Others were sheet steel, or gold, or tin. One near his foot was slate. Most were pasteboard, probably fashioned by humans. Some he recognized. A love card with two hearts bound by rose vines lay on a slope nearby. Others bore images so weird they twisted his mind.

Where had they all come from? Was this where magic cards went when they died? Or were they duplicates of every card ever made? Or had demons and gods fashioned them? And if this was the graveyard of cards, was it also a special hell for cardsmiths? A fantastic idea on this fantastic day.

But most fantastic was the creature perched atop the mountain of cards.

He was fat, fatter than anything Byron had ever

seen. Fat as an elephant, if the flesh of an elephant could be packed on a human frame. But the creature was not human, for the mouth cut halfway through its head, the ears were pointed, and downward-curving horns almost touched a flat nose. His skin was pale white, like a toad's underbelly, and rippled in roll after roll of ugly, lumpy warty fat.

The thing looked old, and tired, and filthy. Lazy, too, thought the cardsmith. Even his eartips drooped. Maybe carrying all that fat was tough work even for a demon, or king of demons, if this was one.

High up, the demon king sat with short bowed legs propping a wide board. He plucked cards seemingly at random from the heaps and windrows around it, absentmindedly laid them on the board in uneven messy rows. He ignored Byron.

The cardsmith cast about. Other than rock and cards and uglies, there was nothing.

As the initial shock wore off, Byron decided this must be hell—the most boring spot he'd ever seen, either in life or death or nightmare.

Then he recalled his former life, his friends far above, and wondered how they fared, whether they were dead yet. Poor sweet Rose, her beautiful soft body he'd enjoyed so much, cut to pieces and tossed as gobbets into pots so that—

Suddenly, he was angry. Angry at the Shinyar for their invasion, at Chancellor Clement for betrayal, at the Bronessans for mercenary greed, at himself for quitting, at this lazy demon for—what had he done?

Never mind, Byron was mad at him, too.

"Hey!" He surprised himself by shouting. Other than the rustle of demons and soft slap of cards, there were no other noises. His voice was sucked up by emptiness. "Hey! What's going on? Why am I here? Is there something you want? Hunh? 'Cause there's something I want, too! I want—"

He stopped, unsure what he wanted. Something to do, perhaps. Didn't priests preach that in hell demons whipped you with burning flails, or hung you by the heels, or forced you to roll tremendous rocks, or submerged you in pools of acid? Or was it blood? Whatever, the punishments kept you busy.

Not here, though. Here you stood and watched a stinky fat moronic demon play solitaire.

And were ignored.

After a long period of grizzling to himself, Byron huffed. Treading on cards, he climbed the mountain on hands and knees.

It took a long time, for every step up he slipped down a little. But, finally, he inched close to the fat demon, who stank like garbage in summer streets.

At last, Byron got his attention. Piggy bloodshot eyes, rimmed by fat and dulled by film, peered. Cards poised in sausage-like fingers.

"Hey. Hello. I'm Byron, a cardsmith. I'm new here. I have a few questions. Like why am I here? And did you fetch me here? And if so, why?"

The demon king swept a fat hand to brush cards from the board. Even the board was ratty, splintered around the edges and dimpled with wormholes. This hell had no class whatsoever, Byron thought bitterly. What a dump in which to spend eternity.

The demon scooped a handful of cards from the piles around him. Then waited.

"What? You want to play cards?"

The demon king pointed a dirty nail at the board.

Byron blinked. Had the king really sicced a horde of fiends on him just to gain a card partner? Why couldn't the stupid demons down below do that? Or had they lost all their cards? Is that where this mountain came from? Cards won by a demon king playing for eternity? But enough questions.

"Fine, fine." Byron shuffled his knees and skidded, kicked, dug with his hands, scooped a seat where he could reach the board. It was strange to dig through cards, like a child in sand or a mouse in straw. He cut his hand on a card made of glass etched with a swan in a snowfall, but drew no blood from the wound. Oh, yes. He was dead. He kept forgetting.

"Fine. We'll play cards." He fished in his shirt, drew his purse. "I've got, uh, thirty or so left, I guess. And I surely don't need them now."

With a thumb and finger thick as lobster claws, the demon king laid a card on the corner of the board. A coiled dragon, Byron saw. What did that mean?

"Um, how do we play? What are the rules?"

The demon didn't answer, only blinked like a toad. His lower lip stuck out so far Byron could have fanned a hand of cards on it.

"Wonderful. I don't know the rules and you won't talk." He plucked a card, a Charm Beast with a ferocious guard dog, laid it opposite the dragon. "But then, you're a cardplayer. Why give hints for free?"

The demon king laid another card sideways. A robin. Byron looked at his cards. One showed an orange tree. He laid it opposite. "What are the stakes? What do we win? Is it my soul? Don't you already have that if I'm here?"

In answer, the demon held up a card. Byron goggled.

The card showed the mountain cave in Thallandia, and the fight he'd just left. Brown-clad Bronessans surged from the left, from behind the card's red border. Shinyar charged from the right. In the middle was Duke Stanwin's party. The duke was upright, bleeding copiously from the forehead but fighting. Rose jabbed at someone with a spear. Cerise hooked her sword blade to block a musketoon. Byron marvelled at the precision of the card, which looked clear as a tiny window.

Then he gulped. From the musketoon barrel gushed smoke. But slowly, by inches. He saw a handful of musket balls like a swarm of wasps, drift slowly from the barrel.

"Slow time! I know that spell!" Byron gabbled. "They're in slow time! Or we're in fast time! The battle's still raging! It's only seconds since I—"

He choked. For the first time, he noticed a blond boy with a bowl haircut, dressed all in black, lying on the floor, curled like a baby. Was that him? He looked so puny!

The demon lowered the card to the board, off by itself.

"Wait! Wait!" How much could be negotiated? "How about this? If I win this card game, I go back! To help win the battle! Is that a deal?"

Neither nodding nor shaking his head, the demon king shuffled cards in flabby fingers and plunked another on the game board. All right, the cardsmith decided, if the demon kept playing, that was tacit acceptance.

But what were the damned rules? What would he forfeit if he lost? He had nothing left!

The demon laid down three cards. A bishop's crozier. An arm with exposed veins in blue and red. A cake sprinkled with pink sugar. What in blazes did those mean?

Byron shuffled cards like mad, pored over them again and again. He peeked at the card of the battle scene. Cerise had tilted the musket barrel back, was driving the diamond-shaped pommel of her rapier at a Shinyar's face. Minutes passed here while seconds crawled there. But could he get back in time?

Shuffling, fumbling, he thunked down cards. Opposite, the crozier, a bishop's shepherd staff, he put the gypsy girl with curly black hair and laughing eyes. Perhaps she'd steal the crozier while smiling into the bishop's face. Next to the cake he put the cup: tea time, he thought inanely. The dissected arm flummoxed him. Opposite he put a palm leaf, a healing card.

Was he winning or losing? He couldn't tell. The demon studied his deck. And what good, Byron realized suddenly, would winning do? Even transported back to the battle, he'd still be useless as before, stuck with worthless cards—

"Hey!" He spoke without thinking, but the battle was boiling. "If every card ever made is here—is that true?—then you must know how to use them. Mustn't you? Shall we say that? Anyway, I've got another offer. If I win, you tell me the tokens for all my cards. Is that a deal?"

For the first time, the demon king hesitated. Then he reached behind—a tough task given his rolls of fat—brought out a card, laid it on the table.

It showed a man. Tall, burly, built like a blacksmith

or dockworker, except he wore rich clothes of black with silver sworls—

"Gods above! Master Rayner!"

It was indeed, even to the slight list to one side, for Rayner had had a bad foot, once crushed by a horse's hoof. The master glared at Byron from under shaggy eyebrows, a look that demanded he stop chatting up kitchen girls and clean pots. The glare was alive, as was the card; touching it, Byron found it warm, pulsing with life.

"Is this—Rayner's soul—trapped on this card?"

As answer, the demon king laid down another card. It showed only the outline of a cardsmith, a young skinny one with a bowl haircut holding up fingers afire.

Byron knew whom that card awaited. It only needed his name at the top, like a tombstone. But if he gave up his soul, he couldn't help his friends, could he? Would he be a zombie? Damn it, magic was so unknowable. He should have become a cobbler like his mother wanted.

"I . . . don't think so." The cardsmith fought to keep his voice even. He wasn't sure how much he could bargain. "I won't trade my soul just for a trip home and the secret of these cards. That's too steep. Make some lesser offer."

Tilting his horned head, shrugging and jiggling with fat, the demon king offered another card. It showed a thumb.

"You want my *thumb*?"

The demon laid the card in the center of the board. Byron wondered what a thumb was worth. Certainly the life of his friends. "Agreed."

With the stakes set—if not the rules—Byron took

the offensive. He laid down a card, Garden Pests Begone. The demon countered with a Frost. Byron put down the Entwined Weasels. The demon laid down a hawk that might carry them off.

Byron had no clue how he fared. He peeked at the battle card, saw Cerise knocked backwards, falling slowly, as a cutlass just missed splitting her guts. Frantically, Byron laid down cards, most unknown to him: a donkey with a seagull perched between the ears, a thorn tree, a boat tossed in a storm. Each time, the demon calmly countered with something similar or else wildly erratic. Byron understood none of it.

Then he ran out of cards.

While the demon sat atop millions more.

"Um . . . I can't continue."

The demon nodded. Nice that one of us understands the rules, Byron groused in his head. The demon king held up the Thumb card in one hand and the battle card in the other.

Byron strove to understand. "If . . . if I affix my thumbmark on the card, you'll send me back?"

A nod made folds of neck fat compress.

Why? the cardsmith wondered. Because he'd won, or come close, or played well, or was a good loser?

"Wait. There's no use my going back without knowing the tokens for my cards. (I get to keep my cards, don't I? I do?) Fine. I'll give my thumbprint for the tokens. *Then* I'll go back. Deal?"

For answer, the demon king reached back far, stretching his fat like rubber, and grabbed fistfuls of cards. Byron wondered how he knew where to reach. How did one sort millions of cards?

With stubby dirty fingers, the demon laid cards

atop Byron's. The Entwined Weasels got a card showing a mouse—and suddenly Byron understood. The weasels represented Friendship: a pinch of mouse fur, the token, would break that friendship as one weasel deserted the other to hunt prey. The donkey-and-bird card got a mug of ale: ah, a Foolishness card, the bird gulling the drunken donkey into a rash decision. The storm-tossed boat got candle wax representing a lighthouse, a beacon to bring someone from danger to safety. The gypsy girl, Infatuation, got a chain of iron, representing a loss of freedom. The two mountains split by water got seawater, the buffoon falling off the bridge got a pot of rock oil, and so on, through all of Byron's cards.

Except the last, the bitten Apple (or Tomato), the smeary card left unfinished by Rayner's death and descent into hell. The demon smiled with yellow fangs, but wouldn't show the token. When Byron insisted, the demon displayed the battle card. Off-balance, Cerise had tumbled against Rose. A pair of Shinyar lunged to stab both with jagged-toothed spears.

Byron still had a thousand questions, but it was time to go.

Grabbing up the thumb card, he pressed his right—no, his less-used left—thumb against the pasteboard. It stuck like a tongue on frozen steel: he ripped his thumb loose and lost skin. Hastily he gathered up his cards.

He grabbed the battle card from the demon's hand. "Come on! Send me there! Quickly, please! For my friends' sake!" Then he remembered his manners. "Um, it's been lovely playing with you. Not that I understood any of it. But it was, uh, different and

instructive. I hope we can do it again sometime"
—What was he *saying*?— "but right now I must
go! Please!"

The demon leaned back, patient as a toad, raised
a card showing a dragonfly, flicked it at the cardsmith's
chest.

When the card struck his black doublet, Byron
vanished.

Chapter 19

Bursting with energy and ideas, Byron uncoiled from the cave floor like a panther. A sheath of ice a fingernail's thickness splintered and crackled and sloughed off him.

Rose saw him, bleated and blinked away tears, but continued to jab at Shinyar. Cerise was sprawled on her rump under a stunned Shinyar that she struggled to push off. "Byron? You looked dead!"

"I was!"

Hastily he cast about. In the gray half-light, the fight had not changed much from the picture on the Battle card. The barbaric Shinyar, near-naked and tattooed and earringed, flailed at the sagging defense, but their numbers and the confining cave walls prevented them surging like a tidal wave. Past the cardmasters' line, the Bronessans poised swords and shields but otherwise hung back, content to let the Shinyar kill and be killed.

With a catalog of cards and tokens filling his mind, Byron thought of thirty ways to attack at once. And minutes ago he'd despaired for doing nothing. By the gods, knowledge *was* power!

Almost chortling with glee, he went to work.

Close by the Bronessans' feet rolled a tin lantern someone had set down and forgotten. With a broken spear, Byron hooked the ring atop the lantern and dragged it past shuffling feet. Coal oil ran out of the reservoir at the bottom. Digging through his purse of cards, Byron plucked out the buffoon-falling-off-the-bridge card and dipped it in the oil.

Rising, he flicked the card over Cerise's head out amidst the Shinyar. None of the raging barbarians noticed its flittering flight or fall, or the flicker of light when it struck the cave floor.

Then a Shinyar slipped and crashed on his face, cutlass pommel banging rock. A woman's feet went out from under. A third warrior slid sideways, grabbed his partner's wrist, and both fell. One by one, then in groups, Shinyar slipped and sprawled and pratfell onto their rumps and knees and faces. Those who landed on their knees were unable to brace against the floor and slid further into tangled clumps with their fellows. A foolish prankster card, Slippery, had proved their undoing.

Cerise rasped, "What *is* that stuff—*whoops!*" Too close to the spelled area, the frontierswoman lost her footing and, jingling, crashed on her butt. Duke Stanwin, his scalp streaming blood, stamped forward with sword raised. "Thallandians! Take the attack to them—*opp!*" He pitched on his chin. Molly, his trainer, had to scoot low, grab his legs, and drag him backwards.

The Shinyar rolled and blundered and scrabbled like fish out of water. None could rise except for a few at the back of the mob, out of range of the spell. They waved swords and stone-studded clubs and shrilled foreign curses. Two of the duke's soldiers leaned out to slash at the struggling Shinyar, but one, too close, skidded on the sloping floor amidst them. Flopping, frustrated barbarians yet buried knives and swords in his back, hacking the man to ribbons.

"This way! This way!" Byron yelled as he held a card aloft. It depicted ships' masts protruding above a harbor-hugging fog. Armed with magic, he faced the Bronessan mercenaries.

In dim light packed with surging bodies, the brown-clad invaders couldn't see the Shinyar clearly, but knew somehow their allies' attack had stalled. Still, they outnumbered the duke's party two to one, so the Bronessans upped shields at a captain's command and prepared for slaughter.

Cerise hollered, cardmasters cheered and jeered to encourage themselves, Duke Stanwin bellowed battle orders. But it was Byron the Cardsmith who acted first.

Holding the card to his mouth, Byron puffed hot breath on it. Immediately, the card began to steam. As he hurled it spinning amidst the Bronessans, it pumped a fine cool mist like a mountain geyser. Leery of magic, the Bronessans shuffled and stamped to shy away from the fallen card. Beads of moisture clung to their oiled swords, ran in rivulets down their sun-painted shields. Wherever they moved, cloudy shreds of mist followed clinging. Fog billowed and swirled waist-high, then chest-high, then full to the top of the cave. Bouncing off the ceiling, fingers of mist curled towards the duke's party, who also recoiled from the strange phenomenon.

Duke Stanwin watched with mouth agape, unsure whether to strike ahead. "What good is that?" Cerise objected, "The fog just makes it harder to see and fight!"

"I'm not done!" Byron crowed. "Here's more!"

In his hand, another card showed a vast yet indistinct wall on the horizon, almost a ghost wall. As if striking a match, the cardsmith stroked the card down the nearest cave wall. The card sparked, crackled, and spat like a child's sparkler.

Shouldering past cardmasters, Byron waved the fizzling card back and forth like a signal flag. When the dead card curled like a dry leaf, he dropped it. To everyone's amazement, he thumped the air and then laughed with joy. "Put out your hands and push! Come on, *push!*" By example, he leaned and shoved ineffectually.

No one had a clue what he meant. But someone gawped and pointed. The mist that gushed along the ceiling suddenly stopped before Byron. Moist tendrils of fog flattened and curled downward, boiling back towards the Bronessans, thickening the murk around them.

While the brown-clad invaders cursed, the defenders laughed and whistled in astonishment. Byron yelled, "Come on! Drive them back to the secret passage!"

Quick to assess and take command, Duke Stanwin sheathed his blood-sticky sword and shouldered beside Byron. Gingerly he extended his hands, involuntarily flinched as a Bronessan leapt forward to chop at the unarmed duke.

The knight's sword thunked something hard and unyielding—and invisible.

Duke Stanwin yelped with joy and relief as his hands flattened in mid-air on something cool. "It's true! There's an invisible shield! Help me push!"

Blood-stained hands rose in the faces of the Bronessans, touched the invisible wall, and shoved. Gasping and grunting, the defenders pushed the wall along the cave floor. Slowly, then faster, the wall moved like a great haywagon stuck in mud.

Two feet distant and wreathed in swirling mist, Bronessans barked and balked and swore. Duke Stanwin laughed at them and pushed harder. Confounded, the Bronessans pushed back, but their labor did no good, for the magic only let the wall move one way. Inch by inch, they were shoved back by the unstoppable magic.

Gasping, grinning, Byron craned over his shoulder to see Rose. Shunted to the back of the party, the girl used her spear to probe the limits of the wall, wary they might be flanked, but the magic clung to the wall like steel spiderwebs. Flushed and grimy, she grinned at his success, proud of him. But then she lost her smile.

The chambermaid squatted, helped Earl Otto hoist the stricken Veronica to his brawny shoulder. The small priest hung limp and bleeding, more dead than alive. Byron felt a pang in his heart. Long ago, it seemed, he and Cerise had first berated and then befriended the adamant priest. But life had dealt her a poor hand at the start and now an early death. The cardsmith shoved harder on the shield wall, determined to save Duke Stanwin lest Veronica's sacrifice be in vain.

Finding the rhythm in their work, the cardmasters and Thallandians trotted the wall along. The magic must have allowed the clinging wall to shrink against barriers, for before long, the murk-clad Bronessans were forced into the hacked-out tunnel, then the inky secret passage. With much grunting and shoving, the invisible wall was forced to fill that space, forcing the Bronessans to retreat through the fireplace niche and down the black stairwell, dragging misty murk with them. Stumbling across the fresh-breeched blocks of stone and dust into the dark bread-oven chamber, Byron yipped in triumph while people pounded his back and hurrahed.

But all along the cardmaster had been timing spells. The mist would fade soon, then the invisible shield would vanish. But, more dangerously, before those two spells winked out—

"The Shinyar!" yelled Rose from the rear. "They're on their feet!" The slippery-floor spell had worn off.

"Let me through!" Byron yelled. He shoved past cardmasters and guards and Duke Stanwin to face the oncoming Shinyar. "Get behind me! I'll stop 'em!"

"Are you mad?" Cerise demanded. Magog barked hysterically. "And what are you doing *now*?"

The cardsmith didn't answer. With a card stuck in his mouth, he fumbled with his breeches.

The card showed two mountains with water between, or so Byron had always thought. But the demon king had shown him the truth. The "mountains" should be painted white with blue tints, and the water greenish for seawater.

Which was also the token.

Byron cursed as he yanked at his drawers. It was one thing, he thought inanely, to *know* the token to a card, it was another to *have* the token at hand. Right now, he was a long way from the sea. But seawater was just brine, heavily salted water. . . .

As he fumbled with buttons, he tried to ignore the horde of howling Shinyar who stampeded from the cavern towards him. "Back into the stairwell, Cerise!"

"Not without you!" Cerise grabbed his shoulder, yelled, "What? Are you *playing* with your *pecker*?"

"No, damn it! I'm trying to *piss*!"

"What? Why?"

"These are *icebergs*, that's why!"

It was hard to make his bladder cooperate when two score mad barbarians howled for his blood, but finally he squirted some urine on the card, and the rest on his legs and hands.

Immediately the card began to quiver and quake in his fingers.

"Cerise! Go!"

"But—"

Clutching his unbuttoned breeches with one hand, Byron flicked the damp card at the screaming Shinyar. A spear clattered near his foot and a war axe thudded on the wall. Whirling, he hooked Cerise and threw the two of them headlong into the secret chamber. But, even falling, he twisted to see if the magic worked.

He looked straight into the face of a Shinyar chieftain not ten feet away. The man's sallow skin was tattooed across his forehead and around his eyes like a raccoon's mask. His topknot was pulled so tight his eyebrows made peaks, his ears were riddled with brass earrings, his nose had a bone thrust through it. He wore only a sheepskin loincloth and battle harness, and he swept high a curved sword to cleave Byron and Cerise in half. Pinned, Cerise cursed and wriggled while Byron whimpered.

Then the magic card on the cave floor sparked.

With a roar like a mountain splitting, a crashing and grinding and screeching that set teeth on edge, the magic seized two opposite walls of the cave and slammed them together.

The forty-odd Shinyar in the tunnel never had a chance. Colliding stone split skulls, shattered bones, pulped organs, crushed ornaments and fingers and weapons alike. Byron saw the war chief smashed to the thickness of a card before his eyes. The victim had time for one short cry before dying, then his blood exploded from the crack to shower the cardsmith with red gore. Other Shinyar behind died as quickly and horribly.

Then it was over. The walls were reduced to rubble. Stones fell and pinged and creaked and cracked and groaned, but the cavern was gone, sealed with rock, the crushed bodies part of the mountain. Byron idly watched a trickle of blood worm across the dusty floor.

Then he rose and turned away.

"Icebergs?" Cerise puffed at him in the darkness.

"Aye. Never sail between them, for they can suddenly drift together and crush your ship."

The Bronessan mercenaries had fled: Clement's retreat, the unquenchable spirit of the defenders, and Byron's dizzying magic had proven too much.

Duke Stanwin was again in possession of his ancestral home and the War Room. As Byron entered, people clustered around to slap his back and proclaim he'd saved the day. But more gathered around a small figure laid on the floor amidst cards and blood. Blonde hair spilled except where the top of her head was tonsured. The front of her blue robe was rags, the fat-footed cross shot away by musket balls and nails, her thin chest and torso pale white skin torn by ghastly wounds that weeped red.

Byron bent over the pale Veronica, who lay with eyes open, glazed and staring towards heaven. He grabbed Rose's shoulder as she tended, asked, "Is she still alive?"

The priest herself answered in a voice softer than dust settling. Bloody foam flecked at the corners of her mouth. "Not for—long, Byron. Thank you— for befriending—me. And you, Cerise. I never had— friends before, or—love. . . ."

"You'll know love, child." Duke Stanwin knelt by the priest's head. "You'll have the love and honor of our dukedom, a living legend for all time—"

"No, wait!" Byron waved a dirty hand. "Don't go, Veronica!"

With shaking hands, the cardsmith shuffled his dogeared pack, found the card he sought, dipped his finger in the girl's warm blood. "Back up, your majesty. Here, Veronica, bite on this."

Near dead, the girl didn't understand, but Rose and the duke held her chin as Byron put the Palm Leaf card between her teeth. Gently he touched his bloody finger to the card. "Duke Stanwin, you all, pray to her gods this blasphemous card saves her life."

Despite his touch, there was nothing to see: no spark, no flash, no puff of smoke. The palm leaf image didn't even flicker, and Byron thought he'd failed. Some cards were duds, some were shams. But it was a shame that this one—

The stricken girl jolted as if kicked. People gasped. Kneeling, Byron carefully plucked the shreds of blue robe from her skinny chest and small bosom lest the rags be bound into the wound.

For magic healed the priest. Blood stopped oozing, smashed ribs knit, and slowly, like the tide receding, the skin over her chest and belly flowed together like wool being spun. The process was erratic, uneven, proceeding in fits and starts, leaving smooth skin alongside lumps of ugly puckered scar tissue. But the wound closed. Byron laid a hand on her breastbone, felt inside a mild churning as internal damage healed. Veronica's breathing, raspy and gurgly before, grew deeper, like a child's falling asleep. Then it steadied.

Above Byron, an old bodyguard with creases in his face and a stringy mustache blubbered with joy, as did many others. Hands settled on Byron's shoulder, not to clap him on the back boisterously, but in simple heartfelt thanks.

Byron felt thanks, too. To his master Rayner, who'd fashioned the card, and to the demon king, who'd shown him the token. It was all right to be indebted to them, he thought, if it could save one life.

For the first time in a long time, Byron took pride in his work. Cardsmithing and magicmaking were tough, incredibly hard, and frightening and life-draining. But used right, magic could be a powerful force for good and not just greed. He'd have to remember this moment, and savor it.

The weary cardsmith sat back on his heels and watched Veronica relax. "Well. Someone ought to inform the bishop that magic cards are good for something, eh, milord?"

But Duke Stanwin wasn't listening. Veronica's head was pillowed on his thighs, and he took care not to disturb her. With craggy grimy bloody hands, he caressed her calm face. "She looks so pretty asleep. Beautiful even. Funny I never noticed before . . ."

And in her sleep, Veronica smiled.

"Clement got away."

Clutching her gloves, Cerise strode into the main hall, rapier swinging at a jaunty angle, Magog trotting alongside with toenails clicking. "Most Bronessans, too, though some opted to decorate the floor with their bodies. But Clement ran first. On a horse, he could be halfway to anywhere by now."

"Maybe he's found a home with the Shinyar," offered Rose.

"I say good riddance." Byron slouched on a bench and quaffed mug after mug of ale. The chambermaid sat by him, as did lords and ladies and guards and cardmasters, all equal in status after the battle. The only one missing was Duke Stanwin, who sat by Veronica's bedside to hold her hand and await her wakening.

"If they caught him," Byron went on, "Stanwin would have to devise some grisly death: whip him to death or tear him between four horses or burn him alive. There's no penalty too horrid for a traitor. Better Clement keeps running, living in fear, glancing over his shoulder and waiting for the axe to fall."

Cerise sniffed but didn't argue. She scritched Magog's head until the giant dog's tail batted the table legs. "Byron, I'm curious. How did you suddenly know the tokens for those cards? You lugged them around forever, then suddenly . . ."

"I'm not sure." Byron waved a laconic hand. "When I flubbed that spell and collapsed, I dreamt about meeting the king of demons and playing cards with him. I dreamed I saw Rayner, my old master, too, sort of. And one by one, I sorted the cards in my mind and somehow puzzled out the tokens for each. I guess I knew the tokens all along from hearing Rayner talk about them."

People goggled at the cardsmith's blasé talk of demons and dead men and magic, but he didn't notice. Shifting, Byron pulled out his smudged purse of cards, idly thumbed them. The deck was smaller, some cards lost in the hurly-burly. "Anyway, it shows the power of dreams. I even dreamt I sacrificed a thumb, or a thumbprint, to learn the secrets, but—"

He stopped, frozen. Shuffling his deck down to blanks, he'd found a new card on the bottom.

It depicted the battle in a cave. Cerise slammed the pommel of her sword into a Shinyar's face while a musketoon blatted overhead. Duke Stanwin laid about with his cut-and-thrust sword. Rose jabbed with a spear. Veronica lay crumpled and bloody, and near her, curled like a baby, was a skinny boy in black with a blond bowl haircut.

Byron stared at the card, flexed it, found it thick, substantial, incredibly detailed, bordered in red. "It's real. A real card. But I got it from—"

The demon king. So *he* was real?

Staring, Byron noticed for the first time his left thumb lacked a patch of skin. Prodding the spot, he expected it would feel sore. But instead the whole thumb was numb. Prodding it produced no feeling.

"What's the matter?" asked Rose. "Your face is so odd."

Byron stared at his thumb as if it belonged to someone else. Or were dead.

"I think . . . I made a down payment on my soul . . ."

Chapter 20

"So all is well?"

"Looks that way." Naked, Byron lay propped against pillows. Rose scooched under the blankets and nestled on his shoulder. With one hand, he idly tickled her hair, the tip of her nose, a rosy nipple, until she bit his hand. "Ow."

"The Shinyar are still out there," the girl mused. It was the dead of night, and for once the castle was quiet. Celebrating had roared for three days, but people were finally wearying of it. Byron and Rose and others, mobbed as heroes, were glad for some quiet time. "I wonder if Clement struck some deal with the Shinyar and was leant a small war party, or if the horde truly plans to invade us this summer? Would they wait now that his plans were spoiled, or forge ahead?"

"Hard to say. Hard to believe a man would betray

his own kind." Byron stroked Rose's shoulder, which glowed with a golden sheen in the light of a single candle on the bedstead. "What could he expect as a reward? If he let the Shinyar pass the keep, they'd let him be duke? Of course, if they overran the entire kingdom, they might let him keep a small piece. Still, he must have been mad. I wonder where he went . . . ?"

"Who cares? You're too serious." Rose ducked her head and bit him on the nipple.

He yelped, playfully caught her nose in finger and thumb, then froze. "Damn it."

As he had hundreds of times in the last few days, he wiggled his left thumb. It would crook and bend, but still had no feeling, as if dead. Rose saw his anxious glance, gently kissed his thumb. "Perhaps you just banged it on the cave wall and didn't know. It will heal eventually."

"No." Byron frowned at the treasonous digit. "I'm afraid it won't. All along I reckoned—prayed—the demons weren't real, just fragments of dreams or idle thoughts plaguing me by night. But then I met their king, and pledged him my thumb, and brought back that card from—" He didn't say "hell."

Wiggling close, Rose tried to distract him by licking his neck. But Byron lay back as if his whole body were numb. "What if the demon king wants more of me? I'm sure he does. Maybe my thumb is just the start, and later he'll take a hand or an arm?"

"Maybe you won't see him again. Maybe the nightmares won't return."

They hadn't for three nights, but Byron wasn't sure they'd disappeared entirely. "No, I think we're linked. First he sent demons to hinder me, but later they helped me. That's a partnership of sorts. And we played cards, though I never understood those rules either. Now he's got part of me and will want more. And besides, he's got—"

"What?" She tilted her head to study his face in the light. "What, Byron?"

"Well . . . knowledge. The demon king knows volumes about magic. He showed me the tokens to all my cards—except the smushy Apple—without even trying. And he has *all* those cards! If I could *study* them, find out how they're made, who knows what magic I might work? I could be the greatest cardsmith *ever!*"

"Byron!" Rose sat up straight, revealing golden curves and uptilted breasts. "You can't bargain with the devil! What are you thinking? Instead of signing your soul over in one lump sum, you'd sacrifice parts? You'd be—more dead than alive! More demon than man! You can't do it!"

"I know." But the cardsmith's heart caressed the idea of all that magic, there for the taking or dickering. Now what haunted his dreams were millions of cards in a heap, and what he might accomplish with them.

For a moment, his mind reeled with the potential. Perhaps dealing with the demon king, he could learn an easier method of creating cards. Or how to make more powerful cards. Or perpetuity: cards that worked more than once. Or, the final, most fantastic secret of all—how to work magic without cards at all!

But with it came new worries. Did all cardsmiths encounter demons? Rayner must have, but Nanette said no. Was that section of hell, ruled by the demon king atop his mountain of cards, a special hell reserved for cardsmiths? Were those hideous demons excardsmiths? Was *Rayner* one? Must a cardsmith sacrifice his or her soul? Did Byron have what it took? For years, he'd worried that he didn't have the brains or guts or talent to be a good cardsmith. But he could snap his fingers and make fire, something no other cardsmith could do. If he were careful, made a few canny deals with the demon king, he might gain untold power.

But better not tell Rose those plans just yet . . .

And of course, lying was the first step to hell, his mother always said.

Rose licked his navel and he groaned. Her distractions were working. Grabbing her shoulders, he kissed her long and hard. She sighed against his lips. "Oh, Byron, I love—"

"Uh . . . yes?"

He pulled back, waited for the rest. Rose sat still with eyes closed and lips puckered in mid-kiss. Gently he shook her. "Rose? Dear? Honey?"

Then he couldn't move.

His hands were locked on Rose's soft shoulders. His arms were frozen in place, his back and neck, his head. He tried to speak, couldn't.

What the hell?

Then he knew. Magic of some kind. But who . . . ?

The tapestry on the back wall flickered. Byron could only move his eyes, saw it bulge as someone slid from behind. Creeping from the servants' hall.

A short man, fat, dressed in fine clothes now tattered and speckled with blood and leaf mold. His round face was swollen from insect bites, his hair frazzled, his eyes pouchy from lack of sleep—and from being hunted.

Clement, ex-Chancellor, tiptoed to Byron and Rose,

poked the two of them with a dirty finger, gurgled a tired laugh. "Ah, the Arrest card *was* valid! You'll be frozen for five minutes or so. Not long enough to sample the little lady's charms, unfortunately." With a scratched hand, he pinched Rose's breast hard. The girl couldn't react, but she felt it.

"But I must hurry." Clement plied the same busy-jolly tone as ever, but babbled as if crazy. Perhaps terror and hiding and suffering insects and cold and sleeping in the woods for three nights had unhinged his mind. "Yes, must hurry. You have something I need, and the spell won't last, more's the pity. Would I could freeze you and that little snippet immobile forever, to suffer like the living dead, like I've become."

Clement picked up Byron's black clothes from the bedstand, rifled them, searching. "Yes, the living dead. That's what I've become. Hated by an entire kingdom, and now even the Shinyar won't take me in! I could have been a lord greater than Duke Stanwin, Older or Younger. I could have been a prince! I could have been *emperor* of these lands after the Shinyar left! But no, *you* had to thwart me with your cursed magic! *You* had to scotch my mercenaries and *kill* my assassins, knock all my careful plans—*years* of planning—into a cocked hat! Now I'm *nothing*, thanks to you!"

Emperor? thought Byron. This fat boob had bigger schemes than anyone could imagine! And his mutterings were scary, turning into personal threats.

Finding nothing in the clothes, Clement turned to the bed, squatted, ran his hand under the mattress, nudging Byron's rump. "Cardsmiths aren't clever. I'll bet—aha!"

He found Byron's purse of magic cards. Shuffling

the deck, he gave another cry of triumph. "Aha again! Look!"

He held the saggy bitten Apple card before the immobile cardsmith's nose. "See *this*? Your master gave his *life* for this card, didn't he? Oh, I know he did! I know everything! But *you* don't know what this card *does*, do you? You little fool! You pissant! You turd! *This* card is what the bishop sought when she raided Rayner's house! This card *alone*! And when she couldn't get it, and couldn't come here without scotching the Great Game, she asked *me* to steal it! As if I'd be fool enough to surrender it! This card will make me *emperor*! And *you* carried it over half the kingdom without even guessing what it stands for!"

Frozen, watching from the corners of his eyes, and sweating, Byron recalled too the demon king had refused to divulge that card's token. Why? Because it was too powerful for a mortal to handle?

"No doubt you wonder what it is!" Clement batted the card against Byron's nose. "Well, too bad! I won't tell you! And you won't tell anyone else!"

Now the cardsmith poured sweat, and under his locked hands, he felt Rose tremble. She was conscious, but stuck with her eyes closed.

Clement drew a long wicked dagger, held it before Byron's nose like the card. "This will be a delicious torment. You'll be able to move soon, but not soon enough. I'll cut your throat slowly—no, I'll cut *her* throat slowly. *Her* blood will gush from her beating heart and drench *you*, while you're helpless to move! Then, when she's dead and you're just beginning to move, I'll prick *your* throat! They'll find the two of you locked in each other's embrace but drained like pigs for the winter slaughter! Ha, ha! And me? Long, long gone!"

Despite his immobility, Byron shivered as if drenched in an ice storm. He wished he could move, to strike out at the mad ex-chancellor, or just move his jaw, to beg, plead, promise anything to spare Rose's life. For she was suddenly more precious to him than anything, including his life. But he was helpless as a suckling pig, and so was she.

"Oh, where shall we start? Oh, over here, I suppose." The chancellor moved to one side to sever Rose's throat in full view of Byron. The knife glinted in the yellow light. Unable to move, Byron watched the tip touch Rose's soft throat where a vein pulsed, and Byron knew she felt it. Her eyes were still closed, her lips a clownish pout.

The knife tip pricked as if testing, drew a trickle of blood—

—and the door crashed open.

"Drop it!" screeched the voice of the frontier.

Though Byron faced the back of the room, he knew who it was. Cerise, sleeping across the hall, must have been woken by Clement's mad shouting and broken down the door. He hoped she'd brought her sword or wheellock pistol . . .

Trapped, a coward again, Clement held up both hands. One contained the long knife tipped with Rose's blood, the other the mysterious Bitten Apple card. The chancellor howled, "No! I'll go! Don't—"

Behind Byron, the pistol clacked, fizzed, and banged. Clement flinched but remained unhurt. Byron knew the pistol wasn't very accurate, but it had clipped something with a thin whisking impact.

"Ruined! Ruined!" Jaw agap, Clement stared at the Apple card in his hand. Punched through the middle, it was destroyed.

Now Byron would never know what it did, he thought inanely.

Then came a puff as the magic in the card ignited.

Clement let out a shriek. He hollered, cursed, prayed, staggered backwards as if assaulted by invisible wolves. As if arm-wrestling in pantomime, he clutched his left wrist in his right hand. Something was wrong with that arm.

It was shiny in the candlelight, glistening golden. And heavy, for it sagged straight down. Why so shiny? Was he wearing a shirt of cloth-of-gold that Byron hadn't noticed? And why so heavy? Had the bullet ricocheted or nicked a tendon so he couldn't lift his arm?

Then Clement's shiny arm fell off.

It tore from the traitor's body and thudded on the floor. Only a stump was left at the armpit, and it pumped bright frothy heart's blood in all directions. But only for a few seconds, then it quit, for the man was drained. White-faced, shuddering, Clement tumbled to the floor and died.

Cerise, in a white nightshirt, padded barefoot to the dead chancellor. With her was Stanwin's combat trainer, the gray-streaked Molly, in a matching nightshirt.

Byron was so surprised his creaking jaw dropped, for the spell had worn off. "Cerise! You and Molly?"

The two women whirled and, amazingly, blushed like schoolgirls. Cerise chided, "Well, you landed a nice girl. Why shouldn't I? Is Rose all right?"

With a slump, Byron's arms fell off the girl's shoulders.

She stirred and opened her eyes, winced as stiff muscles pinged. "Oh, ow! Yes, I'm all right!"

"No, you're bleeding!" With clumsy aching fingers, Byron dabbed the sheet at the puncture on her throat.

But Rose caught his hand and kissed it. "I'm all right as long as I'm with you, Byron." And now the cardsmith blushed, and gave his girl a solid hug.

Curiosity overcame passion, and cardsmith and chambermaid, wrapped in blankets, bustled over to examine the dead Clement. Byron said, "I don't understand! What *happened* to him— Ah!"

"What 'ah'?" asked Cerise drily. "Explain it to us non-magicmaking simpletons, please."

Picking up the fallen Apple card, Byron pointed where the bullet had punched out another bite. "Good shooting, Cerise. Now we know the name of the spell *and* the token."

Three women looked blank, so he explained, "Remember the legend of the king who wanted the Golden Touch? He bargained the power from the gods, turned his couch and statues and plates to gold? Then the spell backfired, remember? When he tried to bite an *apple*, it turned to *gold*! Rayner meant to paint this apple *gold*!"

"You mean," asked Rose with wide eyes, "it's a Golden Touch card?"

"But what's the *token*?" Cerise demanded.

Byron laughed from relief and delight at being alive. "*That* was a joke on Clement! What do alchemists try to turn into gold?"

"Lead," mused Molly, "because it's cheap and almost as heavy as gold."

"Right again! *Lead* is the token. And Cerise's bullets are made of . . . ?"

"Lead!" laughed three women.

"Yes!" Byron's blanket slipped, he laughed so hard. "The lead bullet struck the card and triggered the magic! Too bad Clement couldn't have touched the card to a big rock or statue, anything but his bare hand!"

Snorting at the vagaries of fate, Cerise squatted and picked up the arm. It took two hands and all her strength, for it was solid gold. She examined it by candlelight. "Amazing. It's got veins and little hairs and a crack in the thumbnail and everything. It would fit his stump like a puzzle piece. But no matter. We'll melt it down and split it, and no one will ever know it was somebody's flesh—"

Swaying, a white-faced Rose suddenly grabbed her mouth and ran out the door. A moment later they heard her retching out a hall window.

Fighting his own queasiness, Byron heard Cerise tell Molly, "Some people just don't have the stomach for magic."

A month later, on a day of fine summer sun and fresh mountain air, Veronica, a former priest, walked up the aisle to marry Duke Stanwin of Thallandia.

The bride wore a pale green dress after the House of Stanwin, a long yellow train held by four handmaidens, and a round hat adorned with mountain flowers, for the crown of her head had yet to grow in. She'd abandoned the tonsure and the church in weeks past, after receiving the blessing of the bishop (who'd herself received a generous gift of gold from Duke Stanwin). It was a shame to lose such a stalwart arm of the church, the bishop had proclaimed, but obviously the gods had chosen another path for her daughter, and she'd serve devoutly and well as Co-Defender of the Eagle's Road through the White Bone Mountains.

Hundreds of guests were gathered, many survivors of the "Fired Fair" and the "War Room War" as the recent events were called. Among the crowd were Countess Lenda and Earl Otto, each wearing their own heraldic symbols now surrounded by the broken-chain device of Duke Stanwin. The Great Game had been interrupted and never resumed. After the duke so ably repulsed the enemy and saved their lives, the two lords admitted Stanwin was the best leader to defend the Eagle's Road. They graciously conceded defeat and accepted the yoke of servitude, proving the noblest of nobles when the cards were down. Combining their armies and strategies, the pass was guarded as never before, and the three fiefs could respond faster and stronger to any threat of Shinyar invaders.

The unresolved game had profited all the players. Since Stanwin's team had been ahead, the monies were divided with half going to his team and a quarter each to Otto and Lenda's teams. Most of the cardmasters had then gambled for three days and nights straight, betting furiously. Cerise had collected a small fortune and given Byron a quarter-share for his help. Duke Stanwin had rewarded his followers with money and even lands in the outer reaches of the fief. Quietly, Cerise had a goldsmith melt down Clement's golden arm, then apportioned that, too. For the first time in their lives, Byron and Rose were rich. Thunderstruck by good fortune, they'd wisely banked the money to let the full import sink in. But at night, they interrupted their lovemaking to make plans for the future.

Veronica paraded to the head of the aisle and took Stanwin's arm. The ceremony took place on the old fairgrounds, now raked and bedded with flowers in a great circle, and the vice-bishop from Waterholm stood on a knee-high platform where the bride and groom joined them. Men smiled and women wept and children laughed. Stanwin wore a new green-and-gold doublet, dashing hat with plumes, and flowing cape, and the big man smiled down on the little ex-priest in pure and utter worship. The bishop began to drone in a high sing-song.

Beside Byron, not twenty feet from the couple, Rose whispered, "Do you think he'd have ever noticed her if she hadn't taken those bullets for him?"

"Shhhh! Yes, I think so. You women have a way of making men notice, if you have to trip them and jump on their chest with both feet."

Rose giggled and squeezed his arm. On the opposite side of the aisle, Cerise and Molly stood arm-in-arm as they watched, both unashamedly spilling tears down their cheeks. Byron was glad to see them together, for he suspected a good part of Cerise's taciturnity was caused by loneliness, and he hoped Molly could fill the gap in her heart.

"Byron," Rose's warm breath tickled his ear, "do you think *we'll* ever get married?"

"Hush!" He turned and found her close enough to kiss, so did. "I guess so. But let's survive one ceremony before we start another, shall we?"

So they stood, hands together, and watched and listened. Everything had worked out so well, Byron thought, nothing could spoil this day. Rose sighed, "Oh, Byron! How *could* things be any better?"

"Hist! They couldn't. But beware. Boasting of

good luck is a sure way to make the gods pay attention. And that's something you *don't* want." Unconsciously, he rubbed his cold and dead-feeling thumb.

The bishop droned about love and purpose and happiness and proper worship of the gods, but after a while had to lift his voice. Then shout.

A rumble shook the air, and people outside the circle turned. Someone called, but Byron couldn't hear as the drumming got louder. Everyone craned to see. The bishop frowned as Duke Stanwin towed his bride to the edge of the platform, waved wildly. "Over here! What is it?"

The thunder was hoofbeats. Three weary riders on blown horses plunged across the field and rode to the platform. The lead man had lost his helmet, and his sweaty brown hair stuck up around his head. A flint-tipped arrow protruded through his saddle cantle.

Byron gripped Rose's hand. So much for good luck, he thought. This could be only one kind of news. And it was.

"The pass, milord! It's overrun! The Shinyar charge the Eagle's Road in thousands!"

THE END

To Read About Great Characters Having Incredible Adventures You Should Try 🚀 🚀 🚀

BAEN

IF YOU LIKE . . .	YOU SHOULD TRY . . .
Anne McCaffrey . . .	Elizabeth Moon Mercedes Lackey Margaret Ball
Marion Zimmer Bradley . . .	Mercedes Lackey Holly Lisle
Mercedes Lackey . . .	Holly Lisle Josepha Sherman Ellen Guon Mark Shepherd
J.R.R. Tolkien . . .	Elizabeth Moon
David Drake . . .	David Weber S.M. Stirling
Robert A. Heinlein . . .	Jerry Pournelle Lois McMaster Bujold

Send for our free catalog for more guides to good reading—
then buy the books from your local bookstore!

Please send me a free catalog! ✏️

Name _____

Address _____

_____

Here are my suggestions for "If You Like... You Should Try..."

_____

_____

Send to Baen Books, Dept. CI, PO Box 1403, Riverdale, NY 10471